THE UGLY ROSES

HARLOW STONE

THE UGLY ROSES TRILOGY
CONCEALED AFFLICTION – BOOK TWO

Reviews

The connection and chemistry of these two characters is so strong I experienced it in every word they exchanged. The sexual tension was insane and when they finally connect in an intimate way, I could not take my eyes off my e-reader. **—JB'S Book Obsession**

Nothing is as it seems. What you believe you know is all a lie. **— Obsessed By Books**

Wow, from page one you are thrown into an emotional mess!!! And it doesn't stop until the end!! It's a gripping book and a gripping series **! —Alpha Book Club**

Frayed Rope will capture your heart!!! Follow Elle and Ryder on an incredible journey! Elle is sassy and tells you like it is and Ryder is her perfect match! Be prepared to not be able to put it down!!! Harlow Stone is AMAZING! **—Amazon Reviewer**

THE UGLY ROSES

Copyright

Preface

Ryder has been my light in a hurricane,
but even I know the sun can't shine all the time.
He's made me feel safe, but that doesn't mean he can save
me.
Because someone's still out there.
Hell bent on hurting me.

This journey of mine only leaves me two choices:
Do I continue on my path towards retribution for my family?
Or do I focus on the first man to crack my steel encased soul?
He hurt me, lied to me and broke my heart.
But I was wrong, wasn't I?
So wrong.
I'm at a crossroad.
Crooked cops, a shady mayor and his conniving daughter,
I don't know where to turn.
Ryder or retribution?
Love or loss?
This life of mine isn't a fairytale.
I know I can't have both.

THE UGLY ROSES

Prologue

Eleven months ago

I force my eyes to stay open as I drive. One is completely swollen shut from being hit in the face one too many times. I can barely see. Gravel crunches beneath my tires as I swerve off and on the road with this pissy little car, a clear sign my depth perception is off. The car is pathetic but it's fast, not that I can take advantage of speed right now.

I've been awake for the better part of three days. The wounds on my back keep tearing open every time they touch the back of the driver's seat. I do my best to lean forward, but the tears still manage to open, and the pain still afflicts me. I curse the sick fuck formerly known as Andrew when I feel the blood run down my back.

If I could have just found a phone, I would've called for help and wouldn't have needed to drive. But then deep down inside I think—I know—I would've run anyway. Once the ropes were off of my wrists, come hell or high water, I was not spending another minute in that place.

I needed air.

I needed to breathe.

I needed to get out of the filthy hole that I was beaten in to remind myself that I'm still alive.

Andrew lived on a little road outside of town. I don't know how far I've driven. I've passed a few houses since pulling out of his driveway, however I'm too afraid to stop and ask for help. What if he knows them? What if they aren't friendly neighbors, but sick fucks like him who aided in my capture and subsequent torture? Since I have no trust in anyone but myself

THE UGLY ROSES

I'll drive as close to civilization as I can before I pull over to get help.

I press a little harder on the gas. I know I'm minutes away from passing out. I've lost way too much blood and I still feel the rope around my wrists. I breathe deeply, trying to stop the phantom pain of his hands around my throat.

I press the button to lower the window, hoping the cool breeze will keep my eyes open. I know the only thing currently allowing me to move forward is the adrenaline rush from what I just did.

I need help.

I need blood.

I need a bed.

There's a bottle of water in the cup holder. Not wanting to crash the vehicle, I ease off the accelerator before lowering my blood covered arm to grab it, using what little strength I have left to slowly twist the cap off and bring it to my lips. The first taste of cool water in my parched mouth is heaven. But when I swallow, my abused throat rejects it, causing me to cough.

The tang in my mouth tells me my throat is bleeding. A mixture of blood and water sprays past my lips and onto the plastic bottle making it impossible to hang onto. Not willing to try drinking again, I decide to dump what's left of the cool liquid down my face, hoping to wash some of the blood out of my eyes.

It burns.

Badly.

"Aghhh!" I yelp, my abused throat sputtering out what strangled sound it can.

HARLOW STONE

I grab a corner of the towel wrapped around my neck to clean my face with. I manage to clear a bit of the blood, but it comes back just as quickly. I give up, dropping the towel back into place before focusing back on the road.

When I left the basement, the tattered old towel was the first thing I found that would cover my chest. I tied the ends of the once white—now red—towel around my neck to cover the front of my body. I couldn't put a shirt on due to the lashes Andrew left on my back. It would be far too painful.

I see lights in the distance. There are a lot of them, suggesting it must be town maybe five kilometers away. I can make it! I can get that far before passing out! I continue down the road, passing a few more houses sparsely dotting the landscape. I still don't pull over for fear that they know Andrew; maybe the sick fuck had friends? I know it's a ridiculous notion, but I can't help the fear that I feel at stopping when I've finally found freedom.

Headlights are coming toward me so I slow down, squinting my eyes against the harsh light. I would never want to hurt someone else by causing a car accident, so I do my best to stay on my side of the road driving slower than my father used to on a Sunday.

Which was incredibly fucking slow.

My head starts to get fuzzy, sort of like tunnel vision. I only see the two headlights heading in my direction. Nothing in the scenery. Nothing else in front of me. The edges of my vision get darker and I can't help but stare as two lights turn into four, then four into six.

The sickening sound of crunching metal is the last thing I hear before it all goes black.

Chapter One

Present Day

"I have to head to Chicago soon, beautiful."

I've been quiet these past few days, ever since I found out a psychotic set of twins were out to ruin me.

By ruin, I more accurately mean murder.

The nightmares have flooded back in, and as much as I want to turn to Ryder to make them go away, I can't bring myself to let him that close to me. I've become distant. Not even by choice, it's simply because I'm lost in my head but too stubborn to talk about it.

It's not so much that I've completely reverted into the old me that doesn't speak much. It's just that I have so many things to go over regarding the attack, and how the hell I don't ever remember meeting a set of twins. No matter how much I wrack my brain, I don't remember who 'Andrew' is. Nor do I remember his twin. A girl in college would certainly remember a set of twin boys. Wouldn't she? Wouldn't I?

Either I'm not most girls, or my memory went down the shitter along with my ability to open up to people.

"You do what you need to do Ryder, I'm not stopping you."

I don't say that in a rude way, more like I need time with my thoughts, and I understand he has a life and work to get back to.

No hard feelings.

We haven't had sex again. Not that I couldn't, I could have. I'm just in that mode where I need to be alone to process everything. I need to open up all the ugly of my casework and go through it again with a fine-tooth comb now that I have this new information. I let him hold me at night, and it helps. But I haven't made a move to take it any further and neither has he.

I would love to call Detective Miller and let him in on all I've learned, but for the time being I am going to keep this to myself, mull it over, see what I can do, and what should be done with it before I share with the boys in blue. I doubt it will be easy to convince them of my findings. If they look at the evidence again; they will see the obvious. Andrew's home was only lived in by one person. It had only one bedroom, and the only belongings were that of the one person who occupied that room.

How far will they dig? How much will they want to delve into this mess again to try and figure out if there is an evil twin out there waiting to take my life? Will they even believe me and consider giving it a shot?

I'm almost positive if this case gets solved, it'll only happen if Ryder and I commit a lot of time and determination to doing so. Aside from Detective Miller, my shot at getting any help from the rest of the police department is probably nonexistent.

A weight settles next to me on the couch. I turn to face the handsome man who's planted himself into my life. He hasn't shaved in a few days, but he knows it doesn't bother me. His dark silky hair falls around his ears and brushes the collar on his dark grey shirt. The sleeves are pushed up to his elbows, showing the endless black lines of art that covers his skin. He begins to speak so I settle my green eyes on his beautiful black ones.

"We haven't talked much babe, but I need to know what your plans are. I will help you in any way I can, you know that. However, in order for me to do that, you need to talk to me Elle, let me know what's in your head."

I don't know how to answer that, mainly because even though it's *my head,* I have no idea what's going on inside it at the moment. I need more time, and I need to be alone to do that.

"I need more time Ryder, and I want that time to be alone. That's the only way I can figure this out on my own. I *do* want your help, I just need some time to process before I get into it with you."

A strong hand lands on my thigh, his tell that he not only cares, but that he wants my undivided attention.

"Told you before babe, I'm not going anywhere. As much as I may not physically be here, I'm still with you. What I need to know is if you're coming home. And if you are, when? Because when I'm finished this job in Chicago, I want you with me, beautiful."

If I'm honest with myself, I've thought a lot about when I would go home. Not if, *when.* I know this place in Indianapolis is not home. It's a little ironic considering I've met more people here and speak much more than I did when I was in North Carolina.

I think that has to do with growth, more so than location. I was still numb in my little cottage. I didn't want to meet anyone, so I didn't bother to get to know anyone.

Here in Indy, I have the kind old souls on this street who've brought me muffin baskets and fed my dog over-cooked pot roast. I have Brock and his kind wife Sam, who continue to show me just how amazing people truly are by checking in on me and dropping off baked goods from time to time.

I never had anyone like that in North Carolina, simply because I never put myself out there. I rented a home on a quiet lane with virtually no others, other than Ryder's. I never joined a gym, or went to town for anything other than food and alcohol.

What more did a single, thirty-year-old woman need?

If they say it's a family that makes a home, or the people around you that help create it, then the most logical explanation would be to stay in Indy.

If someone asked me where my cold heart wants to go, it's North Carolina.

I can't help but wonder if my mind and heart would still make the same choice if Ryder were not in the picture. I know I didn't want to leave my little abode in the first place. I simply fled after Ryder saw my scars. But what about now? Will I be happy back there? Will I miss old Greta, and the other friendly senior citizens on this street?

What will I do three nights a week, without Brock as my trainer to help me sleep at night?

I'm not an idiot.

I'll buy more wine is what I'll do.

I also have to ask myself if this will continue to work with Ryder. The man is on my side, I know that much. Seeing as I haven't been deported back to Canada and he's still here with me, putting his dishes away and holding me when I sleep at night.

"I know this place is not my home, Ryder. But that doesn't mean I haven't met some pretty amazing people here. As much as I may not join them for tea, or meet up with Brock and Sam for drinks, it's not going to be a quick move from here like it was from the cottage."

I know I hit a nerve with that comment, but it's the truth. Regardless of the fact he explained his relationship, or lack thereof, with his ex-fiancé Anna. It was still the situation that gave me a quick kick in the ass to get on the road. I was fully ready to stay until he got back from work so that I could say goodbye properly, and in the flesh.

The minute that country club whore showed up on my doorstep and declared herself Ryder's fiancé was the exact minute I threw common courtesy out the window. I called him with little more than a 'fuck you and your bitch of a fiancé too.'

Then I hit the road.

Looking back now I should've gave him the benefit of the doubt. But I'm never one to dwell on things or have regrets. So I live, learn, and move the fuck forward.

"I should only be gone for a few days, a week tops Elle. I know you have a lot of shit going on in your head right now beautiful, but my hope is that you'll try to sort some of it out on your drive back home. I need to head there first, then I'll fly to Chicago. If you have anything you need moved back, you can put it in my truck. More room for Norma, and less for you to have to worry about."

Typical Ryder, even when I want to be a little bitchy with him, push him away so I can be alone with my thoughts, he still manages to say something kind, making me want to throw myself into his arms. I decide to gather more information before I make my decision.

"When exactly do you need to be in Chicago? And when do you plan to leave here?"

He reaches out and tucks some stray strands that escaped my birds nest behind my ear. "Would like to be there and back as soon as possible. Ultimately, I'd like to leave tomorrow for the drive home, which means I could be finished in Chicago by Tuesday. But if you still need me here, then I can wait a few more days."

God, this man treats me better than I deserve.

"I need to find someone to take over the lease on this place. Not that I care if it sits empty, but the pipes are older than the cottage and I don't think it would do it well to sit here unattended for the next nine months."

Ryder seems lost in thought for a moment before he replies.

"That mean you're coming home with me, beautiful?"

I know that pleases him, but I cannot and will not make this move solely for him. I miss the cottage style home, and I know my girl Norma misses it there too.

"It means I'm going back to my little abode in North Carolina, Ryder. I won't lie to you and say that it's me coming home with you. Not to be a bitch, but I'm doing this for me first. You may not understand that right now, but from almost a year ago until now, I've realized that this life is about me. Not anybody else. I need me, and I need to get my shit together. If you want to be included in that, right on. But if it gets to be too much, you let me know before we head any deeper into whatever it is we have going on here."
A strong hand wraps around the back of my neck and pulls my face towards his. Wet lips meet mine and for the moment I'm lost. He pulls back a little and rests his forehead against mine.

"It won't be too much. And you are not 'too much,' beautiful. This is going to work; I'll prove it to you. But in order for me to do that you need to knock down some of those walls. You got so much shit going on in your head and you need to share that with me. I can't help if I don't know what's going on, babe."

"I know you want to help, Ryder, and I appreciate it. But you have to understand that I've been doing this on my own for a long time. At this point, it's all I know."

My eyes and tone are both sincere. He needs to understand that it's not so much that I don't want his help or need it. I just have a hard time accepting it.

"I'm working on it though Ryder, I am. But just like everything else in my life, it takes time."

His dark eyes roam my face before he settles his lips on my forehead.

"I know babe, appreciate that. Speaking of which, I don't want to push you too soon, but I'd like to sit down with you and go over your case file. More specifically, what's missing from it. If that shit's tough for you to look at then leave it with me. Either way babe, I need all the facts I can get so that we can figure this out."

If I show him the rest, that means the photos too. That means revealing the old me to him, the woman with a different face and long blonde hair down to my ass. It means showing him the girl that used to have shining green eyes and a bright smile on her pale face.

"I'll think about it while you're gone handsome, I'm not ready to dive into that shit right now."

Ryder pulls me close beside him so we're both reclining on the couch, my head on his shoulder and his arm around my back.

"I can work with that." He places a kiss in my hair before continuing. "You going to the gym tonight?"

"Yes. I haven't missed a session since I started, and I won't until I leave. Need to talk to Brock anyway, so two birds with one stone."

"I'll come with you. I normally work with the guys on base and get some ring time in or at least a jog."

I know he's referencing the fact that since he started hunting me down, he put his physical health on the back burner. He continues to rub his hand up and down my back, consoling me in the only way he knows how to at the moment. "That okay with you?"

"Yes, that's fine. In the meantime, I have ten bags worth of clothing you have to pack to take with you on your drive tomorrow."

His deep whiskey laugh greets my ears. "I'll pack the whole goddamn house if that's what you need babe, I just don't think it'll all fit in my truck."

I don't want anything else here. It's all cheap shit, aside from my mattress.

"Well, no time like the present. You can pack handsome, and I'll find something to eat for lunch."

I pull myself out of his embrace. Not because I want to, but because I need to keep moving before my morbid thoughts takeover and nothing gets done. I don't tell him that, but I suspect he knows.

Who am I kidding? Of course he knows.

Ryder Callaghan is the most intelligent man I've ever met, and possibly the only one who has ever read me like a book. I can hide behind my sunglasses, and dress in my armor, but at the end of the day I have a feeling this man knows me better than I know myself.

Sometimes that scares me more than my impending death.

Chapter Two

"Fuck babe, your man can fight."

He's not joking.

I've been trying to concentrate on my training with Brock, but now we're both too distracted with watching Ryder take down opponent number three in the ring.

"The man is a machine," Brock says.

He doesn't need to tell me. I already had that figured out when I slept with him a few nights ago.

Twice.

We also made love which was equally satisfying and a memory I'll never forget. After the last few days of celibacy, I'm thinking I'll see just how much more energy he has when we get home.

"You listenin' to me Elle?"

"Huh?"

His deep chuckle washes over me. "I said, I can see why he's so sought after for work. The man's like a high-priced body guard. Vinny in there is one of my best guys, and he can barely get a punch in."

High priced body guard? I knew there was a reason not asking questions would one day leave me confused.

Ryder gave me a short description of what he does a few months ago, but I assumed it was more like he delegated jobs to his men who carried out the work. When he mentioned working for political parties and a few hostage rescues, I pictured his men using their K9 abilities to sniff out potential bomb threats, or barreling into a house on a hostage rescue carrying AK-47s, shooting up the bad guys.

Maybe I watch too much television.

"Pardon?" I ask.

It's all I can manage. Clearly Brock knows more about Ryder's work than I do.

"Babe, not sure how much you two talk, but that man could've been a secret service agent if he wanted to. When Denny left me to work with his company, it wasn't just because he wanted to leave. It was because of the opportunity.

"Callaghan Security has contracts with some very influential people babe. I'm not talking celebrities, I'm talking governors. Word has it he's kept his business small because he doesn't want to be shipped off all over the country for months on end. He chooses what contracts to take, and how many men are needed with each one. High security babe, some of the best."

This is news to me. Not that I didn't think Ryder was capable of such work. I just didn't think that he was so...*important?*

"He only has twelve men that work for him, Brock."

"Like I said, chooses his contracts and stays small Elle. Denny was lucky to get a job with him."

Well, who knew? My neighbor who doesn't even live in a gigantic flashy house and wears Levi's has protected some of the Country's most influential people. He seems far too reserved and laid back for someone with that reputation. Ryder's deep voice pulls me from my thoughts.

"You want a round, beautiful?"

I look up to see that cocky shit eatin' grin on Ryder's face as he stands with his arms rested on the ropes, sweat dripping down his bare chest.

"Nah, I already paid Brock to kick my ass. Might as well get my money's worth."

Brock's laugh pulls my attention back to him. "Ready to get your ass kicked then babe?"

I turn to face the kind man that has taught me so much these past few months.

"Actually, I need to talk to you for a minute first."

Brock nods his head and takes a seat on the bench beside the mats. I follow suit. He takes a long swig of his water before resting his elbows on his knees.

"I know what you're going to say, babe. You're going back to wherever it is you showed up here from, and you're going back with him."

Jesus, when did I become so transparent?

This guy has been the closest thing to a friend I've had in a long time. Maybe even my best friend, seeing as he's taught me over thirty ways to take down an attacker, and the proper way to throw a right hook.

"Not going to lie and say I won't miss you around here Elle, because I will. I'll miss your payments for almost six hours' worth of private classes every week too."

I can't help but give a small laugh. These classes weren't through the roof, but they weren't exactly cheap either.

"What I'm most concerned about though babe, is you. I know enough to sense that you've been through some shit. I'm not going to tell you how to live your life Elle, all I'm going to ask is that you keep in touch and let me know how you're doing. Peace of mind for me babe, it's the least you can do if you're not going to pay me anymore."

This earns him a chuckle from me, and even a small smile. I make a pact to look up at the sky once again when I leave here, to thank my angels in heaven for the wonderful people they have brought into my life.

I take a long hard look at him. His full-tattoo sleeves from wrist to collarbone, his buzzed blonde hair and mass of muscles. It's the eyes that get me. *Baby blues*. The man is built like a mastiff, but loves like a puppy.

"I'll keep in touch Brock. I promise."

I expect some smartass remark from him, or maybe even a gloved punch to the shoulder. What I don't expect however is the hug he gives me.

For once, I actually hug him back.

"Make sure you keep it babe."

I give him a squeeze before I ready myself to let go, but not soon enough before I hear a whiskey gruff voice behind me.
"Time to go, Elle."

I know my time with Brock is not up yet. Or at least, not what I paid for. Brock releases me from his hold before addressing Ryder, not aggressively, but enough to get his point across.

"She knows how to get ahold of me if she needs anything. I'm hoping she won't, and I'm trusting you're going to be the one to make sure of that."

Ryder's eyes get a little harder than they were after he witnessed our goodbye hug, not that he had anything to worry about. I don't feel that way about Brock.

"I respect the fact that you're worried about her Brock. I'm also glad she's had someone look out for her while she was here. But bottom line, she's my business, not yours. She feels the need to contact you, she will. In the meantime, I'll do my best to make sure that doesn't happen. But again, she's my business—not yours."

If there's one thing I hate (amongst a multitude of other things) it's when people talk about me as though I'm not in the room. I could let it slip, but if I did I'd lose a part of myself that I worked way too fucking hard to get back.

"How about this fellas, Elle looks after herself. In the meantime, you both can mind your own damn business," I reply. I grab my bag off the floor and walk up to Brock, giving him a one-armed hug.

"I don't do goodbyes. So, talk to you soon."

I give him a quick peck on the cheek before walking out of the building. I'm sure Ryder is still taking the gloves and tape off his hands. I don't care, and I don't wait for him. I push through the double glass doors and head out to my truck in the parking lot, thanking my lucky stars that I met Ryder at the gym.

He was still busy packing when I told him I needed to head into the leasing office before they closed. We agreed drive separately and meet back at the gym.

I decide to take my time heading home so I can cool off. It's either that or unleash my endless vocabulary of profanity. Brock is off the hook because I'm leaving, and this could very well have been the last time I see him. As for Ryder, hopefully my delayed return home will teach the cocky bastard that I don't like being spoken about as if I'm not there, especially when I'm standing three feet away.

Slamming the door on my black BMW SUV, I think back to the last time I had simple actions taken away from me, the days when I had to ask for things. The days when I was told what to do, and what to say. The dark days of my past still haunting my sleepless nights. I put the truck in drive and can't help but let the bitter memories from almost a year ago take over my thoughts.

"All you had to do was say you were sorry, Jayne. Then I wouldn't have to leave you like this."

I watch Andrew from the small slit that will open on my left eye. The right one is still firmly shut. I don't know what he's talking about, his constant wanting for me to say sorry, but I keep my mouth shut. My head hangs low on my shoulders because I lack the energy to keep it upright.

"Look at you! You're a fucking mess. All you had to do was apologize Jayne, then ask me nicely to go the bathroom. But you're such a stubborn bitch that now you've gone and pissed yourself!"

His sickening laugh grates on my eardrums. I think I've been here for two days now. He controls when I'm awake, when I'm allowed to drink (which so far has only been twice) and when I can use the bucket. I don't know what time it is, or how long I've been unconscious, but apparently it was long enough for me—a grown woman—to piss herself.

The warmth is a stark contrast to the coolness of the concrete under my feet. I try to feel ashamed at what I've done, but I feel nothing. I'm covered in blood—dry, sticky and fresh. I haven't slept or eaten in days. My wrists are raw from the frayed rope holding them above my head, and now I've pissed in the underwear I've been wearing since I left home on Wednesday afternoon.

I'm trapped in a basement with a psychopath—who I have no desire to please.

Not to mention my 'give-a-fuck' broke a long time ago.

Regaining my resolve, firm on the fact that I'll never allow someone to dictate my life, I head for home.

* * *

I park my truck in the garage and turn off the engine. I know Ryder is already here because his truck is parked on the street. I grab the bag of Italian food I picked up off the passenger seat along with my gym bag before getting out of the vehicle.

I'm not two steps toward the connecting door leading into the house, before it swings open and angry black eyes stare back at me. "Did you think to answer your phone while you were out joyriding, woman? I've called you ten times in the last hour."

Ryder is about to learn a little lesson about who wears the pants in this household. As well as who can come home to it whenever they damn well please. I square my jaw and look him directly in the eye.

"Whose house is this, Ryder?"

Confused eyes stare back at my determined ones. I don't give him a chance to answer. "It's my house Ryder. That means if I want to roll in at nine at night, or nine in the morning, that's my fucking business. Now, if you'll step aside my dinner's getting cold."

He doesn't move a muscle.

Doesn't blink.

Just stares at me.

"Let me tell you something, Elle. When I'm seeing a woman, when I care about that woman, and when I'm fucking that woman, I think that gives me every right to know where she is, and when she's going to be home."

I'm not sure whether I want to weep, or hit him.

Being as I do best when I hang onto my anger, I choose the latter.

"Well here's a little lesson for you Ryder Callaghan. When you're with a woman, and you feel like you have rights over her, you best make sure you sit down and see if she's ready for the same thing. You also might want to ask her if she likes to make her own life choices and speak for herself. Because that shit you said to Brock back there at the gym? Not fucking cool Ryder! I'm my own person, and I'll be damned if someone will speak for me. So long as I'm walking, talking and breathing I will continue to make those choices for myself! And nobody on this green earth will ever make them for me. Do I make myself clear?"

Wisely, Ryder steps aside as I plow past him to the kitchen. My girl greets me on the way, so I set the bag on the counter and dig out the container of chicken parmesan I picked up for her. She wastes no time digging into her dinner while I lean against the counter, silently fuming.

I hear Ryder come up behind me, he's quiet on his feet but the squeaky linoleum gives him away.

"Where's all this coming from Elle? Not three days ago you gave me a part of you that I wasn't sure I would ever get. You opened up for me babe, and I'm not just referring to your legs. So tell me, where's this coming from?"

I take a deep breath before turning to face him. Deep down I know he means well, I'm sure he didn't mean anything by what he did at the gym. It's the caveman in him, maybe. The 'me man, you woman' thing that makes him want to look after me? The protectiveness that's ingrained in his being not just because of who he is, but what he does.

The thing is though, I've come out on top more often alone than with someone by my side. I keep thinking about that load, my baggage, which I know he'll help me carry. I know I need to remind myself that he has good intentions, but I also can't help but want to feel like I'm the one with all the power here.

That's the thing about having power stripped away from you. It was gone from me for three days, and I never in my life want to feel that again. That hopelessness. That feeling that there's not a damn thing you can do without asking someone for it first.

So I've become even more independent, not ever wanting to ask people for help. Not wanting to ask them for *anything*. Even when you need to ask if you can have some slack on the rope keeping you bolted to the floor simply so you can piss in a bucket. Well, that's part of what I like to call rock-bottom dependency. I'll be damned if I ever need to be dependent again.

"You spoke for me. You didn't ask me what I wanted, you didn't ask me for my opinion, you didn't talk to me at all, and you just went ahead and did it."

He tilts his head to the side, staring at me, thinking about what I just said. It may sound ridiculous to him, and I hope I don't need to explain it, but something tells me I'll be doing just that.

"I apologize Elle, seeing you with Brock doesn't sit well with me. I know you said you're just friends, and he and I had a talk that night I found you at the gym. That guy loves his

27

wife, I get that. I'm just not sure how I feel about him keeping such a close on eye on you. Especially when he has a wife at home. Not many men I know would put that much effort into looking after a woman he wasn't fucking. More so when he's not getting paid outside of the gym."

I huff. "You idiot! One, I *do* fucking pay him. And two, did it ever occur to you there are some kind people in this world Ryder? Trust me, I'm the last person who would have ever thought there was kindness left in this world, but surely if I can stumble upon it, so can you. Nothing, not now, not ever, has happened or will happen with Brock."

He shakes his head, not entirely agreeing with me. "I trust you babe, just not sure I trust him."

"Well that's big of you Ryder—to *trust* me. But let me ask you something. If you trust me so much, why are you so worried about Brock? If you trust me, you know nothing would ever happen."

"I don't think anything would happen Elle, that doesn't mean I have to like you hanging out with him. Regardless, we still haven't gotten to the bottom of the issue here. Why did you go so off the wall because I spoke for you? I thought we were on the same page here babe, and that means when I spoke, I was pretty sure what I said is what you wanted; to be back in North Carolina, with me hopefully looking after you."

I slam my palms against the counter.

"Goddammit, don't you get it? I don't need to be looked after Ryder! I'm not with you so you can 'look after me.' And for shit's sake, don't speak for me. Ever! I can speak for myself!"

Strong arms grab ahold of my shoulders. He puts his angry tanned face in mine.

"Why Elle? Why is this such a big deal to you? Tell me."

Time to turn the tables. "Have you ever been held hostage Ryder? Have you ever been taken into the hands of someone else and not been given the chance to make your own decisions? Speak for yourself? Have you ever had that taken away from you?"

"I was trained for shit like that, Elle. I've been put through the ringer-"

"No! Talk about 'training' all you want! Have you actually ever, really been taken Ryder? Answer the question!"

"No! I haven't, Elle."

My voice is low and angry when I reply. "Then you don't *know.* You do not for one fucking second know what it feels like to not know what day it is, and not want to ask. You do not know what it feels like to want water, but not be able to ask for it. You *do not* know what it feels like to ask for some slack on the rope that's holding you off the ground. Slack on the rope that's bolted to the floor and too far away from the bucket you were given to piss in.

"So until you know what it feels like, that you actually have to *ask* to take a fucking piss, you do not speak for me. Until you know how it feels to have your ability to make such small decisions taken away from you, don't you ever speak for me. Because from today until the day I die, I will decide when I sleep, eat and piss. I will decide when I need help, and who it will be from. *Nobody* Ryder, not even you, will be given the go ahead to speak on my behalf or make decisions for me."

I push his hands off my shoulders and head to the fridge. Opening the door, I reach my hand in blindly and grab a bottle of wine. By the time I turn around his hands are on the counter and his head is hung low in defeat.

THE UGLY ROSES

I don't stick around to speak with him anymore. I have nothing else to say at this moment. The only thing that is going to calm my nerves and make me even the slightest bit approachable is a round with Brock. Since I just left and I'm still incredibly pissed, I settle on a bath.

I shut the bathroom door and begin my ritual of calm, with an iPod plugged into the docking station, wine bottle opened—no glass—and some coconut oil in the water. I remove my sweaty gym clothes and sink down into the tub. I rest my head against the back, feeling the cool porcelain against my neck. I take a few deep breaths, followed by a few mouthfuls of wine.

I stare at the once white now beige ceiling, removing myself from the confrontation I just had with Ryder, replaying the scene in my head.

There are a few different ways that conversation could have went, and unfortunately, I know that that one was not the best. My anger gets the best of me at the worst of times. I'm aware I have a temper and also aware that speaking is not always my strong suit.

A few times during our rant, I know I could've calmed it down and not made it so much about something that he'd done wrong but more something that I've not dealt with. That's going to be the toughest part about this thing I have going with Ryder, having not had to share my shit with anyone in a long time, especially with a man I'm attracted to, physically and as emotionally as my cold heart will allow.

I could look back on my old life and compare this to the other relationships I've had in the past, but the kicker is that nothing ever measured up to this before. I have never, not once in my life felt about someone the way I feel about Ryder. And if I'm honest, that scares the ever living fuck out of me.

How many times do women, not just myself but as a whole, go through life wanting someone they can lean on, and more importantly count on? I know down to my bones that Ryder would be someone that I can count on. He's not the kind of man I should've just thrown that bit of my life to. I should have sat down with him on the couch and calmly told him that I have issues with trust, and therefore issues with people speaking on my behalf as if they know me better than I know myself.

Coming to this conclusion I tell myself that after my bath and wine is done, I'll apologize for dropping that on him like a bomb, and try to tell him about my issues in an adult manner, not like the miserable bitch I was just a few moments ago in the kitchen.

Ryder deserves answers, I know this and plan to tell him so.

I pull the plug and grab my robe off the back of the bathroom door.

No time like the present.

Chapter Three

I exit the bathroom in search of Ryder. He's not in the kitchen or living room, so I make my way down the hall to the bedroom. He's not there either.

I begin to panic, walking quickly to the front door to confirm that his truck is still parked on the street. It is, so my racing heart calms a little, and even more so when I hear his deep voice behind me.

"I was out back with Norm. I told you I wasn't going anywhere beautiful, but if you want me to, I'll leave. Not sure how much more of this up and down shit I can take, Elle."

Now would normally be the time that I would spin around and tell him if he can't fucking take it, then get the fuck out. I know he doesn't mean it in a bad way, but my anger issues and lack of patience are obviously getting to him. I clear my throat before I speak to him, as calmly as I can.

"I speak my mind Ryder, that's one thing you can always count on from me. That being said, if I wanted you to leave I would tell you to."

I turn around and face the man who is beginning to mean a lot to me. His hair is a mess. Obviously he didn't bother to shower after his rounds in the ring at *Fist*. Not that it bothers me, his black t-shirt and shorts leave more skin for me to stare at. The man's calves are as big as my thighs. Not that that's huge, but he's all muscle and I very much enjoy looking at it.
I take a long hard look at his handsome face before walking up to him, slow and a little cautious.

"There's going to be a lot about me that I can't tell you right now Ryder. Not because I don't want to, but because I can't. The reason I can't is because I don't know myself some days, so we're literally learning this new 'me' together. A few things I can tell you is that I have a short temper, and also lack patience. Neither of those are new things. They are just more amplified now after my attack.

"I'm not sure how many more outbursts I'm going to have, or how many times I'm going to lose my shit because you do something that indirectly reminds me of something I'd rather forget. I know it's not your fault Ryder, but realistically it's not mine either. I'd like to say I know the woman I've become, but I don't.

"You're a good person Ryder Callaghan, I know that. You're kind, you're patient and you think things through before you act. I'm a miserable bitch that doesn't have many good qualities left, but I'm trying to get them back. Do you think you're willing to work with that?"

His eyes soften midway through my speech. He wraps me in his strong arms, my head resting on his shoulder.

"You forgot that you're stubborn, babe."

This earns him a small chuckle from me.

"I told you a while ago beautiful, I'll work with what you can give me. But what you need to get from that is that you need to *give* it to me. I know you're strong, I know you've been looking after yourself. What you need to understand is that I want a part of that Elle. I know you'll always want to be independent- nothing wrong with that, babe. But it's okay to need someone, too. And I want that person to be me."

He places a kiss in my hair before continuing. "I told you I trust you, but the million-dollar question here is do you trust me? Or can you learn to trust me? I know a little of what you've been through, and I can't imagine that's going to be an easy thing to give. But if you don't think you'll ever be able give it to me, then we're only working ourselves towards a

cliff, waiting for the moment when we both go over the edge."
He shakes his head, "I can't fly, Elle."

I pull my head off his chest to look him in the eyes when I
speak next. I reach both of my arms up and frame his beautiful
face with my hands. His stubble is rough against my palm, his
hair silky against my fingertips. The outer part of his black
eyes glow when I touch him, they're almost silver when the
light hits them at the right angle. I see nothing but acceptance
when he looks at me, and it makes me feel like a fraud because
there's still so much he doesn't know about me.

"I know you can't fly handsome. What I'm most worried
about is when the things I've kept in the dark finally come to
light, you won't look at me the way you are right now. I also
worry about when you finally know every little detail of my
life that you won't be standing here anymore."

Those dark eyes of his absorb every feature on my face
before he leans down and places his lips on mine. It's a small
kiss, but full of promise. "This is where we get to the cliff
babe. If you're worried about me not standing here, then we
need to sit down and go over everything. Your life, your case
and what's going through your head. I don't see me going
anywhere. I chased you down, didn't I? You mean something
to me beautiful, I just hope I mean enough to you that we can
rip off that band aid, and get it over with."

I lean up on my toes and kiss him on his neck. I let out a
sigh of relief and close my eyes for a moment before I
respond.

"No band aids tonight Ryder. Wait until we're back home."

Strong hands move down my back and over my behind. He
gives a small squeeze before he reaches a hand around each of
my thighs and lifts me up so I can wrap my legs around him.

"That's all I needed to hear babe. Now, if you have no objections I'd like to take you to bed."

I eye the Italian that still sits on the counter. I'm starving and I haven't eaten since lunch. Ryder follows my eyes and gives me a smug grin.

"I'll feed you after I feed me. That work beautiful?"

I know exactly what he means, and boy does that ever work.

"Then you better hurry up, it's getting cold."

Ryder needs no more incentive before he carries me down the hallway. He smells so good and I can't help but stick my tongue out and taste his neck. Sinking my teeth in when I get below his ear.

"Fuck beautiful," he rasps.

My legs are pulled from his back as he tosses me on the bed. Those beautiful black eyes stare at me a little longer than necessary before he reaches for the sash on my kimono robe, unravelling me like a present. The silk is smooth against my skin as he slowly drags the material over my sensitive nipples to uncover me.

"I could look at you all day."

His eyes are tender and sincere. I know down to my bones that he means what he says. I watch as he slowly lowers his head, taking one pert nipple into his mouth. His tongue circles and his teeth tease the outer flesh.

"Hmmmm, that feels so good."

"You taste so good," he says, dragging his tongue between my cleavage so he can pay more attention to my other breast.

THE UGLY ROSES

His hands skim down my body, his thumbs brush the outside of my breasts before they skim down over my ribs. He pauses in the hollow of my pelvis and when he reaches my hips he adds more pressure.

"Bend your knees, and put your feet on the bed."

I do exactly as he says, watching as he kisses a path down my torso. Stopping to pay extra attention at my bellybutton. I reach my hands out to run them through his dark silky hair, grazing his scalp with my fingernails as his mouth worships my body.

His stubble feels like light pin pricks on my over sensitive skin, causing goosebumps to form wherever his face has touched. He trails his tongue down further, teasing my hipbones with small nips of his teeth.

"Handsome, please don't tease me."

Ryder pays no attention to me as he commences the same torture over my thighs. Starting on the outside, and then teasing his way up the inside. I reach out to grab a firmer hold of his hair so I can force his head to where I need him most.

"Please!" I beg. Not at all ashamed to admit that I need what he can give me more than I need air at the moment.

I'm on the verge of agony as I watch him stand up and tear off his shirt. His shorts are kicked off next, and he moves to join me on the bed.

"I think two birds with one stone would be best," he says.

I have no idea what he is talking about until he puts his hands under my arms and hauls me to the middle of the bed. He stretches out beside me in all his naked, tattooed glory.

"Now spin around and climb on top, beautiful. I'm not going to last long once I get a taste of your sweet pussy."

Completely on board with his plan, I move fast doing exactly as I'm told.

He eats first, then I do too.

An hour later, we finally heat up the Italian.

* * *

The warm cocoon I'm currently wrapped in feels like heaven. I might even enjoy it a little more, if it weren't for the constant vibration sound coming from Ryder's side of the bed. He stirs a little in his sleep, then settles before the vibrating starts up again.

"Ryder."

"Hmmmmm?" His arms tighten around me and he settles once again. "Ryder!" I say a little more forcefully this time before he finally comes to, eyes wide and worried.

"What's wrong?"

I bury my head back in the pillow, keeping my eyes closed while I speak in my own whiskey rough morning voice. Not seductive or caused from smoking, but an after effect of being strangled half to death.

"Nothing's wrong if you bought me a new vibrator that just happened to turn on by itself. But if you didn't then I think your phone is ringing."

He let's go of my body and reaches over to the nightstand to pick up his phone. He doesn't answer it but sends it to voice mail and begins typing.

I crack my eyes open, noticing he looks stressed, or maybe like he didn't get enough sleep. I didn't either but I'm definitely not complaining. Ryder really could put the energizer bunny to shame. We went to bed shortly after eleven but didn't go to sleep until two.

Once again, not complaining.

"Everything alright, handsome?" I ask as I snuggle back down into the bed.

I realize I didn't have any nightmares last night. Most likely my workout at the gym combined with my workout with Ryder kept me comatose for the better part of the evening. I'm looking forward to going back to sleep until Ryder speaks again.

"I need to get on the road, Elle. Chicago can't wait any longer."

I understand that he needs to go, and as much as I was hoping for time by myself, I'm suddenly not looking forward to it. Even though he put down his phone he still hasn't looked at me like he normally does when we wake up in the morning. Instead, he stares blankly at the ceiling.

"I don't ask much about your work, what kind of a job is it anyway?"

Ryder scrubs his hands down over his face and takes in a deep breath. "Mayoral election bullshit."

I think for a moment. Not that I know much about elections, but I thought I was certain it was over.

"Isn't that finished by now?"

Ryder stares at the ceiling for a few moments before answering. "Not quite, I still have a few more things to wrap up. I'll be back by Tuesday if I leave now."

He finally faces me and his eyes are a little sad. I'm not sure why, and I don't plan to ask him. Not that I don't care, but if he needs to leave there's no sense getting wrapped up in a conversation that we don't have time to finish. I also hate pushing for information from him when I'm so reluctant to give it up myself.

"No worries. I have a lot to do, and I think I'll get more done without you here," I joke. Not that it's an absolute lie, the man sure is distracting.

His hand reaches out to push the hair away from my face. He runs his fingers down my cheek. It's an intimate moment, and by that I mean it's harder for me to withstand his kind touches than it is to sleep with him. I've never been good with commitment, or full exposure. The thoughts of giving both of those things to him terrify me.

"I want you to call me if you need anything. If I'm not around or you need help with anything, I can send one of my guys over. They're in Jacksonville."

His serious eyes cause me to pause, but I give him a light smirk doing my best to lighten the moment.

"I'm a big girl handsome, but if I need anything that I can't look after myself, I'll give you a ring."

He leans over and places his lips to my forehead, breathing in my hair. "I mean it Elle. The more I know, the more I worry about you. Don't make me worry anymore please. And for fuck's sake when I call, please pick up the damn phone."

THE UGLY ROSES

I lean in and place a kiss just above his collarbone.

"I'll answer handsome. Now, get out of my bed and make me coffee." I'm greeted by a deep laugh, followed by a firm smack on my sheet covered ass.

My sharp intake of breath does not go unnoticed by Ryder. Not that I'm surprised, he misses nothing.

"I'd say if you don't answer your phone, I would punish you. But the way you just reacted to me slapping your ass, I'm thinking it wouldn't be much of a punishment."

I'm no stranger to different fetishes in the bedroom. I've tried a little bit of everything since I lost my virginity to Will Cooper in his parents' minivan when I was sixteen. The only difference now would be that bondage could be a serious trigger for me. Spanking however, I think I can manage.

"We'll discuss this when I'm caffeinated, and back at the cottage." Ryder leans down across the bed and places a quick kiss to my lips. Turning around to leave the bedroom, he speaks again.

"We won't be discussing anything when we first get back to the cottage, Elle. We'll be fucking."

I don't get a chance to respond before he's gone, but I don't think I needed to. Obviously when it comes to priorities, we're both on the same page.

* * *

I stand at the door watching Ryder load the last few bags of my stuff in the back of his truck. I feel like something is missing between us, he hasn't quite been himself. Sure, he's cracked a few jokes and acted like everything is normal. But I can see it in his eyes; something's been missing in them since he woke up this morning. Every time his phone rings he either leaves the room or scowls at it while he texts whoever is on the other end.

I've never been one to over analyze things in a relationship, and I hope I'm not doing that now. I've always been a 'go with the flow' type of gal, and if things don't seem to be working out, I move on. Rarely can I say I've ever had regrets in this department, but I can also say I have never really let my emotions get too involved in it either.

Ryder has melted a little bit of that ice around my cold heart, and where normally I would brush it off, at this moment I want to ask him what's wrong. I want to know what changed since we went to bed last night.

He begins making his way back to the front door for his own bag. When he gets close enough, he bends down to pick it up and moves so he's standing just inches in front of me. He studies my face for what feels like hours before he finally speaks.

"Tuesday, Elle. If I'm going to be any longer, I'll call you."

Distant.

That's what he is right now. Perhaps he's having second thoughts about that band aid we're going to rip off when he gets back.

"Tuesday," I confirm.

He leans down and presses his lips to mine and wrapping his hand around the back of my neck to hold me there, he speaks against them. "Let me know when you make it back to the cottage."

I nod my head. "I plan on leaving in a day or two."

41

THE UGLY ROSES

He studies my face in the oddest way before he too nods.

"Text me when you leave, and when you get there please, babe. I'm gonna be busy and won't always be able to take your call. But at least text me so I know you made it there alright."

I give him one last kiss before bidding him farewell. This moment is awkward and I'm not sure how to handle it. "Drive safe, handsome."

Giving me a small smile, he backs out of the house. I stand and watch like the fool I am until he's in his truck. Not liking goodbyes, or watching people leave, I shut the door and head back to my room. It's only seven and after last night's activities and this morning's odd behavior, I need to rest my body, and hopefully my mind.

Chapter Four

I'm cleaning out my fridge when there's a knock on the door. I managed to get a few more hours of sleep this morning, and its early afternoon now.

I make my way cautiously to the door and peek out the side window finding Greta standing on my front step, along with Mrs. Butler and Mr. Clemens. It's not Sunday, but old Mr. Clemens has what looks to be one of his wife's famous over-cooked dinners in his hands.

"Is everything alright?"

Always my first concern with these old people. You never know who's going to bust a hip or have a stroke. Their clocks are ticking, that's for sure.

"Oh Miss Elle, we just wanted to say our goodbye's before you leave."

This comes from Greta, the ol' bitty pack leader. As per usual, she's dressed in pressed slacks with nude stockings and open-toed shoes. Mrs. Butler's outfit is the same, only she's wearing full out sandals with the nude stockings.

"How did you know I was leaving?" Mr. Clemens pipes up at this. "That young man told me when I was out in the yard yesterday. Nice boy, and he's a Marine. We had a good talk about my time in the service."

This is news to me about Mr. Clemens past, but I don't exactly sit and have long conversations with these people. Quick hellos, and helping out the odd bit when I can. Greta and Mrs. Butler's voices cut through my thoughts as soon as I hear the word marriage.

"Now Miss Elle, you shouldn't move in with that boy until you get married. "Greta cuts Mrs. Butler off. "He has those tattoos, I told you most of them get those in the *prisons*. I worry about you Miss Elle."

"Greta, not every boy gets tattoos in the prisons. I told you my grandson has one, and he was never in the prisons." Greta shakes her head at the words that just left Mrs. Butler's mouth.

"Well that grandson of yours is thirty-five and still single. Now my Randy, he's a good boy, no tattoos-"

"Alright! Greta, Mrs. Butler—both of your grandsons seem like nice men. I'm not moving in with the man that was here, however I am moving back home. I plan on leaving tomorrow."

Mr. Clemens gestures to the food in his hands.

"I thought I would bring over Mary's pork chops for Norma, a last supper. Sure going to miss sharing these with her," he says.

Henrietta Butler feels the need to put her two cents in, snickering toward Greta. "That's because Mary couldn't cook a microwavable dinner."

Greta snickers in return.

"Thank you, Mr. Clemens, I'll let her out and you can feed her yourself if you'd like. If there isn't anything else you guys need, I should finish packing."

Greta reaches out and grabs my hand lightly, giving it a small little shake before backing away.
"We're going to miss you around here Miss Elle. You be safe dear."

If she only knew that this life of mine revolved around safety. I shake my head and give the sincerest smile I can manage to the kind old people. "I will Greta. And thank you all for stopping by. Take care of yourselves."

They each give me a shaky hug before making their way down the driveway. As they walk away, Brock comes jogging up to the house. Greta eyeballs his tattoos in distaste, clearly assuming he's a criminal. Kind Brock does his best to wave and smile at them, but sadly very little is returned.

"I don't think your neighbors like me, babe," is the first thing he says when he reaches my front step.

"Nah, they just associate tattoos with former prison inmates. Wear some more clothes next time, and maybe a pair of loafers."

Brock's deep laugh graces my ears. "That's not gonna happen."

"Ya, I didn't think so. What's up? I wasn't expecting to see you again."

"I wanted to see if you were still here and give something to you."

I'm hoping it's some of Sam's sugary sweets from the bakeshop, but he pulls a piece of paper out of his pocket.

"Two things actually. One is, Vinny from the gym just split with his woman so he needs a place to stay. You mentioned the lease on this place not being up, you find anyone to take it over yet?"

"No. I stopped by the leasing office yesterday and they said I could pay them to look after it until they found someone to take over the lease. No calls yet on them finding someone."

"Okay, well if you want you can tell them Vinny will take it over."

I sigh in relief, thankful that one obstacle can be taken care of.

"I don't care who takes it over Brock, I don't like the idea of paying them extra to look after this place."

"It's settled then. If you want to give them a shout when I leave, I'll send Vinny over there to fill out the paperwork."

"Sounds good. Now what's number two?"

Brock reaches out and hands me the piece of paper.

"My buddy Denny finally called. You know, the one that went to work for Callaghan? He says he's been working mostly out of Virginia but moved down to Jacksonville last weekend. I told him I was going to give you his number, that way if you need anything and I can't help out, he'll be around."

"I appreciate that Brock, but I'll be fine."

He runs his hand over his short blonde hair.

"I'm sure you will Elle, but piece of mind babe. He also offered to continue my training with you, if you're up to it."

That is one of the things I was going to miss most about not being here anymore, and to be honest I look forward to keeping up with it at home. So long as I can connect with this 'Denny' person, and not leave him bleeding on the floor like I did when I first met Brock.

"Thank you, Brock. I'll be honest though, if I don't feel comfortable with him, I won't be able to train with him."

Brock looks at me with soft eyes. He understands. I knew he would.

"I get that babe. But I'm being honest when I say Denny is one of the most solid guys I know. He may come off as a miserable bastard, mostly because he is, but he would do anything to protect the people around him. He's a good guy, Elle. Ryder gave the boys a week off, so my guess is he's drowning in whiskey and women right about now, but I told him you'd get in touch with him next week if you were interested."

I didn't catch much beyond '*Ryder gave the boys a week off*'. I'm too busy wondering why he'd be off on a job by himself, while his men are obviously living up their vacation time.

"He gave them the week off?"

Brock looks at me skeptically before responding.

"Yes. Ryder told Denny and the boys there was no work this week and to take some time off before they start some training shit near the base in Jacksonville. You alright babe?"

No, I'm not alright. But I'm not about to tell him that. I could very well be jumping to conclusions, but one would think he would want to be here, ripping that band aid off with me and sending another one of his cronies to do the job.

"Ya, all good. I just have a lot of shit on my mind, and more packing to do."

I know he can tell I'm not being completely honest with him and I hope he doesn't push me to answer. We don't talk about our personal lives so I see no reason to start now.

"Told you not to bullshit me, Elle. But if you don't want to talk about it, I won't push."

"Thanks."

He braces both hands on the doorway and leans in.

"But if you need help to pack, I'm here. Unless Ryder's helping you, not sure I need to spend more time with him."

I know they have a mutual dislike for each other. They both share a small amount of respect for what the other man does for a living, but that's where it ends.

"Ryder took most of my shit when he left this morning."

This perks Brocks ears up and he's quick to come back at me. "Why was he in such a hurry if the boys have the week off?"

I don't feel like lying right now, even though I'm damn good at it. If Ryder is up to something, I need to know about it. I could ask him, and I will when he gets back. But to say I'm intrigued as to why he ran off for work when the rest of the crew has time off would be an understatement.

"Job in Chicago."

Brock stares at me for what feels like an hour before he finally speaks again.

"Not going to tell you how to live your life, not that you'd listen anyway. But something doesn't sit right with me when it comes to him. I know as far as Denny is concerned, he assumed Ryder was still here with you. The only reason he knows that is because he's tight with the tech guy on their crew whose job it was to track you down.

"I'm all for a man tracking down the woman he loves, but babe, something is not right there. Not sure what, but do me a favor and keep your eyes wide open."

His speech makes the hairs on the back of my neck stand up. I know this feeling, it's like the calm before the storm. Soon enough, the proverbial shit will hit the fan. Not often is my gut feeling wrong, I knew something was up with Ryder this morning.

Not wanting to deal with this any longer, with Brock no less, I change the subject.

"I need to get back to packing Brock. But I promise you, I'll keep in touch and keep my eyes open."

My answer seems to placate him enough that he reaches out and pulls me in for a hug.

"You do that babe. Then you put Denny's number into your phone and call the rental office for Vinny."

I give him a quick squeeze back before letting go.

"I will. And thanks."

"No need to thank me. Safe travels babe."

He puts his fist out for a bump, which I reciprocate, before he leaves.

I watch the man who's taught me more than I will ever be able to thank him for walk down my driveway. I'm left hoping to hell that moving back to North Carolina doesn't come back to bite me in the ass.

* * *

"Come on Norm!"

THE UGLY ROSES

I holler from where I'm standing near the truck. We pulled off the highway in West Virginia so I could stretch my legs and Norma could get some exercise. I wandered around for what must be half an hour by now, watching her sniff around the trees and drink from a small pond near the rest station.

There are a few other families milling about. I'm thankful this rest stop includes a canteen, so I grabbed Norm and I each a burger when we got here.

Double patties for my healthy girl, single on mine.

I've wandered aimlessly just watching my dog and thinking about Ryder's trip to Chicago. I texted him when we left this morning, but I'm not sure if he got it because he never responded. I understand he said he would be busy with work, but I can't help but wonder why he's off working with some mayor when the rest of his guys are supposedly boozing it up in Jacksonville.

He has no reason to lie to me, or at least I don't think he does. I just can't shake the feeling that something is off. I'm not often wrong when it comes to my gut feeling either. Something's not right, and it hasn't been since he woke up yesterday morning. I think about the effort he put into searching for me when I first left, and it calms me a little. That is until I think about how he hasn't contacted me since he left, especially after he made such a big deal of finding me in the first place.

I've never been one to worry or over-analyze anything, but this new life of mine causes me to do both of those things. I can't stop now because it's what's kept me alive this long.

After my thirty or so minutes of wandering around, I come to the conclusion the only way I am going to get answers is if I ask him. Knowing that's not something I want to do over the phone, I get Norm in the truck and continue my trek toward the cottage. It'll be late when we get home, even though we got on the road after dawn. I'm emotionally and physically exhausted. I know it'll be straight to bed for me when I get there. Hopefully tomorrow my head will be clearer.

Chapter Five

"Jayne, it's me, Mrs. Anderson."

At least she knocked this time before she came in. Yesterday when I woke up in this lumpy hospital bed the snooty bitch was perched on the chair beside me, hoping for a chat. Having never met the woman in my life, it would be a huge understatement to say that I was pissed to wake up finding a stranger not only staring at me, but touching my arm.

After the hell I've been through this past week, you'd think that a psychiatrist of all people would understand my need for privacy. You would also think she understands the concept of space, meaning I don't enjoy strangers being within touching distance, and I don't appreciate being stared at.

I told her all this, along with a few carefully added curses which ended up being something like "don't look at me, don't sit near me, and definitely do not fucking touch me."

Her voice pulls me out of my thoughts from yesterday's encounter. "Jayne, how are you feeling today?"

She doesn't wait for me to ask her if she'd like to join me, but wisely she sits near the wall opposite my bed a good ten feet from me, not that I want her in the room at all. I also don't want to speak with her, so I keep my eyes trained on the window overlooking the parking lot. Not that I can see it, being that the bed is down flat, but it's the same thing I've been staring at for two days. Why change now?

"Jayne, other than your outburst with me yesterday, your doctors and the nurses mentioned that you haven't spoken since you were brought here. We know that although there's swelling in your neck and around your vocal cords, they are still functional. I'd like for you to use them today Jayne. The

police will be here again soon, and it's my job to make sure you're in the right frame of mind to speak with them."

I remain silent.

What is there to say? I don't want to talk about what happened to me, I don't want to talk about the weather and I have absolutely no desire to get to know this cold woman in a business suit in front of me.

She told me yesterday on her rant after I told her to get out, that she's been the psychiatrist on call for this hospital for years, and basically that she needs to find out whether I'm in my right mind, or if I need to be sent to the ward on the third floor.

At this point I don't care where I am, or what I'm doing. I just want silence. Peace and fucking quiet. Mrs. Anderson gets up out of her chair. Her dark hair is graying. Too much Botox leaves only her eyes and mouth to judge her mood by. Her grey suit is crisply pressed, more like something a lawyer would wear.

The sour expression on her face tells me she hates her job but likes the paycheck. This is most likely why she's the on-call psychiatrist for the hospital. Not one person in their right mind would pay this woman to pick at their brain. She's a bitch, I could tell from the moment I woke up yesterday.

She doesn't have a high-ranking practice of her own somewhere. She's paid by the province to be on call for fucked up people such as myself that end up in the hospital for medical reasons and who end up needing their heads checked before they can be sent home.

I'm no doctor, but I think it's fair to say that someone in my position is allowed all the fucking crazy they want after being held in a basement by a psychopath.

THE UGLY ROSES

"Alright look Jayne, if you let me do my job you can get out of here quicker. Your doctors informed me that you'll be held for at least eight more days. Thereafter you'll get a home nurse to change your sutures. However, that cannot happen until you speak with me. We need to verify where you're at mentally so that the police can determine what happened at the residence you were kept in."

In my opinion, Andrew's shrine of me speaks for itself— pictures of me at lunch with friends, at home raking the yard and at the park with my beautiful little girl. The blood, the knife, and the frayed rope left hanging from the beam tell the rest of the story. Self-explanatory really, aside from the two dead male bodies on the floor.

Only one deserved it.

"Jayne, I know what you've been through-"

I cut the cold bitch off, I've had enough. I'm not certifiably insane, I'm fucking miserable. There's a big difference! Why the hell would I want to talk about it? And who in their right mind would want to hear about it?

"You know? "I ask in my low raspy voice, slightly shaking my head. I can't fully move anything because my body hurts too badly. "No, Anderson, you don't know. And until you do, until you've hung in a basement for three fucking days, don't you dare try to tell me 'you know'. I'll speak with the police, I will not speak with you. Now get the fuck out of my room."

My outburst hasn't shocked her, because the bitch presses on. "Jayne, if I believe you're mentally unstable or mentally traumatized, I will invoke my right to keep you here under observation. The police have questions regarding the deaths that took place where you were held, and I need to determine if you're mentally stable to answer those questions."

"I'm breathing, I'm alive and I can see daylight. That's as stable as you're going to get right now, Anderson."

She huffs out a long breath and begins flipping through some papers in her binder.

"Very well, Ms. O'Connor."

She jots down some notes on a piece of paper before tucking the binder under her arm and looking at me. If her job was to truly assess me, if she was really concerned about my well-being, she wouldn't give in so easy. This woman is like a pill dispenser. A doctor who would rather prescribe you a medication than diagnose what the true problem is.

She signed off on my paperwork, therefore she'll get her paycheck to fund the next round of Botox injections and her weekly dry-cleaning bill.

"I'm finished here unless the detectives need to speak with me. I'll send them in on my way out."

I don't respond, and I don't watch her leave. I lie here and stare out the window, appreciating the silence, although it's short lived.

"Ms. O'Connor, we'd like to ask you a few questions regarding the incident that took place in Bakersville two days ago."

If I never heard his voice again, it would be too soon.

Detective Braumer.

The last time I heard it was after my mother, father and little girl were taken from me. I now know that Andrew, my attacker, and the man who kept me captive was responsible for their deaths. If one good thing can come of speaking to the detectives, sharing this information might be it.

THE UGLY ROSES

"Andrew was responsible for the death of my family."

I finally turn my head to gauge the reaction of Detective Braumer, as well as his kind partner Detective Miller, who jumps in to ask questions.

"Did Mr. Roberts say that Ms. O'Connor?"

Braumer cuts him off. "We're not here regarding the death of your family Ms. O'Connor, we're here because there are two dead men in a basement, and one alive and breathing woman lying in a hospital bed. We need answers and an explanation of what happened two days ago."

This sack of shit excuse for a detective has no empathy at all. Not that I expected it, but I at least would like him to acknowledge what I just said.

"My memory is fuzzy, the doctor said this is to be expected." I'm lying, but I'm also exhausted. My speech is slower, most likely from the automatic morphine drip connected to my arm. My surgeon told me that I have one hundred and sixty-two stitches in my back, three broken ribs, a fractured jaw and cheekbone, a broken wrist, dislocated shoulder and a fractured collar bone. Four units of blood were administered on arrival and I've slept for thirty-eight hours of the past forty-eight that I've been here.

"Ms. O'Connor, a forensic team has been through the basement, and we're looking for answers to put this case to rest. We need to talk about your purpose in that basement, as well as how Andrew Roberts ended up in the morgue."

I'm not coherent enough to come up with a proper story that I can remember, not that I care much about my fate at this moment so long as I can see daylight. I discreetly press the nurse call button on my bed and answer Detective Braumer.

"I told you it's a little blurry after I lost half my body weight in blood. I also just told you he admitted to killing my family. How about you look into that while I rest. Then, we'll talk more when my memory comes back."

Miller speaks up, he has a lot more compassion for people, and it's not just the good cop-bad cop routine.
"Get some rest Ms. O'Connor, we'll come back later."

Braumer apparently doesn't like being told what to do, and he tells him so. "I'm not finished yet Miller. We need answers, and I'm here to get them."

My kind old nurse with perfect timing comes bustling into the room. "Alright, everyone get out. I need to change Ms. O'Connor's sutures, and then she needs more rest. She's not going to get it with you pickin' at her. Now go."

Miller gives me a kind nod, while Braumer eyeballs me. If looks could kill, I'd be a dead woman. This man still hates me, and if I cared what people thought about me I'd look into it to figure out why. However, since I still give no fucks about that, I eyeball the miserable fuck right back before thanking my nurse.

"Thank you, Reta."

She lifts the paper cup of water to my mouth, giving me a sip before tucking me in much like a grandmother would. She's a bigger woman in her late sixties I'd guess, and clearly takes no shit from people.

I respect her immensely.

Reta folds the blankets gently around my body as I lie on my side. It's too painful to lay on my back. She adjusts something on my IV machine before leaning down close, for some reason it doesn't bother me for her to be near. Perhaps it's the age, or the eyes.

THE UGLY ROSES

Maybe both.

She stares at me kindly for a moment, not at all making me cringe. Her worn old eyes study me closely before she speaks.

"I don't know what happened exactly dear, but I can take a good guess after seeing you, and the man who took you. I was in the operating room when they brought you in, never seen anything like it in my forty years as a nurse. After we fixed you up, I went down to the morgue. I had to see him for myself."

Kind Reta puts her hand on mine and gives it a gentle squeeze before she continues in a determined way only a woman of her age could get away with at such a time.
"You fought well, dear. That's why you're up here, and he's down there. Don't ever think it should've been different, and don't you dare ever feel bad about that."

She gives me a firm nod before patting my hand and leaving the room.

She didn't change my sutures—it wasn't time to.

* * *

I take a deep breath before I open my eyes.

Water.

That's what I smell, along with the sand and the few evergreen trees outside my window. It's crisp and clean, and exactly what I missed while I was in Indy. I lie here staring at the ceiling, listening to the birds, absorbing it all.

A calm settles over me, much like when I'm in the bath. I feared coming back would revive memories of my last time here with Ryder when he saw my scars for the first time. To my surprise, I felt nothing but calm. The kind that relaxes your muscles and eases the tension in your neck.

I glance at the clock on the nightstand and see it's eight in the morning. We got in just before ten last night and I went straight to bed. Despite the dream about my time in the hospital, I feel quite rested.

I throw off the covers and stretch out my body that's a little stiff from the long drive yesterday. I take in the gold walls I painted myself, and my black furniture that definitely needs dusting before I make my way to the bathroom to start my morning routine.

Coffee on my back porch. That's all I want right now.

* * *

The weather is beautiful. The sun is shining, and Norma hasn't left the water since we came outside this morning.

It's the little things in life, and this is one of them. I'm on coffee number three and haven't had the urge to do anything other than sit here. I'm thankful I packed up most of the contents of my fridge before leaving Indy. Therefore, I don't need to leave the house today for things like milk or coffee. I can just sit and enjoy the view from my lounge. Breathing in the fresh air, exhaling the anxiety.

My phone ringing from the kitchen forces me to remove my ass from the lounge and head inside. Only two people have my number, Ryder and Brock. I look at the call display to see it's Ryder calling. In too good of a mood to be a bitch, I answer with a mild smile on my face.

"Morning, handsome."

"Morning, beautiful. I'll take a guess you're still drinking coffee and haven't left the porch yet."

Apparently my routine is predictable.

"Your guess would be correct."

His whiskey chuckle rumbles through the line. "I don't have much time, just wanted to make sure you got settled in alright."

"All good here Ryder, and thank you for bringing my bags of clothes in."

I hear voices in the background, but not close enough to make out what they are saying. Ryder begins speaking to someone but obviously covers the mic on the phone because his voice is muffled.

"Got to work. Glad you made it home babe, I'll talk to you soon."

Short, sweet and straight to the point. Normally this is a quality I like in people, being as I'm still not one to sit around and shoot the shit, but in this case it displeases me.

"Alright, bye Ryder." That's all I manage, hearing the dial tone immediately after. I know something is up and I'm determined to find out what it is when he gets back. Until then, I'm going to drink the rest of my coffee which will soon be switched to wine. Regardless of Ryder's aloof behavior, I'm happy to be back, and I'm damn well going to celebrate.

Chapter Six

*"I don't care if you lay here all day. I don't care if you
don't shower for a week. But for shit's sake you will eat
something Jayne! You can't sustain your life with only water,
and I'll be damned if I let you die on me now."*

*I stare blankly at the cream-colored wall as Laura
continues to plea with me from the doorway. I'm not listening
to her, but instead I'm wondering why I never bothered to
paint it something brighter. Was it because I knew that one day
I'd need something to focus on besides the fact that my family
was murdered and I was held captive in a basement for three
days?*

*Or did I do it because I knew this was not going to be my
forever home. It sure felt like it was at the time, but maybe the
mind knows what the heart doesn't yet understand. I know in
this moment I won't stay here. It once held the happiest
memories of my life, but now I realize the memories can come
with me. I don't need this tainted house that was photographed
repeatedly by my stalker.*

*The house is now contaminated, poisoning me from the
inside out. I'll never be the same and I'll never feel the same.
But regardless of what's happened, this place is no longer my
home.*

*"I'll fucking force feed you Jay and you know it. Now eat
the goddamn soup." I shift my eyes to the doorway, taking in
Jimmy for what feels like the first time in weeks. He looks the
same, minus the light that's normally in his eyes. His brown
hair is messy and a little longer than usual, just brushing the
tops of his ears. The stubble on his sharp jaw is longer than
usual, giving away his distress over me being captured and
beaten. His brightly colored tattoos are on display, and his
jeans are covered in paint, letting me know he's been self-*

medicating with long work hours and less sleep. I feel like cracking a joke at him, but I soon realize I don't have it in me to do so. I don't have it in me to do anything.

I don't want to eat.

I don't want to sleep.

I just want to stare at this ugly wall and remain mute for the remainder of whatever the fuck this is I'm going through. I have no idea how long I've been out of the hospital. I don't know what day or what time it is.

I just don't care.

I hear the door opening downstairs, and I register that at some point Laura got fed up with me and sent Jimmy to take her place. I don't want either of them here, but I don't say that. I would do the same for them, and I know they are only trying to help.

Jimmy pushes off of the doorway and moves to lean against the wall, blocking my line of vision to the ugly beige paint. It pisses me off because it's been my focal point since I came home. His right thigh is blocking the crack in the plaster that looks like a fucked-up letter 'L'. The 'L' has kept me awake because it was the first letter of my daughter's name. Angrily, I pull my eyes from the wall, ready to tell him to move out of the way and stop blocking the 'L'. I need the 'L'! It keeps me here, it's my focus. I no sooner open my mouth before a small cry comes from the bottom of the steps, followed by the quick thud-thud-thud-thud of someone running up the stairs.

Jimmy pushes off the wall faster than I could tell him to. I'm thankful yet half-concerned at the weeping coming from the hallway outside my bedroom.

"J-J-Jimmmy."

He is at her side in an instant. "What the hell, Laura?"
"H-he-he's n-no-not d-d-d-dead."

For once in what feels like a lifetime, my body and mind react at the same time. I twist my neck, trying to avoid tearing open the stitches on my back. I push myself up on my elbows so I can face my terrified friend who's the closest thing I have to a sister. I stare blankly as she trembles, dropping what's in her hands to the old wooden floor.

I blink my eyes; certain I must've seen it wrong. I'm not so fortunate as I register the black petals that have fluttered to the floor.

My mind flashes back and his voice grates on my ears, like it was just yesterday he spoke into them. He spoke the words that only now make sense, the words I ignored at the time.

I open my mouth and speak them from memory. At the same time, Jimmy reads the note card, his eyes snapping to mine. Our voices blend together as we say the words that'll send me away from the place I once called home.

"Black flowers for a black heart."

They aren't just black—they're dead. I allow myself one last look at the ugly roses, allowing them to seal my fate.

Jayne O'Connor died in Andrew's basement. Whoever I am now needs to go.

* * *

I've been home for a few days. It's now Monday.

I haven't heard anything else from Ryder, so I'm not sure if he's coming home tomorrow or not.

THE UGLY ROSES

Yesterday I dug out most of my casework and started searching for any signs indicating that Andrew had a twin brother. I looked through the few photographs the police took from his home, not that there are many. After going over each of the pictures with a magnifying glass I noticed there were no photographs in any of the rooms of his house, much like my home here where there's nothing personal—almost unlived in.

One thing that stood out to me was that there was no computer, only a desk where there should be one. If I were a detective, this would've stood out to me, but there was no mention of it in the case file.

I stayed up until two in the morning trying to wrap my head around it all again, trying to come at it from a different angle; the angle that there were two brothers, not just one. The only conclusion I have is the obvious one: if Andrew Roberts does indeed have a brother, then perhaps the mother separated them at birth, and the grandmother that raised Andrew didn't know about the other twin. If she did, surely you'd think she would've taken both. What grandparent would separate her twin grandsons?

But *why*? And why in the first place did the *mother* separate them and give them up? I don't get it.

Deciding my mind needs a break, I grab my burner off the counter. I tossed and turned last night and after finally falling asleep the nightmares came flooding in. There's only two ways I've learned to burn off enough steam to sleep. Since Ryder isn't here, that only leaves me one option. I put the phone to my ear and wait.

"Black."

I wasn't expecting him to pick up on the first ring, or answer with his last name. Since it's just barely been a week since Brock spoke with his friend Denny, I don't elaborate when I respond.

"It's Elle."

He clears his throat and his rough voice responds. "Wasn't expecting you to call so soon."

Since he's not trying to bore me with pleasantries, I assume he must be my kind of person. Either that or Brock mentioned I don't do small talk.

"Well, I need to get back to the gym. Are you free to meet with me today?"

He cuts straight to the chase. "Our team has a room rented in the Mannick building, it's off Eighty Third on the south side of the city. Use the west entrance. It's on the second floor, room 201. I'll be there around seven if you want to meet."

It's only four now. As much as I was hoping to meet up with him sooner, I'll take what I can get at this point in hopes that I'll sleep better tonight.

"I'll be there."

* * *

Not wanting any questions thrown at me right away, I put on a light long sleeve sweater to wear to the gym. Once I get some gloves or tape on my hands, Denny won't notice the marks on my wrists. I put a light layer of bronzing cream on my already tanned neck to cover the strangle marks and wear a dark short sleeve top so if any rubs off on my shirt it won't be noticeable.

I have no trouble finding the Mannick Building in Jacksonville. It's about six stories tall and mostly made of glass. I enter the west entrance and use the directions Denny gave me to find room 201. This whole building seems dedicated to health and wellness. Most of the rooms are private, but I noticed the main gym, which was visible through the floor to ceiling windows, is located on the ground floor.

Thankful for the privacy beyond the first floor, I open the door to room 201 and see a familiar setup to Brock's gym. There's a boxing ring directly in front of me, the space to the right is filled with weights and a few workout machines. The entire left portion of the gym is mats, like I used to work out on with Brock. My body would have been bruised from tip to toe without them.

I hear a door open from behind the ring and see a giant headed in my direction. I thought Ryder was a big man. Sweet Jesus, not next to this one. Denny is the definition of big. He's probably an inch or two taller than Ryder, and has an extra twenty pounds on him. His skin is not as tanned as Ryder's and I can tell from this distance that the blue of his eyes has probably melted *many-o-panties* off the ladies. His longish dirty blonde hair is tied back at his neck and I only notice one visible tattoo on his arm. Writing of some sort that I plan to read once he gets closer.

"Elle."

The incredibly deep voice suits the man. I nod my head. "And you're Denny Black."

He extends his hand toward me and I get a closer look at the writing.

Grace.

"Denver. Friends call me Denny. Nice to meet you. Brock told me a little about where you guys were at with your training. He also told me this might not work out, you and me doing this. What's your take on it?"

I love a man that gets straight to the point. I'm not uncomfortable around him yet, so I assume I won't be later.

Knowing he's a friend of Brock's, and also an employee of Ryder's, I'm ready to give this a shot.

"Only one way to find out."

He looks me over from top to bottom before nodding his head.

"Good answer. How about you get your training gloves on and I'll meet you on the mats."

Denny turns around and heads toward the room he came from while I head over to the bench beside the mats. I take out my tape and gloves and work quickly getting myself ready after I take my sweater off. I throw my dark hair up in a messy knot on top of my head to keep it out of my face.

I begin warming up with some stretches when Denny comes out of the back room with punching pads and a bottle of water. His muscles strain against his black shirt. He's removed the jogging pants he had on and changed into red gym shorts.

"Alright Elle, let's start out with some basics so I can get a feel of where you're at, we'll go from there."

I nod my head and get lined up with him before he raises the pads. I study the faint haunted look in his eyes until he gestures toward my hands, "You know the drill girl, hit me."

I give it everything I've got, for some reason wanting to impress this man instead of look like some pussy wanting to prove a point. I've worked my ass off these past few months with Brock, and I hope it shows.

I begin punching at the pads, and surprisingly quick, we develop a rhythm. Judging by his face, I assume he's a little caught off guard that I'm not the weak little duckling he presumed I might be.

THE UGLY ROSES

"That's good, Elle. Leg work now."

I nod my head and jump right into the leg work, starting with knee jabs up into the pads, and moving into full out kicks. We continue this pattern for about ten minutes before he tosses the pads to the side of the mats.

"When Brock told me you two had only been working together for a few months, I wasn't expecting you to be this far ahead. Did you train with someone before then?"

I take a swig of my water before answering. "Nope."

He too takes a drink of his water before studying me. "Good way to get your anger out then."

I look at his incredibly blue eyes and nod my head. "That it is."
We silently stare each other off for a few moments, me taking in his chiseled face and broad shoulders, and him trying to figure me out before he breaks the silence.

"Hand to hand. I want you to use your arms more. Your legs will get someone down, but you need more upper body strength."

This isn't news to me, I recall Brock saying the same thing. My jogging keeps my legs in great shape, but I don't do much with my arms other than when I was training with Brock.

We practice a few of the moves I'm familiar with, and to my surprise I feel like I'm back in Indy at *Fist*. Obviously these two developed a technique together because their moves are quite similar.

I see Denny's right hand coming at me. *I know this move.* He's going to fake out and use his left to grab my arm and spin me around before it forces me to my knees. I move quickly and dive low, bringing my left hand up to block his move and jabbing my elbow back into his stomach.

Clearly he could kick my ass if he really wanted too, but that's not what this is about. I don't wait for a second to pass before tugging on his arm and bringing my foot down on his leg.

"Fuck. Damn Elle, you're full of surprises." Denny chuckles.

I know I didn't hurt him, but I'm thankful I got him down to one knee, even if he wasn't giving it his all. I brush the hair out of my face and the sweat off my forehead.

"You and I both know you could've kicked my ass by now."

Denny stands up and uses his shirt to wipe the sweat off his brow. As much as I enjoy going to bed with Ryder, I'm not dead. I move to sit on the bench and discreetly admire the black ink that is partially hidden behind his shorts while he cleans himself up.

"Yes, I could have. But I'm not most men, Elle."

No, he definitely is not.

"I make a living doing this, you pull on a regular man what you just pulled on me, and he'd still be lying there."

"Yes, let's hope so," I say in a low voice, not meaning to but it just came out. I ignore his questioning gaze and quickly change the subject. "I appreciate you doing this Denny. I'm not sure how often you have time, I used to train with Brock three nights a week."

He runs a towel over his face again before tossing it on the bench.

"Well that explains it. Most guys went three times a week. Women only went for the self-defense classes a few times a month."

I shake my head as I recall the group woman I hope to never see again. "Well, I'm thankful I never have to work out with those PTA moms again. What's your schedule like, and do you want the same fee I paid Brock?"

Denny rubs the back of his neck before he looks at me. "Not sure the boss man wants us making cash out of this room, Elle. I'm doing this as a favor to both Brock, and Ryder."

That gets my guard up.

"I don't want any favors Denny, and I don't do handouts. If you have a life to live and this is taking up that time, let me know. I came here because I thought this is what you were doing while you guys were out of work, not because you owed someone something."

He holds his large hands up in a placating gesture.
"That's not what I meant girl, but either way I'm here most nights anyway. Or at least I have been since we got back to Jacksonville."

"Well if I had of known that I would've come sooner. Brock said you guys had the week off, or at least until tomorrow I assumed when Ryder gets back, so I didn't want to disturb you."

He looks at me, a little confused. "Thought Ryder was with you? In Indy?"

This is more confirmation that something isn't right, I can feel it in the hairs on the back of my neck.

"He left early for Chicago."

Denny averts his eyes from mine and stares at the boxing ring for a moment before speaking again. "I'm here a lot Elle, you want to work with me just call or text when you want to come in. Mondays, I usually work out in the morning. Today was an exception. Other than that, I spend a lot of nights here."

He seems lost in thought, so I don't disturb him or ask more questions. My questions will be saved for when Ryder gets back. I take off my gloves and grab my bag.

"Thanks. I'll be in touch."

He nods his head and grabs his own gear before heading to the back room.

I make my way toward the exit wondering what in the hell is going on with Ryder Callaghan that even his men don't know why he's in Chicago.

I get in my truck, very much on auto pilot and nearly hit a pedestrian on my way out of the lot. I curse my thoughts of Ryder, and force myself to focus on the fact that I've found someone else to add to list of people I can trust.

My time with Denny may have been short, a little over an hour. But it only took me five seconds to determine whether he was a good person or not. It's all in the eyes, and a little in the way people carry themselves. After experiencing both good and evil, I think I'm a bit of an expert on character.

I spent a few summers in university taking a psychology class so I could get to know people on a deeper level. Trying to understand what makes them who they are, and what shapes them into who they become. I'm not sure whether I should be grateful for the classes, or for my experience to allow me to be such a good judge of character, but either way I'm thankful for having met Brock West, and in turn his leading me to Denny Black.

Chapter Seven

Ten Years Ago.

"Counseling on Campus. This is Gina speaking, how may I help you today?"

Week number five here at the center and I already want to drop my psychology class. I chose to take it as a bit of a filler, to eat up some of my downtime in the summer. That and my curiosity toward people as a whole made me interested in studying them on a deeper level.

I've always believed I have a natural ability to read people. Not often am I wrong, or at least I haven't been. I assumed volunteering at Counseling on Campus would enable me to put some of these skills to good use.

No such luck.

So far I've dealt with calls like, "my boyfriend of two months dumped me, and since he's in most of my classes I need to change my major because it's too hard to look at him every day." And then, "I went to the spring mixer last weekend and ate a bad batch of mushrooms that put me in the hospital for two days, so I couldn't finish my essay. Do you think I can submit it late? You know, since I was in the hospital?"

No! You dumb shit! You put yourself in the hospital!

Of course I can't say that. No, I'm here to help. No matter how ridiculous your complaints are. So here I am answering the phone, hoping I can actually help whoever is on the other end of the line.

"Hi Gina. It's Matty again. I asked for you specifically, I hope that's okay?"

Ah, Matthew. He's one of the sweeter ones that call. The guy sort of reminds me of the slightly dorky kid in school that gets a bad rap, but he's actually incredibly sweet and very intelligent.

I'm sure Matt is not his real name, much like mine is not Gina. When you work in the center they ask you to use an alias, that way the students feel more comfortable, and so do you in the event you did run into one another.

"Hey Matty boy, what's shakin'?"

This is probably the sixth time I've talked to Matt. He calls frequently, always unsure of himself. Always asking if 'that's okay' in regard to his decision making, always needing a second opinion. Or maybe it's reassurance? Either way the kid has no self-esteem. He's very polite and if I could guess I would say he either grew up with a father who never gave him a pat on the back, or he grew up without a family at all.

I know he doesn't have many friends. He told me so. Matty prefers to do as much work from home as he can, taking most of his courses online.

"I just wanted to tell you that I had a really good day today, Gina. Someone made an anonymous donation to my scholarship."

"What? That's awesome Matty! Congrats! I still don't know what it is you're going to school for, but either way that's pretty exciting. Are you going out to celebrate?"

I am certain the answer will be no. Matty doesn't do crowds, much less people.

"No Gina, I have a lot to do. I haven't been working as hard, knowing I wouldn't be able to finish. Now I have a lot to get caught up on."

THE UGLY ROSES

Poor Matty. Such a sweet kid. Makes me wish I knew who he was so I could take the poor lad out and buy him a beer.

If he's even nineteen.

"Well Matty, my recommendation would be to go and treat yourself to a good meal and a cold one at The Tap." *I reference my favorite watering hole, hoping the kid takes the hint and gets out more. I would even offer to buy him a beer, if I were allowed to meet up with the people that call in here.*

"Thanks Gina, but I think I'm just going to stay in and get caught up on my school work."

This is where some of these kids go nuts. I'm all for dedicating time to your studies. I've spent the past three years with my nose buried in the books here. However, one thing I realized over time is that we all need a break. Otherwise you're bound to pull your hair out.

"Matty, you do whatever it is that you need to in order to sleep at night. But let me remind you, as much as I believe that school is a necessity in order to get a great job, it's also imperative you take some time for you. Remember that Matty. I know you've had a bit of a rough month. You had a few family issues, and then lacked the funds to continue your education. Just remember it's totally okay to take five and do something for yourself. Okay Matty?"

He's silent on the other end of the phone for a few moments before he replies in his usual soft, timid voice.
"Thanks Gina. Maybe if I get a little more caught up tonight I'll take some time tomorrow for myself."

That's Matty. He could never outright say 'no' to anyone. If I told him to go and rob a bank right now, he'd probably do it. The entire time he would know it's the wrong thing to do, but he's a people pleaser. "Anyway, I just wanted to share some *good news with you for once. I'll call you back soon, okay Gina?"*

"Okay Matty, you take care of yourself. Talk soon."

* * *

I feel warmth on my face, followed by the movement of a hand. Not used to waking up with someone touching me, and knowing I went to bed alone, I jackknife up from the bed while shoving my hand under the pillow for my gun.

"Elle, it's me!"

I whip my head around to find Ryder sitting on top of the covers on the opposite side of the bed. I let out a huge breath and shove my gun back under the pillow.

"Tip for you Ryder: do not wake me up like that when you didn't sleep here the night before, unless you want a bullet in your body."

I'm heaving. My heart is racing fast and I can feel the angry tears threatening my eyes. How dare he, and how the hell did he get in here?

"Jesus, I'm sorry. I just got back and wanted to see you." He pleads with a mildly irritated look on his face. He probably thinks we're past my jitters and jumpiness. It will take a lot more than a few nights together before that changes.

I turn away from him and climb out of bed, heading toward the bathroom. I shut the door and lock it behind me, then do the same to the other door that connects to the hallway. Not wanting to hear anything else he has to say at the moment, I turn on the shower and strip out of my sweat soaked clothes. Hands shaking the entire time.

THE UGLY ROSES

Once again, this is the norm. I expect it whether my nightmares are full of fear, or just memories of the past. What I didn't expect was to feel someone touching me when I woke up.

Feeling his hand on me reminded me of my past. When I woke up in Andrew's smashed up car, an old man had his hand on my shoulder, gently nudging me. Trying to wake me up.

"Easy there dear, you hit the hydro pole. You stay still, now. I called the po-lice, help is on the way."

I don't know what I hit, or what I did to him when he woke me up. I just clutch the blood-soaked towel to my chest, ignoring the pained expression on his face as he registers my beaten body.

I grab my shampoo and begin to lather my hair, thinking of the person who helped me. He was a kind older man. He wanted to help when I escaped Andrew's basement and crashed his car, only I lost my shit when I felt his hand on my shoulder. In that moment, I didn't remember escaping the basement and crashing. I felt like I was still in there, in that cold damp place and he was waking me up to torture me again. It wasn't the old man's fault and I feel awful for the way I screamed at him, but it was out of my control.

My body may have escaped the basement, but my mind was still there.

I get under the hot spray, washing away the filth and the memories, preparing to put my armor back on before I leave the bathroom. I know it's not just my memories that are making me pissed off right now, it's Brock's comments about Ryder and Denny's confusion when I mentioned that Ryder was in Chicago for work.

I get out of the shower and proceed with my hair and make-up. I don't bother flat ironing right now, so I settle for a blow dry and leave my dark hair in loose long waves. I put on my robe and venture through my room toward the closet. Ryder is not in here, which I'm thankful for, so I continue and get dressed in a long black cut-off sleeve top, paired with black Capri tights. I put on my wrist cuffs and find a pair of heeled gladiator sandals with a wide band around the ankle that cover my marks. I tie it all together with a light scarf around my neck.

Armor on, ready for confrontation.

I smelled the coffee from the shower, so I know Ryder is still here. I make my way toward the kitchen and find it empty. I glance through the screen and see that he's on my back porch so I head for the coffee maker.

I make my morning brew and step outside. Ryder is sitting at the small table by my barbecue. Knowing I can't let this stew any longer, I head over and sit down. I take my spot facing the water. His chair is beside me, facing toward his own home.

He's dressed in a pair of black dress slacks and a white button down shirt, not any usual attire I've seen on him before. I don't take Ryder for the type of man that dresses to impress people, but I'm not ready to ask him about that either. Thankfully, he breaks the silence.

"I didn't mean to scare you, Elle. I have a key to this place, have for a long time. I knew you were still sleeping. Not wanting to wake you up, I used the key. I wanted to see you, but if that's what's going to happen when I let myself in, trust me I'll knock next time."

I take a sip of my coffee and light up a smoke. Every time I think I'm closer to cutting back I find an excuse to light one back up again.

THE UGLY ROSES

"It's not about you using the key Ryder. If I had of known you were coming back while I would still be in bed I would've expected you and not have attempted to shoot you."

His head whips around to mine. "I told you I would be back by Tuesday, Elle."

I shake my head at him. "You didn't tell me you'd be waking me up on Tuesday morning Ryder. Because you never told me a time. You said you would keep in touch and let me know. I've not heard from you since the morning after the night I got back here." I shake my head in exasperation, "Look, I'm not a needy woman Ryder, never have been. But don't think for one second that you kept me in the loop, because you did no such thing."

He scrubs his hands over his face, indicating his frustration. "Fuck Elle, I'm sorry alright. I'm sorry. I didn't mean to scare you beautiful, I promise you that."

I take a good look at the handsome man in front of me. He looks tired, worn down. Like Chicago kicked his ass. I calm myself and my voice before speaking to him again. "What was so important in Chicago, Ryder? And please don't lie to me."

He doesn't look at me right away, or even acknowledge that I've spoken. He stares across my property toward his own. I take the opportunity to admire his profile. His strong jaw has two days' worth of stubble. His hair is messy from the wind and I assume he hasn't had a shower this morning. The whiskey voice I've grown to love pulls me out of my ogling.

"Been working that job on and off for over a year, Elle. Sometimes people expect things from you after you work with them, they expect *more*. I try to make everyone happy but it doesn't always work out that way. It's done now; I don't need to go back anymore."

I study him for honesty. If he looked me in the eye, I would be able to get him a whole lot sooner, but he's not. Eye contact is a necessity for me when it comes to respect, which ultimately means trust. He's giving me neither at the moment and speaks again before I can question it. This time thankfully he looks at me.

"We all have to do things we don't want to sometimes, Elle. Running a business isn't always easy babe, but it's *my* business. I need to keep people happy, in order to keep working. That's what Chicago was about."

He looks torn, like maybe he needs to sleep for the next three days before he can give me a straight answer.

"As I said, I'm not a needy woman Ryder. I never will be. It's not my style. That being said, I can't give you a piece of me that I don't get in return. You asked to know where I was when I was late getting home in Indy. You made a big deal about finding me, only to ignore me for the past week. You talked about not being able to take my 'up and down shit'. Well I can't take your 'hot and cold' shit.

"One week you're racing across the country, you've got my bank transactions flagged and you're hunting me down at the wine store. The next week I hear from you once for all of twenty seconds and your MIA again. So like I said, I'm not needy, but don't you dare expect something from me that you're not willing to give in return."

Ryder puts his elbows on the table and rests his head in his hands. I don't know what it is about this Chicago job that has him so put out, but if I were him, I would've dropped that contract a long time ago if this is what happens to him. Brock mentioned he picks and chooses his work, if that's so I'd start picking somewhere else.

THE UGLY ROSES

"It was selfish of me to say that Elle, I know. But I worry about you, more than you need to worry about me. Does that make sense?"

I think about it for a moment and have a question before I answer him truthfully. "No Ryder, it doesn't make sense to me. Because I think if you truly worried about me, you would've been calling me every day. Not that I want that, you know I barely have shit to say on a good day unless we're arguing about something. But if your reason was because you worry more, you'd think that you'd be burning out the ringer on my phone every morning and night. Wondering if I woke up and wondering when I went to bed."

His sad eyes meet mine, knowing what he's going to say but not speaking yet. I study him. His hair looks like it still has product in it. I study his pressed shirt and slacks. His dress shoes. This is not the man I met months ago. Or it is but boxed in different packaging.

"When I found Norma that day, I asked the guys to bring up the GPS trackers on all the BMW SUV's that were on that street and send them to me. There was only one that frequented that address where Norm was. I didn't disable the notifications, because when I was busy working in Chicago, it gave me piece of mind seeing your vehicle was parked at home every night, even if you were out through the day. It let me know that you were okay, and home."

I slam my coffee mug down on the table and push my chair back. Ryder grabs the arms of it to prevent me from escaping. "Don't Elle. I never, not once kept that to invade your privacy. I just didn't fast track the process of disabling it. There is someone in this world hell bent on seeing you dead, so if when I'm working and don't have the time to call, I was damn fucking thankful that I at least had a way of knowing you were alive. I didn't look where you went or check your bank records to see what you did. All I looked at was that the vehicle left the house and returned back home. I'm sorry Elle if that upsets you, but you need to understand that when I know someone out there wants to harm the woman I care about, I will feel no fucking guilt for doing what I could to make sure she was okay.

"Ultimately babe, I would outfit the piss poor fucking security in this place and put two men on your door at night. I know you won't go for that so please, give me this. Let me know you got home at night."

I don't know what to say to him right now.

I'm pissed.

I understand a little where he's coming from, I get why he wants to know that I'm okay and I'm almost thankful for it. After all, at the end of the day he's the only person in the USofA that knows a little of my story, so if I were to find myself dead with the identification of Elle Davidson on me, not a soul would know that I'm also Jayne O'Connor.

I turn away from him and light up another smoke. He lets go of the arms on the chair, knowing I'm not running from him.

"I can understand why you did what you did Ryder. But it doesn't mean I like it. What I don't understand is why you couldn't just shoot me a text like a normal person. Because ultimately Ryder, in the time it takes you to read my GPS whereabouts, you could read a text. That's the part I'm not understanding right now."

He reaches his hand out and puts it on top of mine.

"I'm not used to this shit, any more than you are, beautiful. I'm not used to wanting to know where someone is, or caring about them enough to do so. What I know is tracking people; it's all I've known for a long time. I'm not saying that to condone what I did. I'm telling you that because we're learning this new 'Elle' together. We're also learning this new 'Ryder' together. I'm thirty-six beautiful, and as much as you may think my relationship with Anna was conventional, it wasn't. I didn't ask her what she did, and she didn't ask me. I was overseas. I didn't have the ability to talk to her every day."

"Yes Ryder, and this here is the difference. I'm not saying I need to speak with you every day, but you weren't exactly in Afghanistan either. You *chose* not to. That's the difference Ryder."

He turns his chair toward mine, pushing our knees together until we're face to face. His deep, dark, silver rimmed eyes stare back into mine before he speaks.

"I fucked up, beautiful. I get that. I apologize. Now fucking forgive me and let me learn from it, just like I forgive you with your up and down shit. We're learning here Elle, can't learn until you make the mistake. Forgive me."

I take a long hard look at the beautiful man in front of me. Whether the old bird's think his tattoos make him look like a prison inmate or not, he's the most attractive man I've ever laid eyes on; his dark hair and black eyes, his tanned skin complemented with art. Ryder is an incredibly perceptive man who has sacrificed his life for others without a second thought.

My father may not be alive today, but he'd be proud of me sharing my life with someone such as Ryder Callaghan. He's selfless, and he's caring, regardless of the shitty ways he's proved that. If there were a way for my father to track me while I was a teenager, he would've done so. However, cell phones were still incredibly new back then and GPS trackers in vehicles were null and void.

"I don't ever want to be referred to as 'the old ball and chain' Ryder. That's not my goal here. I also don't want you to think of me as the woman who sticks her nose where it doesn't belong. What I need you to understand is that you're the only person in this whole damn country who knows who I really am, so when you take off for a job that your men are not even aware of, well that puts up a few red flags for me. The biggest flag being I'm not ready to go back to Canada yet, and you could very well send me back there.

"I'm still wanted for questioning Ryder, and when I don't know what you're up to, and your men don't, that makes me wonder who it is I can trust. It makes me wonder who's lying and what is really going on here."

He puts his hand on my leg and looks shocked at what I've said.

"What do you mean 'my men'? Who's been around here Elle?"

I'm a little shocked that this is his question. Regardless, I answer. "Nobody has been here Ryder. I spent some time training with Denny, he mentioned you being with me in Indy, and I informed him you left before I did for work in Chicago. To say he looked surprised would be an understatement. However he never elaborated on the subject at all and I didn't ask. I saved my questions for you."

Ryder pushes his chair away from the table and begins pacing the deck, one hand on his hip, one scrubbing his face. I hate second guessing myself, and I know he's a good man. But I have every right to ask what I did. I'm practically here illegally; I've certainly been here long enough. I know little of his work or this mystery job in Chicago. His explanation seemed legit enough, but I'm still curious as to why he was so secretive about it.

"Is this how it's going to be Elle? You not believing what I say, and you asking my men my whereabouts?"

I too stand up out of my chair and stomp over until I'm standing in front of him, pointing my finger at his chest.

"Don't you fucking dare. I just told you I didn't want to seem like I'm sticking my nose where it doesn't belong. I didn't prod Denny for information, I answered a question that he asked. Or more like a statement, seeing as he said you were 'with me in Indy' to which I corrected him and said you left early for Chicago."

Angry eyes stare back at mine. "Well I was in Chicago, I didn't fucking lie to you Elle. I'm not always going to be able to share my work with you, seeing as the majority of it is confidential. And I won't tolerate you talking about me with my fucking men, Elle."

I stand as tall as my sandals will let me before I lean into his face. This conversation is getting us nowhere.

I thought I had anger issues? I'm not the only one.

"Remember that part of me telling you I didn't want you to think I stuck my nose where it didn't belong?"

Since he's still a lot taller than I am, he leans down so our faces are inches apart.

"I'm not fucking deaf, woman."

I seethe at his words, spitting my own right back. "Good, because you won't need to worry about that tonight when you go to bed. Alone."

I turn away from him and head for the house. I reach out for the door, swinging it open as I look over my shoulder. He's standing there, fuming, staring back at me.

"And take that fucking tracking shit off of my truck."

With that last parting shot I slam the storm door and lock it. I know it won't do much good considering he has a key, but after this morning he'd be pretty goddamn stupid to surprise me again in my own house, unless he wants a bullet planted in his ass.

Chapter Eight

I slept like shit.

I tossed and turned all night regardless of the amount of wine I drank. One bonus to that I suppose is when I don't fall asleep, I don't have nightmares.

Knowing I can't put off the grocery store much longer, and not wanting to lie in bed and stew over my argument with Ryder, I pull my sorry ass out of bed and head for the bathroom. I don't want to sit on my porch this morning, I just need to keep busy.

I'd like to say I'm genuinely upset that I slept alone last night, but I'm not. Being alone is something that I'm used to. Do I enjoy a warm body to sleep next to? Of course. However, that body belonging to someone who tells lies is something I won't tolerate.

Ever.

The day is mild but cloudy, so I throw on a pair of torn skinny jeans with my high brown boots and a loose black top. Once again, my attire is paired together with cuffs, a knife in my boots and a gun in my bag.

I put on a pair of hangover sunglasses and give Norma a pat on the head as I exit the house, travel mug in hand filled with my morning brew. I descend the steps, scanning my surroundings on the way to my truck. Ryder's big Ford is not parked in his driveway, not that I expected it to be. If he and his men were in fact getting back to work today, it would make sense that he's not home. With that in mind I head for town. I plan to contact Denny today to see if we can make alternate arrangements for working out.

As much as I was comfortable working out with him in room 201, he did say that it's rented out to his crew. That means Ryder must've done the renting. Not wanting him to get his panties in a twist because I'm working in his room with his men, I hope to make other plans.

I turn up the heavy rock station on my stereo and begin the drive toward town, trying not to fret too much over how much of a prick Ryder was yesterday. The thing that really gets me is he knows I don't just sit around and 'shoot the shit' with people, much less ask about their personal lives, so his blow up about me speaking with Denny confuses me.

What about when he got pissed at me for picking up and leaving the first time? All that shit he spewed at me about not actually asking him for an explanation? He was furious I took his ex-fiancé Anna's words over his own.

So, shouldn't he be giving me some sort of credit now? Seeing as I sat him down and asked him about Chicago, as opposed to jumping to conclusions? I may have done so in my mind, but I definitely gave him the chance to explain himself. Which he did, a little. Just not enough for me to believe that he's actually telling me the whole truth. Especially after his blow up. To me that just screams guilty conscience.

I pull into the Green Grocer and grab an abandoned cart from the parking lot. I've pretty much exhausted my supplies at home, so I begin at the first isle, working my way through them all to pick up what I need. I grab everything from ketchup to eggs, then somewhere between the papayas and bananas I hear his voice, only he's not speaking to me.

"You'll need to find someone else. I have contracts lined up here on the East Coast that can't be put off."

I don't mean to eavesdrop, but I can't help but overhear the conversation taking place from somewhere behind me. I turn around to see how far away he is and recognize the back of his head by the meat counter.

THE UGLY ROSES

"I did what you wanted me to do. Our contract is finished."

He pulls his phone away from his ear and sticks it in his pocket. Not wanting to linger any longer, I toss my handful of bananas into the cart and head for the checkout.

I'm loading my seven bags of groceries and two bags of alcohol into the back of my SUV when his voice washes over me.

"I turned the tracking notifications off."

I close the hatch on my truck and begin to steer my cart to the return spot, but not before glancing through my sunglasses at Ryder. He's dressed in jeans, a dark t-shirt and boots. I may be pissed at him but I can still admit he looks good.

"Good to know."

I park the cart and walk toward the door of my truck where Ryder is standing.

"I shouldn't have been angry with you like that yesterday, Elle."

His hands are in his pockets and his sunglasses are on his head. I like that I'm able to see his eyes, and I appreciate him apologizing. The only problem is I just don't want to deal with it right now.

"No, you shouldn't have. I guess we both have anger issues."

I reach the handle for the truck, opening it and climbing into my seat.

"Elle, I'd like to talk."

I close the door and look at him through the open window. I let out an exasperated sigh and slightly shake my head. Maybe I can't do sex *and* emotions? As much as I thought I could make this work between us I realize I'm losing sight of what's most important, which is finding the other twin and solving my case.

It wouldn't be the first-time sex has clouded my judgment, as well as my priorities. It is the first time however that emotions have been in the mix. The only way I'm going to get this straightened out is by solely working with Ryder and not sleeping with him. It's obvious I can't do both, or at least not right now.

"Ryder, we only do one thing well together, and it's not talking. So either we stick with fucking each other senseless, or we only remain friends. It's clear we can't do both."

He reaches out and places a hand on the side mirror.

"I think you're wrong, Elle."

"Well then Ryder, you have a few days to figure out how to prove that. Not to be a bitch, but I'm tired and I don't want to deal with it right now."

He eyes go soft before he replies. "You having more nightmares?"

I shake my head and put the truck in gear. "You going to tell me more about Chicago?"

He nods his head reluctantly, not willing to answer, and moves away from my truck. Clearly he too has shit he needs to work on, if yesterday's outburst is any indication.

* * *

THE UGLY ROSES

"Damn, you don't fuck around."

I watch Denny take in the beauty that is the third floor. After Ryder's blow up the other day, I took it upon myself to call and book my own room at the Mannick Building. I discovered that the third floor has smaller rooms but cater to a classier clientele.

The size of the room is only about a third of the one that Ryder's men use downstairs. To the right when you walk in is a counter with fresh fruit and juices, accompanied by two comfortable black chairs and a table. The middle of the room is made up entirely of mats, and the left side holds a few workout machines and a weight set. It's not what I'm used to, but it's more than I need. The furniture smells new, and the glass wall behind the table and chairs gives a great view of the water.

It's perfect.

"I'm a straight shooter Denny. I told you on the phone that Ryder could have an issue with us working out together. He doesn't want me anywhere near his work life. So, if at any time you feel like this could fuck up your work relationship with him, you let me know. I rented the room. You're supposed to be off work hours, so I'm hoping we can still make a go of this."

Denny turns around from checking out the juice bar and leans back against the counter, crossing his arms over his broad chest. He's in a white short sleeve shirt and long black shorts. His biceps are bigger around than my thighs. Oddly enough I still have no fear around him.

"Not sure what's going on between you two, and it's not my business. Much like what I do on my free time is not Ryder's business. I respect him Elle, and I enjoy working with him. But what I do outside of work is my choice to make. Not his."

I take a long hard look at the good looking, large man in front of me and nod my head. "Good answer. Now, let's hit the mats so you can kick my ass. Brock used to leave me with bruises. You barely gave me an excuse to have a bath last time."

A deep laugh graces my ears, not quite as beautiful as Ryder's, but enough to make me smile a little.

"Alright girl, center of the mat. And don't bitch if you can't walk tomorrow."

I think about the last time I couldn't walk, but it involved being pounded into a different type of mat with a different man.

I pull my mind out of the gutter and proceed to getting my ass kicked.

Chapter Nine

If my stiff and sore body is any indication, Denny well and truly kicked my ass yesterday. I don't regret a single minute of it, seeing as I slept like a rock without any nightmares.

Ryder texted me last night while I was in the bath, asking if I was ready to speak with him. I told him when he saw me awake and on my porch in the morning that he could come over.

I brush my teeth and wash my face before heading out to the lounge with my coffee. I haven't been smoking as much recently, but I bring them out with me knowing this conversation with Ryder could spark my need for them. Pun intended.

I sit down on the lounge and watch Norm waddle her way toward the water. The sun is out today but the weather is a little cooler, a sign that fall is approaching. The lower temperatures don't bother me much anymore. It gives me the opportunity to dress in clothing that completely covers my body, avoiding the need for decorative scarves and bracelets.

I hear footsteps approaching and turn my head to see Ryder making his way toward me, coffee in hand. He's dressed in loose running pants and a white short sleeve shirt that makes his tan skin stand out. His long dark hair is bedroom messy, which will make this conversation more difficult as I remember waking up with that same hair in my bed not too long ago.

He climbs the steps and comes to sit on the lounge, not up beside me this time. He sits at the foot of it. I appreciate the small moment of silence to memorize his profile again.

"You want to start, or do you want me to?" he asks.

Typical Ryder, well, typical on a good day. Thinking about me, and what I'd like first.

"I think we have two options Ryder. I need your help, you know I do. I don't ask for help often, so please don't take that lightly. The other option is for you to distance yourself from my personal life, and me from yours. Meaning our relationship would be that of neighbors who occasionally fuck each other."

His head whips around fast to face mine. "Not fucking happening, Elle."

I sadly shake my head. "There's no other option for you Ryder. I'm going to be selfish about this and tell you that I need your help, more than I need your dick. You said it yourself we're both learning this relationship stuff, so let's put it on the back burner while we figure my case out. We've already proven we can't do both without tearing each other's heads off. Keeping myself alive is more important than sharing a bed with someone right now, Ryder. If that doesn't work for you then we toss it all aside and just share each other's beds while I figure it out on my own."

His frustrated black eyes stare back at me while he shakes his head, his posture tight. "Why do you get to be the one to make the decisions here Elle? Why do you get to give me ultimatums?"

I soften a little, and settle my greens on his blacks.
"Because my life has an expiration date Ryder, and it's not like yours that includes wrinkles, grey hair and grandchildren."

His eyes close and he tilts his head down. This man has looked defeated in front of me so many times, I'm starting to wonder if I'm doing him more harm than good. Surely a regular woman with a normal life couldn't put this much stress on a man.

THE UGLY ROSES

I remind myself he too has left me stressed, and that whatever way we move forward will be for the better. At least right now.

"I don't like it Elle, I don't. But it doesn't sound like you're giving me any other option."

I reach out and put my hand on top of his. "This is the way it needs to be right now, Ryder."

He grabs my hand and brings it up to his mouth, placing a kiss on my palm. "I still think you're wrong, and you never said I had to agree with you, because I don't. I hope to prove you wrong, Elle. I fucked up the other day and I'll probably do that a lot."

He takes a deep breath and runs his hands through his hair before continuing. "I'll help. You know I will beautiful. But don't think it's going to be easy for me."

I know what he means, and this is what it comes down to. Sex. It's what it always comes down to. This is his way of letting me know that he'll have a hard time not getting it from me, and maybe even that he'd find it somewhere else. Or at least I assume that's what its all about. Maybe it's more, maybe less, either way I stay focused. It's no longer my place to ask him exactly what he means by that so I give him a small, reassuring smile. "I think this is the time we rip the band aid off, so if you don't have plans today, I suggest we dive right into it."

He studies me a few moments longer than necessary before standing up. "No plans. I'm going to go grab a shower and a bite to eat. Meet you back here in an hour?"

I nod my head.

"Sounds good."

Chapter Ten

I sit at the old wooden table that Tom Morgan and his dear late wife used to share dinners at. They probably smiled and told each other about their day around this table, most likely over a nice home cooked meal.

There will be no smiles around this table today.

Ryder is sitting in his usual spot at the head of the table, and I'm to his right, facing out the window toward his house. The mood is somber, and despite my want for a glass of vodka to accompany the task ahead of us, I know I need to keep a clear head.

"I'm not going to dive right into what happened in the basement, because at this point I don't think it's relevant. You'll see enough from the photos and you've already seen my body."

Out of habit he reaches over to squeeze my leg, but it ends up being more of a pat before he corrects himself.

"What I think is important is for you to look at all the information gathered so far, and do whatever it is you'd normally do to try and figure out who the second attacker is. My being wanted for questioning back in Canada is a moot point at the moment. I'm not asking you for help to get me out of that, I just need your help to find out who's after me."

I push the two-inch-thick folder containing the rest of the things he hasn't seen toward him. The things he noticed were missing when he first discovered my dark secret spread out on my old kitchen table back in Indy.

"I'll do what I can and use whatever resources I have to help you, Elle."

THE UGLY ROSES

I absorb the sincerity in his eyes before nodding my head, and letting the folder go. He gives me a small, reassuring smile before opening it up.

Ryder heaves out a long breath deep from his lungs and rests his hands on the table, now clenched tight into fists.

I know what he's looking at, the first photos are of Andrew's shrine. A wall approximately twenty-feet long by ten-feet tall covered in photos of me, along with notes of my schedule. When I went to work, who I hung out with, what time I usually went to bed at night.

The first few photos are of the full wall. The next photos he'll see are the close ups on that wall. I wait for him to turn the pages and see the woman I once was; the one with the big smile on her face. The one that walked around without a care in the world. The woman who once swayed her hips when she walked, not because she wanted to flaunt herself, but because she had pride in who she was, what she did.

She was a hard worker, a good mother and a damn good friend to those closest to her. She was pale-skinned, with long wavy light blonde hair and sparkling green eyes. She was everything this new miserable bitch is not, and her name was Jayne O'Connor.

I watch him look at photo after photo. I watch his hands clench and unclench. I watch him grind his teeth, and fidget in his chair.

He turns the page and I see the photo of my daughter and I playing on the swing set in our backyard. Both our smiles are big, we were laughing at Norma who wouldn't stop barking every time Lilly squealed because she was being pushed so high. Next to that photo is one of me at Frank's bar, dancing with a man I used to spend time with.

They were both nice photos, if it weren't for the words 'dirty whore' written over both of them. This is where I noticed a pattern. The candid shots of me meeting with work clients, or photos of Laura and I at lunch, didn't have those two words angrily written across the top.

I note the silence in the room and glance up at Ryder, who's now staring intently at me. It's not pity in his eyes. It almost looks like longing.

"You're beautiful Elle, so was your little girl."

I nod my head slowly and try to put his focus back on what's in front of him. "That she was. But she's gone and I'm not that woman anymore. Let's keep going, I don't like to look at this shit any longer than I have to."

He reaches out and places his hand on top of mine.

"You're *you*, babe. That's what I like best. I don't give a fuck what color your hair is, not then, and not now when I've seen who you used to be. Remember that."

I nod my head in mild understanding, not wanting to make this any more personal than it has to be.

I continue to watch Ryder as he studies the photos intensely, taking notes on a pad he brought with him. I know when he's getting close to the real ugly, not because I know this file like the back of my hand, but because his breathing has grown heavy.

I look down at the file and see the photo of Cory and Andrew's bodies lying lifeless on the floor. I see that awful rope, and the filthy blood soaked blanket in the corner. My eyes drift toward the bucket I was given to piss in and I turn my head away.

THE UGLY ROSES

No matter how long it has been, when I see it, I *smell* it. It's like this awful thing that has permeated so deep in my brain that seeing that photo takes me back there.

I can feel the rope on my wrists again, the blood running down my back. I can smell the putrid scent of that goddamn bucket, stale with piss and the man that didn't shower for three days.

I push back from the table and walk briskly toward the bathroom, not slowing at all, knowing that if my head doesn't get to the toilet soon, I'm going to have one hell of a mess to clean up.

I make it to the bathroom and fall to my knees, I reach my hands up to try and hold my hair, but two larger hands beat me to it as I empty my stomach of the coffee and toast I consumed this morning.

I don't want him to see me like this.

Head in the toilet.

Weak.

I don't have a chance to object because I can't stop heaving. Everything from today and whatever was left from last night comes up. It's a torrent of hell that that photo brought back to me and it doesn't stop until my stomach is completely empty.

Ryder reaches in front of me and puts a cool cloth to my forehead. I take it from him and he begins to rub my back. I'd love nothing more than to put the nightmare on my kitchen table to rest and just have this man hold me for a while so I could sleep it off. But I can't do that. I need to push forward, no matter how much it pains me to do so.

"Maybe we should take a break, Elle," Ryder softly says, always seeming to know what I need, even if it's not technically what I want.

I shake my head.

"No."

I reach out and flush the toilet, and Ryder helps me stand up. I don't bother looking at him as I make my way to the sink and proceed to brush my teeth. He stands silently in the doorway, waiting for me.

I rinse out my mouth and wash my hands before looking at him. He's leaned in the doorway, wearing a dark grey long sleeve shirt and worn out jeans. Dressed—or undressed—Ryder Callaghan is a beautiful sight.

"Let's finish."

He gives me a long hard look before nodding and following me back to the table. I stop on the way to get a glass of water before taking my seat.

"His photos of you started near university, is that right?"

I nod my head. "Yes, but there were only a few from that time. Then there was about a year gap before it started again, and from then on they were pretty consecutive. No more gaps."

He looks up from his notepad.

"What happened during the first gap? After university?"

It's not hard to forget, they were some of the best memories of my life. "The curly haired brunette in some of those photos is my best friend, Laura. We spent close to a year traveling. Everywhere from California to Italy. We'd fly somewhere for a month, spend a few weeks at home and then fly somewhere else. It wouldn't have been easy to know where I was, unless you were a close friend of mine."

Ryder nods his head, deep in thought before looking back to the photos and notes.

"Only the photos that are taken with your daughter, or men, are written on. I'm not a profiler Elle, but any idiot could assume that either he has strong religious views and didn't like the fact that you had a child without being married, or he envisioned himself being the one to give that to you. Did he mention anything about that?"

Not wanting to think back on that time right now, I tell him so.

"I'd prefer if you would just look over that file, and make your own assumptions. Then maybe tomorrow we'll sit down so I can answer your questions. You're going to have more than just that one Ryder, and I would rather hash it all out at the same time after you've gone over the whole thing."

Knowing that my suggestion is the best course of action for me right now, he nods his head and gets back to it.

"Sure, beautiful." The endearment comes out naturally, but I don't acknowledge it like I usually would. Purely platonic, and strictly business at the moment is my game plan. I try my best to shut down my emotions and remain at this table like an outsider looking in. Not letting my heart or my head get too caught up in the mess that is my past.

After a short while of silence, watching Ryder go over everything with a fine-toothed comb, I get up from the table and head to the fridge in search of the makings for sandwiches. My stomach doesn't necessarily want food right now, but I know if I don't eat I'll pay for it later.

HARLOW STONE

I make us each a chicken club and grab a few bottles of water before sitting back down to eat. Ryder is currently looking over the notes from the forensic team regarding lists of items found in the room. *Steel pipe, two-by-four soaked in blood, four-inch combat knife, etc*. He studies everything with a trained eye, writing a lot of notes down on paper.

I take our empty plates to the counter, knowing what's about to come. I don't need to look at it again, I see and feel the proof of it every day. So I don't turn around when I hear the shattering of glass against the wall, and I don't follow him when he storms past me to head out the door.

I don't need to check the file on the table to know which photos he just looked at. I was barely conscious when they asked to take them. The close-ups of my face are not the woman I am today. My eyes were swollen shut and the entire right side of my face is virtually black. My light hair was stained crimson, and I had a feeding tube inserted through my nose because it was impossible to swallow anything thicker than water down my abused throat.

The photos of my back show the one hundred and sixty-two stitches holding it together. I don't remember much from arriving at the hospital, and I assume I was in too dire need of medical care to take all of the photos on arrival.

There are also pictures of my wrists and ankles, followed by the close-ups of my black and broken ribs. I might as well have been a dead person, because that's exactly what I looked like in those photographs.

I finish cleaning up our lunch mess, and look out the window to see Ryder pacing the beach in front of my house. Norm is not far behind, giving him a little space. I decide not to bother him. He needs a moment alone and I don't think there are words that'll make him feel better.

I turn on the radio to a mellow alternative station and sit back at the table to wait. He'll come in eventually, he just needs time. I send a text to Denny letting him know that I'd like to meet at the gym tonight, and within five minutes I get a response telling me that he's free. I gave him the code for the private room, so if he gets there before me he can let himself in.

Twenty minutes later, Ryder comes back in the house. He heads straight for the fridge and grabs a beer before sitting back down at the table. He cracks it open and takes a long pull before staring straight ahead and speaking.

"What Andrew Roberts did was not because he loved you, or wanted to be with you. It was a punishment. He may have wanted you at one time, but this, these photos Elle, are that of a man who wanted you to pay for something. That payment being your life. I don't for one second believe the detective's notes stating this was an act of obsession and love to be the truth. This man didn't watch you because he loved you, he did it because he fucking hated you, Elle. What we need to figure out is why."

I stare at him the entire time he speaks, and I want to be offended he hasn't yet looked at me. Perhaps it's hard? A combination of seeing what I used to look like, along with seeing me in the hospital. I'm stronger now. Deep down I know he knows that. I just hope his eyes don't judge me differently because of it.

"I agree with you Ryder, but they didn't see it that way. The rest are the accounts of injuries and causes of death, along with a few more witness statements and some of his background information. Why don't you take it home with you? We can sit down tomorrow afternoon and I'll answer any questions you have."

His troubled eyes finally meet mine and it takes everything in me not to jump out of my chair and plant myself in his lap. I want to hold him, I want him to hold me, but I remind myself this is about getting justice, about finding a killer that could potentially be out there harming other women. This isn't about just me, or Ryder, or my desire to want to be with him. This is about tying up loose ends, and I can't do that when my judgment gets clouded with sweet words and strong hands.

"This isn't easy for me Elle. Actually, that's an understatement, this is really fucking hard."

He downs the last of his beer and heavily sets the bottle back on the table, not losing eye contact.

"I'll do whatever the fuck I can to find this piece of shit Elle, I promise you that. My only hope is that when I'm finished, you'll drop this 'work and no play' act you've enforced and realize you still want me right now just as much as I want you."

I go to open my mouth, but he cuts it off with a firm slap to the table, causing my eyes to blink. His voice is surprisingly soft when he speaks again.

"Don't lie. Better yet, don't speak. I'll prove it to you." He doesn't say anything else, or even try to touch me as he folds up the file and walks out of my house.

What have I gotten myself into?

Chapter Eleven

"Elbows in! Tuck 'em in girl, fists up! Come at me!"

I do everything Denny says, punching with every bit of energy I have left in my body. Physically, I wasn't exhausted when I came in here. Mentally—that's a different story.

I had four hours after Ryder left before I got to work out with Denny. I came in an hour early, simply so I didn't have to sit at home, pacing the floors. My mind is mostly here tonight, but it's the anger behind my punches that are really keeping me present.

I'm not angry at Ryder. I'm not angry with my life at the moment. I'm angry because I had to share what I did with him, and regardless of the circumstances I hope he doesn't view me in a different light. That thought alone pisses me off because normally I live life by the rule that I won't give two fucks what other people think of me. Now, all I worry about is if he sees me as weak and helpless after seeing those horrid photos of me.

I lived for three days with someone viewing me as weak, and I never want to feel that way again. I don't want someone to think they need to look after me. I don't want Ryder to become some vigilante and get a wild hair avenging my attack and almost death.

I want a clean break from it all. I *need* a clean break from it all. I want to find the other person responsible, and as much as I once wished death upon that person, at the moment I'd settle for him to spend life in jail.

It's funny how our perceptions change after people touch our lives in a positive manner. As pissed as I was at Ryder for his outburst and the words he said, I know at the heart of it he still lives his life to protect people.

I know at this moment, throwing punches with the gorgeous man in front of me, that people come into our lives for a reason, and there's always a lesson to be learned, some sort of wisdom passed on. Be it good or bad.

I know even if things don't work out with Ryder, I'll forever be thankful for his help. If I find out he's been hiding something from me, I'll still say thank you and move on. Perhaps that's what his lesson will be to me through the friendship we've had; learning to move on. Although I don't believe I'll ever fully recover from losing my family, I can move forward from the attack and hopefully prevent someone else being harmed in the process.

"Fuck," I mutter when I catch a blow to the chest, courtesy of Denny.

The tall Viking of a man wipes the sweat off his brow before placing his gloved hands on his hips. "Lost your head there for a minute." He's not upset about it, judging by the smirk on his face.

"That I did," I say as I scrub my hands over my face, silently scolding myself for once again letting thoughts of the past and thoughts of Ryder mess up my game.

"We've been at this long enough Elle. I'm not sure whether you need one of those protein boost smoothies over there, or a beer at O'Dooles. You pick."

The smart decision would be the smoothie, but after today a beer sounds a hell of a lot better.
"Beer it is, big man. I need twenty for a shower first."

Denny takes his gloves off and shoves them in his gym bag before slinging it over his shoulder. "Me too. Meet you in the parking lot when I'm done."

I grab my own gym bag and head toward the shower at the back of the room.

"Sounds good."

* * *

I make my way down the stairs toward the exit. My shower was quick. I'm thankful it's like my own and when I rented the room exclusively for myself, I stocked the shower and bathroom with some of my essentials.

I dressed in the same clothing I wore to the gym. High black boots, black tights, long black top and a plum scarf. All the rest of my armor is in place as I push the door open into the parking lot.

Denny is waiting beside a black suburban, which is parked a few spots down from my BMW.

"You want to walk down? It's only a block away."

I nod my head as I unlock my vehicle. "Sure, just let me toss my bag in the truck then I'm good to go."

I put my gym bag on the passenger seat and double check my messenger style purse.

Gun?

Check.

Nothing else really matters, so I lock up and fall into step beside Denny. The silence stretches, but it's not uncomfortable. I sense Denny is not big on pointless conversation either and that pleases me.

"It shouldn't be busy at this time of night, just let me know when you're ready to leave and I'll walk you back."

"Thanks Denny."

It's a mild night, and I'm thankful that I put my bird's nest in a giant messy knot on top of my head, allowing the small breeze to cool my neck after our workout. I'd feel better without the scarf, but my comfort is not the most important thing when venturing out in public.

Denny opens the door and allows me to enter first. My initial take on O'Dooles is 'homey'. There are a lot of dark wood, worn in benches and a twenty-foot bar with padded black bar stools. The pub is long and narrow. The bar runs a good portion of the left side, and there are many booths and tables along the right. The end wall is made up of a small stage with a dance floor in front of it. All of it looks worn in. All of it makes me feel at ease.

This place almost reminds me of Frank's back home, only the majority of the clientele here are dressed in camouflage. There are about a dozen men in here and I notice a flock of Gingers near an old jukebox at the back, and a few other stragglers near the bar.

Tits out, thong straps visible.

Classy, ladies. Classy.

Denny gestures to the bar but I angle my head toward the booth, not wanting my back to all of these unknown people in a new place.

He glances around before making his way over to a booth that's about midway in the pub. I sit with my back facing the door, more interested in being able to see the patrons.

The booth is nice, dark burgundy leather and ebony stained wood. It's warm enough to be inviting, and dark enough that I fit right in.

THE UGLY ROSES

I notice a waitress leaving a table near the back and put my hand up, signaling for service. Her eyes roam past me as if I didn't just ask for a goddamn drink. She begins stomping toward the bar and goes to grab her tray off the top, moving her eyes back to my table. As soon as she notices my good-looking companion, she adds a mighty sway to her bony ass (if that's possible) and plasters a wide grin on her face.

She's the only waitress I can see at the moment, so I'm not sure if her clothing is mandatory. Her top barely holds her fake tits in. It's bright pink and matches her nails. Her black skirt is barely visible underneath the apron she has on and her bleached blonde hair completes the ensemble.

Maybe she's a nice person, and I shouldn't judge too quickly. Maybe she's a single mother and this is the dress code for the establishment. Maybe she has no choice but to work here in order to put food in her children's mouths.

I reign in my bitch factor a few notches and wait until she gets to our table. The whole 'hips swaying, big smile' act for Denny could be because he's a very good tipper.

Miss skinny finally makes it to our table. She puts her tray under her arm and her hand on Denny's shoulder.

"Hello stranger, long time no see." Denny visibly cringes and shrugs her hand off his shoulder.

"I'll take an MGD, Elle?"

She looks offended he didn't join in on her mild banter and moves her eyes to mine. "I'll take the same."

She jots them down on the notepad resting on her tray in case she forgets the complicated order and turns her eyes back toward Denny.

"You haven't been here in a while. Maybe we should get that drink sometime soon if you're back in town."

I watch as she runs her pointy fingernail down the sleeve of Denny's shirt, jutting her pointy hip out in an effort to look enticing. It fails considerably seeing as not only is he sitting at the table with another woman, she should be inquiring about an extra meal or two, not a drink.

"I told you we weren't having drinks Shannon. Not before, not now."

She takes her hand off of his arm and cocks her head to the side. "It's Shawna!"

Denny leans back into his side of the booth and looks at her directly before speaking. "I'll be blunt. You've fucked Finn, Maverick and Hunter. They're like my brothers, so no. We will not be having that drink anytime soon. But while you're searching for your next victim, you can bring me mine."

"You're such an asshole Denny Black. I don't even know why I tried."

Denny shakes his head. "Neither do I."

She stomps off toward the bar without looking back. I look over at Denny with a small smirk of my own. I take in his white Henley and massive form. Can't blame that girl for trying.

"You know, as much as I enjoyed watching that encounter, I sure as hell hope you didn't just earn me spit in my beer."

Denny leans his elbows down on the table. "She doesn't have the balls darlin', and this is the usual around here with most of the waitresses."

"Didn't picture you as the type of man to turn a woman down."

THE UGLY ROSES

Denny looks back at me with piercing, serious eyes before he speaks in his usual low and deep voice. "I like women Elle, most men do. But when those women have already spread their legs for half the men you work with, and the majority of this bar, well let's just say they're not my type."

Two beers get slammed down on the table in front of us before Denny speaks up again.

"Keep 'em comin'."

She stomps off and I can't help the small chuckle escaping my mouth. I take a long swig of my beer and relish the cool bubbles as they make their way down my throat. I may love my vino, but a cold beer after a long day is a thing of beauty.

I glance at Denny and notice him staring at me. It doesn't make me uncomfortable, but I hate to be stared at, especially when I worry if one of the marks on my body has become noticeable. I adjust my scarf and clear my throat in preparation to speak.
"How long did you work for Brock before you came out here?"

Denny too takes a long pull from his beer before beginning to peel at the label. Not a sign of insecurity, but a sign he doesn't want to reveal too much in what he has to say. His beautiful blue eyes glance up into mine.

"Brock and I basically started *Fist* together. He was more into it than I was. I enjoyed it, don't get me wrong, but I knew I wanted something more. So, after about five years I made the trip east and hooked up with Callaghan."

I nod my head, not sure which way I want this conversation to go. I sense that I could sit here in silence and Denny would be totally okay with that, but at the same time I crave to know him a little better.

Deciding the best way to get someone else to reveal something about themselves is to share a bit of your own history, I press on.

"Brock was an awesome teacher, and a good person. I'm glad I found him."

Denny stares off into space for a few moments before agreeing. "He's a good friend, won't steer you wrong. I have to say, I was surprised when he called me about you. Brock has never done one on one with women outside of the self-defense classes. Tell me, how did you get him to swing that one?"

The beer, going down rather well, is now empty. I push the bottle to the side of the table, signaling for another before I answer him.

"I swung that one after I left him with a bloody nose in the fetal position, holding his balls like they would've fallen off if he let go."

A deep, boisterous laugh graces my ears. It's a head thrown back, full on belly laugh. In this moment I realize I'm becoming obsessed with male laughter, or perhaps laughter in general seeing as I haven't had a good laugh of my own in close to two years.

I can feel a small bit of wetness coating my eyes, not from anger, but from a happiness that still resides somewhere deep inside me. I look up to clear them and slowly bring my eyes back down to Denny's. He's staring at me, not like he was before, but with a small sadness in his eyes.

"Don't get out much, do ya darlin'?"

I hear the mild slam of a bottle next to me and grab the fresh brew, taking a sip and contemplating what to say. "I'm not much of a people person."

I give him a small, pathetic smirk before returning to the bottle.

I'm good at that.

Denny's wide torso leans forward and he rests his forearms on the table, leaning in closer as the music has gotten a little louder. "Chicken Caesar or a burger? It's the only shit that's worth eating here at this time of night, and I'm starving."

Trying to lighten the mood, I crack a joke. "Damn Denny, had I have known you were going to invite me to dinner I would've dressed my best, and maybe put in a little more effort than a ten-minute scrub."

This earns me a big toothy grin, and his teeth are perfect. "Ten minute or five minute darlin', I think you're the cleanest woman in this hole."

I return the grin. "Or you could rephrase that, after your description of the women earlier I think I could accurately describe myself as the cleanest 'hole'. And I'll take a burger."

This earns me another deep belly laugh before he flags down a younger girl cleaning tables. I'm assuming there's no dress code since she's casually dressed in black pants and a short sleeve black top (tits completely covered).

"Hey sweetheart, can we get two burgers."

The sweet younger girl pulls a pad out of her apron. I'm guessing she's maybe eighteen. Cute, long brown hair and very petite.

"Sure. Everything on them?"

Denny nods his head and gestures toward me.

"Everything but onions, and a side of gravy for the fries please."

She nods and scurries her little body back through the kitchen door.

"She seems a little young to be working in here."

"Ya, her father was the owner. He died on a mission overseas. She and her mother mostly look after the place. Callaghan knows them; he introduced us to this place. The regular waitresses are shit, but so long as the family running the place keeps the doors open, food will be on the tables."

I lose myself in thought for a moment, knowing exactly how that young girl feels, losing someone so close to you.

Denny's voice pulls me out of my thoughts. "Want another?"

I eye my now two empty beer bottles on the table, knowing if I drink much more I won't be able to drive home.

"I do, but first I need to ask how hard it'll be to get a taxi back home?"

"They won't get busy until after one in the morning around here."

"I take it you've had to use the service a time or two? Brock said you guys were most likely on a bender while you were off for the week. Do you all live around here?"

"No. Ryder is the farthest. I actually rented a place between here and there. About ten minutes out."

That means he's not even ten minutes from the little cove that Ryder and I live in.

"Well then, bring on the beer. Taxi it is."

Chapter Twelve

"I'm impressed, didn't expect you to pack back that plate, Elle."

I wipe off the leftover gravy, and whatever else accumulated on my face on my napkin.

"I'm not about the salad, Denny Black."

I'm about six beers in now. I'm not drunk, but definitely feeling good. I feel safe having a few, or many beers in public with Denny. I know already he wouldn't let anything happen to me.

"Not salad?"

I shake my head in mock exasperation before continuing. "Nope. How many women have you had to dinner who only ordered salad?"

Denny pauses to think for a moment.

"A lot," he says so seriously I can't help but laugh a bit, mostly due to the beer.

"Ha! Yes, and then she goes home and gorges on potato chips and ice cream, trying to make up for the lack of protein and carbohydrates in her meal. I'm not salad. I like it, but I'd rather just eat what I want to eat and not give two fucks what you think about me while I do it."

Blue eyes stare back at mine.

One,
Two,
Three.

"You're not salad."

He gets it.

"I need to hit the ladies."

Denny sits, slightly stunned. Suddenly realizing that perhaps his previous encounters with women all failed because they couldn't bring themselves to simply be *themselves* on a date. Not that I think Denny really dates, but I'm sure he doesn't go home to a cold bed every night.

I stand up and sway a little, steadying myself before making my way to the back of the bar where the washrooms are located.

I open the door and head straight for the stall, assuming I must've been dehydrated if I'm only now just making it to the washroom after six beers.

I finish my business and open the stall door, walking toward the sink. There are five, and three are taken up by various women in stages of undress. Fixing their makeup and plumping up their tits. I take a short look at myself in the mirror.

Marks are covered, no mascara running down my face, good to go.

I wash my hands and hear a catty voice coming from the handicap stall at the end.

"I don't know who she is. I've never seen him in here with anyone before."

I recognize the voice as the waitress who brought us our beers. "He said he didn't call me because I slept with three of the guys he works with. If he finds out I've slept with five of them, I'm screwed. I want that one Amy, oh my god why does he have to be such a fucking tease."

I begin to dry my hands off, thinking about her comment regarding that she has slept with five of them. Does that mean Ryder too?

If it was before me, it's none of my business.

I turn around, throwing the paper in the trashcan before the waitress recognizes me, but I'm too late. She comes to a halt about five feet away. I don't like wasting my time or breath speaking to bitches such as this. But I can't help but dig the hole a little deeper for her since she's obviously a lying whore. So, I straighten my spine and confront her directly.

"It's called the clap."

Her head swings back, and her face sours. "Excuse me?"

"The clap. It's why he won't sleep with you. They have regular health checks at Callaghan Securities, you could cost him his job," I say, deadpan.

I can see the red start to overtake her neck. I probably would've noticed it sooner if it weren't for the seven layers of makeup on her face.

"You bitch, I do not have the clap!"

I pay her no mind and walk around her, reaching for the handle of the door. Once it's firmly grasped in my hand I turn my head giving her a quick but thorough head to toe. I shake my head before regaining eye contact.
"I'm not into pussy sweetheart, so you're telling that to the wrong person."

I don't give her another glance as I walk out the door, smirk on my face.

Wench.

I do a slight weave around a few drunk and dancing patrons before tilting my head back up, looking toward our table. There are three new men seated with Denny at the large booth that seats six. All are big, boisterous and a little rowdy, if I can judge by the loud voices coming from that direction.

I walk slowly, not liking the thought of meeting other men. Denny notices me and waves a hand, gesturing me forward. The men look slightly familiar, and as I get closer, I recognize them as the men Ryder had at his bonfire and the same men he was jogging with all those months ago.

Feeling a little more comfortable, I reach the table and go to take my seat. Denny wastes no time in making introductions as I assess the new men around me.

"Elle, this is Finn, Hunter and Cabe."

I give a small salute to the men and let out a small reassuring breath. I don't see these men as a threat. Denny is obviously close to them and that's enough for me. I give him a small smile letting him know that I'm not offended by the company. But I don't have much desire to engage with them. He motions to two of the younger men on my bench.

"I'm pretty sure you heard me talk about two of them earlier. Cabe's not a bad guy though."

This prompts the tall, tanned and brown haired Hunter to speak up. "Fuck you, dickhead."

He follows this statement by throwing one of my fries at Denny. "Let me guess, Shawna's working tonight?" the other man named Finn asks. He's almost identical in looks to Hunter.

THE UGLY ROSES

I'm guessing they are brothers. They both look to be in their late twenties, both with dark hair, blue eyes and built more like quarterbacks than linebackers.

Denny nods his head. "You'd guess right."

Finn pipes up again. "What? I haven't seen her yet. Where is the hooker? I haven't had her in a while."

I polish off the rest of my beer and answer the question. Not just for Finn, but for the table.

"I told the *hooker*, that Denny wouldn't sleep with her because she had the clap. So if you're looking, she's probably in the bathroom checking her twat to see if it's just a rumor."

The man I now know as Cabe lets out a laugh. He's an attractive man. There's definitely a bit of Mexican or Latino in him. He's darker than Ryder, not quite as beautiful but not hard to look at.

"I told you sorry bastards you'd catch something. That why you've been itching your balls all week, Hunter?" Cabe asks.

"Fuck you, Rodriguez," replies Hunter.

Denny cuts off the banter. "Alright, enough. Everyone, this is Elle, who I was having beers with until you useless shits interrupted. Pipe down or move the fuck on."
Hollers and profanity are exchanged before I butt in.

"Actually Denny, I'm going to get that taxi. I'm sure my dog needs out by now."

I look at my watch and see it's just after eleven.

"Who's on call tonight?" asks Denny.

Cabe answers. "I am, these shits couldn't stay sober long enough."

"Alright man I need a ride, so does Elle. You cool with that or do you want to sit here with the kids?"

Cabe moves to get out of the booth. "Black suburban, brother. Parked out front."

That's all the answer Denny needs before shuffling us out of the booth.

"Try to keep your head out of the toilet fella's," I say with a small wave over my shoulder.

I get a few waves back and make my way toward the exit. Tonight was good, and in all honesty I could've drunk more. But I'm thinking it's better to leave it where it is and get home. That was technically my first night out drinking, socially, with someone who's an almost friend.

Denny opens the back door and I get in. He closes it for me and climbs into the front seat with Cabe, all of us buckling up before hitting the road.

"I can bring you back to get your truck tomorrow morning if you want, Elle."

I pull my eyes away from the gadgets adorning the dash of the suburban and look at Denny. "Thanks, just shoot me a text. If I'm not awake yet I'll just get a taxi to bring me back in."

I move my eyes back to the dash and all its buttons, which aren't standard in most vehicles. "Do you have all this fancy gadgetry in your suburban too, Denny?"

He turns his head to look at me in the back seat. "Nah, just Cabe and Finn. He's the tech guru of the group, and Finn helps when he's not buried in whiskey and women."

THE UGLY ROSES

I gathered that, noting immediately that Finn and Hunter seemed like the younger, wilder of the bunch tonight. Cabe and Denny seem to be about Ryder's age, in their mid to late thirties. The other two? I'm guessing late twenties.

I roll all this over in my mind and lean forward between the two front seats to speak, mostly addressing Cabe. "None of you asked who I was tonight or looked surprised to meet me. Seeing as Denny didn't have a lot of time to talk about me before I got back from the washroom, that tells me you must have been the tech man who not only located my SUV in Indianapolis, but also continued to send my location to Ryder?"

Cabe visibly stiffens and curls his hands around the steering wheel. I understand what position I just put him in; Ryder is his boss. His loyalty is to him, not me.

I didn't mean to ask him to be rude; perhaps the beer has made me a little more brazen. But I'd like to think I'd ask him regardless. I like to know who has their nose in my business and how much they know about me.

Cabe makes eye contact with me in the rear-view mirror, and I dare him with my own to lie about it. He remains silent.

"Your lack of response is all the answer I need."

I sit back in my seat and look out the window.

"Ms. Davidson I-"

"Don't Cabe. And don't 'Ms. Davidson' me please. It's Elle, and you were following orders from your boss. Not your fault, and also not your problem. Forget I asked."

Cabe solemnly nods his head. "The GPS notifications were deactivated, Elle."

"I know, he told me."

The rest of the drive is silent. I could feel guilty for ruining the moment, but I don't, mostly because I rarely feel much of anything at all. Before long, we pull onto my lane. I don't bother asking how he knew where I lived, seeing as I already know the answer. I look to the west and notice Ryder's truck in his driveway. The lights are still on in his house. I look at the clock on the dash and see it's close to midnight.

Not forgetting my manners, I thank Cabe for the ride and unbuckle my seatbelt when he puts the suburban in park.

"Anytime, Elle."

Denny opens his door and hops out of the truck.

"I'll walk you to your door, darlin'."

I give a small wave over my shoulder at Cabe and make my way toward the front steps of my house. I do a quick sweep of the perimeter and ascend the steps to my porch. I'm not two steps up before I notice the shadow of a man sitting on my deck.

"Jesus!"

I put my hand to my chest and feel Denny rush past me, taking the four steps two at a time until he comes face to face with Ryder. He throws his hands in the air and angrily runs them through his hair.

"What the fuck boss, you scared the woman half to death."

I take in two deep breaths and quickly realize that in my panic I'd reached in my purse for my gun. It's not pointed at anyone but is mostly pulled out of my purse and in my hand. I know they both saw it, but I really don't give a shit right now.

THE UGLY ROSES

I shake off the fear, that stiffness that enters your body when you're scared to shit that someone was about to kill you.

"Ryder, I told you once, and I shouldn't have to tell you again. Unless you want a goddamn bullet in your body, don't fucking surprise me like that!"

I hear Norma barking and don't waste another minute before climbing the rest of the steps, crossing the small front porch and storming into my house.

I left most of the lights on; a habit to make people think someone was still home. The stereo is still on, playing some old rock music. I give Norm a quick scratch and head toward the fridge in the kitchen.

I grab a bottle of vino and rocks glass, because I'm classy like that. I hear Ryder yelling at Denny though the front screen door, not that the old main door would've blocked the noise. He's arguing with him about priorities, and women, and a small speech about 'his woman'. I just had my first what most would consider a 'normal' night out. I didn't have a panic attack, I didn't freak the fuck out, and most importantly it's Denny who I have to thank for that.

I don't walk toward the door, I don't yell. But I speak firm and loud enough they can both hear me.

"Ryder, is he on the job right now?"

Angry eyes stare back at mine through the screen.

"No, he's not."

I top up my rocks glass with wine at the island, not taking my eyes from his. "Then what that man does or who he has drinks with is not your business right now. So instead of scolding him, thank him, and Cabe too, for making sure I got home safely."

I grab my wine off the bar, and head out the back door to my lounge. My girl comes with me, happy that I'm home and eager for some attention.

* * *

I've settled in and enjoyed the silence for about ten minutes now. I'm lighting up a smoke when three male bodies come out my back door.

"Elle, we need to talk."

Not the words any woman wants to hear. I take in the abundance of testosterone invading my space. They're all like Rambo in street clothes (minus the bandana). On another day I might have a fantasy about this but right now I can sense the mood is going to become even more serious than it was when I almost shot my neighbor.

"If you want to argue Ryder, go home. If you want to talk, then just speak. I'm tired and was planning on heading straight to bed when I got home. Not nearly killing someone."

Ryder shows his telltale sign he's frustrated and scrubs his hands over his face before sitting down at the foot of the lounge. Cabe moves to lean against the railing and Denny moves toward the table on the other side of the deck.

"It might not be a good talk, Elle."

I look up from my drink at Ryder's solemn eyes. "Then you better grab the rest of my wine, and if they're staying for this conversation then get the guys a beer."

Ryder reaches out and squeezes my leg gently before heading into the house, coming out seconds later with refreshments. He sits back down and reaches for my pack of smokes, lighting one up before he starts to speak.

"They both know, Elle."

I contemplate his words for a moment. Not sure exactly what it is he is talking about.

"They both know we spent some time together? They both know we fucked? What exactly do they *know* Ryder?"

He takes a long pull of his beer. I notice he brought two out for himself.

"No beautiful, they *know*. Not everything, but some shit. I needed help when you took off, these two were my help."

I look up at Ryder's face and realize he's not joking. He told my life to some guys, who may be good guys, but none the less guys I don't know. I'm sure he can tell I'm prepared to lose my shit because he quickly tries to calm my raging thoughts.

"Hear me out babe. I was fucking lost for clues when you left. I couldn't find you on my own, which is not something I'm proud of considering what I do for a living. The bottom line is I needed help, Elle. These are my men and they helped me find you."

I glance over at Denny and Cabe, and notice they both look uncomfortable. I'm not concerned about Cabe, I want to know how much Denny knows. We've only worked out together a few times, but for him to know anything about me and not let me know, for him to continue on like we were strangers would piss me the fuck off. I need to know so I waste no time in asking.

"How much Denny? How much did he tell you about me? How much did you know?"

Denny straightens up from leaning against the table and looks to Ryder. "Ryder, don't do that man."

He shakes his head slightly at him before looking at me. "All I know darlin' is that Ryder was trying to find a woman named Elle Davidson. I couldn't find shit; tech crap is not my gig. So when Cabe returned from a job, Ryder got him to tap your bank records and locate your truck. When Brock called me, I put two and two together after he mentioned Callaghan. Long story short I said I'd train with you and pick up where Brock left off. Aside from that I was only given the information that you might be in trouble, and to look out for you. I don't know shit about you Elle, and I haven't asked. That's your business darlin', and not anyone else's unless you choose to share it with them."

His last comment is directed toward Cabe and Ryder. Cabe visibly flinches and Ryder picks up where Denny left off. "I'm sorry, but I'm not Elle. I told you I'd help you, and in order for me to do that I needed help. Cabe is my best tech guy, and Denny is good muscle. I knew you were training with him, I just didn't expect you to show up at home so late with the two of them."

I take a long hard look at the men around me. I hate secrets. I have a lot of them, but they are mine to share. I didn't like when Ryder spoke for me at Brock's gym, and I don't like that he kept from me exactly how much he knew and who he chose to share it with.

"Enlighten me Ryder, how much have you shared with Cabe? And how much has he figured out on his own? Because if he's avidly typing my goddamn name into a search engine, you could be putting my life at more risk than it already was to begin with. Do you realize that?"

I move to stand, but a firm hand to my thigh stops me.

"Dammit, Elle! I'm not a fucking idiot. You remember me telling you I do this kind of shit for a living? Cabe covers his tracks."

I swat his hand away from my leg, and look to Cabe.

THE UGLY ROSES

"How much do you know?"

Cabe sets his beer on the railing, crossing his arms.

"I told Ryder what he needed to know to find you, but I didn't tell him everything I found."

He looks to Ryder, apologizing with his eyes. I make a motion for him to carry on, thinking he can't know any more than what I've told Ryder.

"Elle Davidson, thirty years old. Spent time waitressing. Never went to College. Never did anything. But you drive a BMW. You live in a nice cottage and you have enough money to pay for most things in cash. You have no living relatives."

I look to Ryder and give him a small nod.

"Well that sounds about right."

Cabe's voice tears my gaze from Ryder's.

"All of those things don't add up, mostly the money. I gave Ryder the info to find you, but then I kept searching for myself because something didn't sit right with me. I like my boss, most of the time. But I wanted to know what kind of woman he was chasing after who has more cash than she ever would've made at a bar, even if she took her clothes off."

His dark eyes search mine, asking if it's okay to continue. I can't imagine he found much, so I motion for him to carry on and he gives me a small nod in thanks.

"So I ran your photo through a facial recognition program focusing hits in the United States. There were a few similarities, but nothing concrete. When I widened the search, I came up with twenty-seven hits in total, ten of those being here, which I ruled out, and a few belonging to Canada.

Narrowing my search to women with money in the bank only gave me one hit, Elle. Her name is Jayne O'Connor, and her late father was the owner of O'Connor Inc. It was a leading construction and architectural company in the area where she lived in Ontario."

I try to breathe, feeling the tears sting the back of my eyes. It's been so long since I heard anything about my old self or my family and it sends a sharp pain through my chest. I swing my legs over the side of the lounge and hang my head. Ryder places a hand on my back trying to soothe me but I shrug it off and speak through my pain to Cabe.

"Finish it, Cabe. What else?"

"You're *Jayne O'Connor*, Elle. You inherited over eight million dollars from your father's company when he passed away. Your parents were Gary and Susan. They both lived middle-class lives when they could have had a larger one, and saved most of what they made, not wanting to live the big life, just enjoying the work they did. Other than your trips after university, you mostly paid your own way. I won't go into detail about the loss you've experienced, or the attack, but yes, I know about those too. I haven't shared that with anybody."

I look down at my shaking hands and move them to wipe the dampness from my face.

"If you could find me, he can too. I need to move."

Cabe moves his hands out in a placating gesture.

"Elle, I have access to just about every government database. I assure you, unless the man, or men, involved are high security, there's no way they will find you."

I put my smoke out in the ashtray beside the lounge and stand up.

"That's enough. We'll talk about this later. Until then, do me a favor and keep your mouths shut."

I move to open the screen door and feel a hand on my shoulder. I don't need to turn around to know its Ryder's.

"Elle, wait."
I shake my head in defeat. "I can't talk about this anymore. Go home, Ryder."

I don't look back as I let Norma in and shut both doors behind me. I walk toward the front door and close and lock it as well. I shut off all the inside lights, leaving the outside ones on so the boys can find their way back to their truck.

I carry my still-full glass of wine down the hall and go into my bedroom. I sit on the edge of the bed, setting my drink on the nightstand. Removing my boots and scarf, I collapse onto the pillow, not worrying about anything else.

I lay and stare at the ceiling, remembering times when life was easy. Like when I went to school and had nothing to worry about other than studies and who was buying the first round of drinks on Friday night. Or when I was a leader for an amazing architectural firm known as O'Connor Inc. and would spend my days designing and helping to build some of the most visually appealing landmarks in our area. Now my life is nothing but complicated, living a lie and hoarding my secrets.

I've made it almost a year, living in my reclusive bubble.

Now I feel like it's burst, and since meeting Ryder Callaghan there wasn't a damn thing I could do to stop it.

Chapter Thirteen

"You bitch! I just paid your rent, and this is what you turn around and do to me? Sleep with that lazy fuck from across the hall?"

Laura and I try to avoid listening to the conversation as we stumble our way toward my apartment building beside campus. We've lived together in a little two-bedroom abode here for the past year. It's small, but it's ours.

The couple we're passing obviously isn't having as good a night as we did. We spent the first portion of our night at our favorite Italian restaurant, and closed it off with shots and martinis at The Tap. Typical Friday night for us when we're not too busy with school work.

"You idiot, I've been fucking him for months! You're just too blind to see it! Always too worried with your brother, and your computer! Well fuck you!"

Laura loops her arm through mine.

"Oh my god Jayne, I feel bad for that guy. What a bitch."

"You got that right, what's the rule?"

"You want to sleep with someone else? Have the decency to leave the one you're with first," she says.

"Yup! And if she had done that, he'd still have her rent money in his pocket. Poor guy."

We watch as a security guard approaches and tells the drunken whore to head home. She's the irate one, waving her hands around in the air, spewing profanities at the poor guy sitting on the bench, head in his hands muttering about how much he hates women. I don't see his face, only his back. He looks to be about our age, maybe a year or two younger. It's possible he just got his heart broken for the first time and he may very well be one of my calls at 'Counseling on Campus' next week.

We continue walking, but as we pass the bench I reach my hand out and set it on his shoulder.

"We're not all that bad, give it time and you'll find a good one. I promise."

Laura gives an 'Amen, Sister' beside me, and I let go of his shoulder and continue walking toward our apartment.

I don't know how long that poor guy sits there, but I do reflect on my own life when I go to bed, reminding myself even though it may make me feel a little shallow, I'm confident that when I enter into a relationship with people I let them know from the beginning it's completely casual and not to expect more from me. I won't sleep with other people, and I also make that clear to them. It may not be the most ideal situation for a young woman, but I'm more interested in myself and school than having to worry about getting dinner on the table and putting a bun in my oven.

* * *

I've been beating the shit out of this punching bag for about ten minutes now. It feels good, but at the same time I'm exhausted from my lack of sleep.

I've been having a lot more dreams about my past recently, as opposed to the nightmares. It's as though once I got the majority of them off of my chest, they subsided, allowing the memories of mundane things to filter back into my mind.

Perhaps my recent dreams of university and my time with Laura are because I miss the days when things were *simple*, when I didn't have to worry about much other than myself. Of course, it's not the way I have to worry about myself today. All I had to worry about back then was that I got my ass to class on time and kept food in my fridge. These days I need to worry about who knows what, how many people I've lied to, and when are they going to eventually catch up with me, ultimately leading to my demise.

I rest my head against the bag, hanging on to the top of it. I let the sounds of Chris Cornell's voice singing about 'Black Days' wash over me. That's what today feels like. One big black day, or perhaps black years. I slept and vegged as long as I could this morning before realizing I just needed to get out of the house and beat the shit out of something. It was too early to drink and realized I didn't want to. I need to get rid of the pent-up energy inside me and hopefully clear my head.

I've avoided Ryder and I didn't call Denny before I came into the gym today. It's only four in the afternoon, and truth be told, I just wanted to be by myself. I didn't respond to his text when he offered to come pick me up. I just took a taxi with my gym clothes stuffed in my oversized purse and came here alone.

I take in a deep breath and let it out as I let go of the punching bag. I wipe the sweat from my brow before opening my eyes, my body going stiff as a statue when I take in the man sitting at the small table near the juice counter.

My small table.

In my private gym room.

I note the placement of my bag out of my peripheral vision, not wanting to take my eyes off his. My gun is in that bag, about seven feet away. I step back from the punching bag, still not taking my eyes off the distinguished man in the crisp grey suit.

THE UGLY ROSES

"You're not what I expected," says the strange man.

He's arrogant, I can tell that much. At the same time, I respect the *I don't give a fuck* attitude that's coming off him in waves. I don't say anything, and I don't move any further. If this man wanted to kill me, it would've been done already. That's not why he's here. He takes a long hard look at me before he speaks again.

"However, I can see why he turned me down."

I take a long look at his face. Strong features, grey but well-kept hair. His suit probably costs more than I pay in rent here each month, and his shoes are most likely custom made. He screams money, in every form of the word.

I notice movement through the frosted window of the door and he's quick to answer the unasked question. "That's my associate, assuring we have privacy. I'd prefer if my little *visit* here be kept confidential."

I put my hands on my hips, showing him I'm not afraid of his presence before I speak. "Assuming that your little *visit* is going to be a quick one, would you mind getting to the point? Seeing as I've not one single fucking clue as to who you are, or what you're doing in my private room."

The suit straightens himself in his chair and clasps his hands together.

"Ah, a woman who gets straight down to business. I appreciate that, Miss Davidson."

I cock my head to the side. "Your name is?"

"William Becker," he replies, smugly.

"Well, Mr. Becker. I do not for one second believe this visit is strictly for 'business', once again seeing as I've never met you. I'm also not one for idle chit chat. So cut the shit and get to the point."

Mr. Becker stands, buttoning the front of his suit, clasping his hands in front of him. "A bit of a firecracker you are, and one hell of a right hook. Although that may appeal to him, it's not in his best interest at the moment."

I pull my glove up to my mouth, undoing the Velcro and tossing them toward my gym bag.

"Do me a favor and quit talking in riddles. You have two minutes before I do make your little visit known."

I reach down and grab my long sleeve shirt off the floor, pulling it over my head in an effort to give me a little more armor and cover the marks on my wrists before he gets close enough to see them.

"Ryder Callaghan. You've been a distraction and now I need you to stand back so he can continue what he started."

The hairs on the back of my neck stand up. I hastily pull my shirt into place trying to think of how to respond.

"Two things I'm going to say to you Becker. One is that Ryder Callaghan is nothing but my neighbor. Two, what he chooses to do or *not* do, finish or *not* finish, is not my business, or yours for that matter because he's a grown man. You have a problem with that? Then you're barking in the wrong direction."

Sensing this man is not an immediate threat, I take my eyes off of him to grab my bag off the floor. I pull it over my shoulder, resting my hand on the lower part of the strap so it's closer to my gun.

THE UGLY ROSES

"Miss Davidson, I've known that man for a few years now. Not once has he ever turned down a job offer. That is until *you* came along."

I shake my head in exasperation. "Once again, not my problem. You want him, he's yours. I'm not holding him back, any more than you can force him to work for you."

He stuffs his hands in his pockets and takes a few steps closer. Not in a menacing way, but enough to tell me he means what he says and won't stop speaking until he gets his point across.

"Let me be clear *Elle*, his presence is essential to me at the moment. That cannot happen with you in the picture, as he has already proved."

I huff out a breath.

"Like I said, I don't control him. What is that you do anyway, *William?*"

I throw his first name back at him, as he did with mine. Since he has more pressing issues to deal with, he shrugs the jab off and continues.

"I can gather from your barbaric beating with that punching bag that you do not spend much time in front of a television or reading newspapers. You probably don't spend much time in circles of higher stature either, judging by the ramshackle home you live in, and your measly life as a bartender."

I'd love to throw my education, as well as my money in his face right now. But I don't. I'm the bigger person here, and ultimately this man's opinion of me doesn't matter.

"Politics is a high stakes profession, image is everything. I've been a prominent figure in Chicago for many years now, but as with any line of work our aim is always higher. I need Ryder to help me achieve that."

Chicago?

The hairs on the back of my neck come to attention once again as I try to piece together what little bit of information I have regarding the subject. But I realize I have virtually nothing. I just want to get away from him now and the quicker I finish this up, the sooner I can leave.

"Well William, there are plenty of G.I Joe's running around this town. Head about two blocks west of here and I'm sure you'll find someone to take a bullet for you."

Becker shakes his head in a condescending way, studying me as if I'm no more than shit on the bottom of his shoe.

"You misunderstand me, Miss Davidson. However, I suppose education was not your top priority, therefore I'll make this easy for you to comprehend. *I* do not personally need Mr. Callaghan, however my lovely daughter does. You see, when I enter the public eye with my family, it isn't easy for people to see past my daughter's indiscretions. She is your age, and single, only much more intelligent if I do say so myself."

Of course you would you self-righteous prick.

"The media in Chicago has taken a liking to the man that guards my back, and even more so when he was spotted out with my daughter. This pleases me Miss Davidson and works very well in my favor. I would get the type of security his company provides, and he would keep Claudia from any more public indiscretions, since she is quite taken with Mr. Callaghan."

I'm quick to snap back at him, not thinking it may give away the feelings I have but fail to acknowledge for Ryder.

"Perhaps Ryder doesn't want your job, Becker? It's also possible he's not interested in your daughter. Ever think of that?"

If he could look anymore smug, he does.

"I always have eyes on my daughter, and judging by the amount of times I'm informed of her presence in his hotel room, I would suggest that's not the case."

I feel the proverbial kick in the gut as he delivers those words, but I don't dare let them show on my face. I straighten my back, looking him directly in the eye and thanking the cold heart that takes residence in my chest.

"For the last time, I don't control Ryder Callaghan, any more than you control me. You want him? Go talk to him yourself. I won't tell him to leave and work for you, and I won't ask him to stay either. Good luck."

I turn my back to him and head toward the door. I don't quite get there before I hear commotion in the hallway. It swings open and I come face to face with a very pissed off Denny, and an even angrier looking man about half the size of him, and much older.

"You alright, Elle?"

Denny looks over my head and into the room, scowling toward Becker, apparently they know each other.

"Ah, Mr. Black. Pleasure to see you again," the smug fucker behind me says.

I look up at Denny, taking in his stoic expression. If these two have met before, that means he would've known what type of work Ryder was up to when he went to Chicago. It also means he probably knows about Claudia Becker. That would explain his body language when I mentioned Ryder was in

Chicago, while Denny and the rest of the crew were here in Jacksonville.

His loyalty lies with Ryder, not me.

I lift my head high once again, refusing to feel like the dumb bitch who doesn't know what's going on around her.

"Lock the door when you leave," I say walking through the little bit of space there is, seeing as he takes up most of the doorway.

I don't bother with any greetings to Mr. Becker's associate in the hallway, probably because I don't believe he deserves it.

As I walk down the hallway, I think about how I always hated politics, and about how I hate them even more now. That arrogant prick Becker thinks he walks on water, and his associate out here in the hallway probably helps him stay afloat no matter what lengths they need to go to.

I jog down the steps and out toward the parking lot. I don't do the usual check of my surroundings, just a quick scan before I haul ass across the lot and get into my truck. I shove the keys in the ignition and pull out of the stall buckling my seat belt on the way. I don't want to stay around here any longer than I have to, and I don't want to talk to that arrogant man again. I just need to move, go, get away from here and figure out what the hell just happened up in that room, and what the hell Ryder is hiding from me.

I'm not a stupid woman. He was hiding Claudia fucking Becker. That's what this was all about. I didn't ask for Ryder's half of the story when it came to Anna because I was leaving anyway. I knew I was, I used her as the excuse pushing me out sooner.

I don't want to use Claudia as an excuse this time. Perhaps I should talk to Ryder about it. But for what? I know he lied! It was written on Denny and Becker's faces. He could say he has nothing to do with Claudia, but how does that explain Chicago? Especially when I know there wasn't an election going on.

It doesn't explain it. And for once I don't think Ryder can explain this either. My gut is never wrong and something here is telling me he fucked up.

I pull onto the freeway with my raging thoughts and loud music. I don't drive in the direction of home, I just keep driving west.

Chapter Fourteen

I pull into the parking lot of a grocery store about an hour from home. I don't know if what I'm about to do is incredibly stupid, or just plain fucking dumb.

My decision may be rash, and it may be because of the anger and other emotions I don't care to admit running through my body. I hate that I *feel* anything right now, but in a sense, I feel like I've just had so much shit dropped on me all at once that it's time for a change.

I can't keep running.

It's impossible to hide from Ryder, and I have exhausted my energy in wanting to do so. Sometimes the best decisions are made under stress, not that I'm stressed right now. I'm just...done?

Yes, that's it.

I'm done.

The finality of that statement helps me breathe a little easier.

I reach into the glove box and pull out one of the burners I bought when I was in Indy. Yet another way to send them off the trail when it comes up nowhere near there. I open the dinosaur of a flip phone and punch in the number that's burned into memory and wait while it rings.

"Miller," his sleepy voice says over the line.

I smile a little at the thought of him with his guard down. "You must be on the night shift."

I hear rustling, most likely him throwing the covers off. "Jayne?"

Hearing my given name sparks something inside and I lean my head back against the seat, closing my eyes.

"Yes, it's me."

My voice is quiet, my mood is somber. I'm mentally exhausted, tired of running. Tired of lying, tired of hiding. Tired of being lied to by people I thought I could trust. The voice from my past pulls me out of my head.

"You gave me a little hope Jay, last time we talked. I didn't expect it to be so long before I heard from you again."

I take in a deep breath and dive right in. "Don't cut me off when I tell you this, and please don't jump to conclusions."

He clears his throat. "Alright, I promise."

Detective Miller is a good guy, I know that. But when I left he didn't have a lot of pull in the department. He was respected, but so long as Braumer put his two cents in everywhere, Miller didn't stand a chance in defending me. So I ask him, "Andrew Roberts was adopted, right?"

"Yes, by his Grandmother."

I brace myself for his reaction to my next question.

"How possible is it the reason only one set of DNA was found in the basement is because he's an identical twin?"
There's a long pause so I push on. "You there? Or are you calling the nuthouse from your landline?"

Miller stutters through the phone. "I- Fuck! '*Them*', she kept saying '*them*'. Fuck, it makes sense now."

He's not talking to me, he's talking to himself.

"You said 'them' Miller. What are you talking about?"

He nearly shouts, "I interviewed her! Or tried to. She wouldn't talk much, strung out on god knows what."

"*Who,* Miller?"

"Andrew's biological mother! I tracked her down about a month after you left, off duty. Braumer didn't see the need in investigating her, seeing as she apparently had no contact with him since the day she gave him up. I found her Jay, and she said '*I couldn't keep them*' over and over again. But in my mind I guess I thought she meant '*couldn't keep him*', or if she did say them I assumed she meant she gave up more than one child over the years. She was a mess Jayne, all ninety pounds of her. She practically lived on the street. I could barely understand a word she said, and then she just took off. Spooked and higher than a kite."

I take in everything he said and for once have hope that perhaps my case can come to a conclusion, one that doesn't involve me being insane.

"What's her name, Miller?"

"Shit Jayne, you know I'm not supposed to share this shit with you. It's bad enough I gave you a copy of the files, which no one has figured out by the way."

"Don't worry, being on the run doesn't give me the opportunity to run to the authorities to let them know I have a document belonging to the Ontario Provincial Police."

I hear him let out a huff, but he gives in. "Lucille Roberts, but she changed it to Lucy Greer shortly after she gave up her son. That was her mother's maiden name, the mother who raised Andrew Roberts."

A lot of questions run through my head.

Why would she want to change her name?

Why didn't she have contact with her son?

Why separate them?

Most importantly, why couldn't anyone else figure this shit out!

I ask him, "you going to look into the twin thing Miller? Or are there no more tax dollars left for that?"

"Dammit Jayne, you know I did everything within my power to help you out. Even went behind Braumers back."

I'm being hard on him, I know. I'm just pissed it has taken so long for me to figure this out, or more accurately, for Ryder to figure out there was a twin. I open my eyes with a new sense of purpose and determination to get to the bottom of the nightmare still haunting me.

"I'm coming back, Miller. Whether you help me figure this out or not is up to you. But with or without your help, I'll find him."

"Jayne, if you come waltzing back into town, the first face you're going to see is Braumers, and it'll be on the other side of an interrogation desk."

That fat lazy fuck won't leave me alone.

"Did you tell him I called you a few months ago?"

"No."

Of course he didn't, he's too kind to me.

"I won't ask you to lie for me again Miller, and I won't tell you exactly when I'll be back. But I'm coming. I'll let you know when I'm ready to talk. Until then, do me a favor and find that woman so we can figure out where her other kid was sent to, because if you don't, it's possible he'll find me first. We both know how that ends."

There's silence on the other end of the phone for a moment. I know he's still there, he's just contemplating what I said.

"I'll do what I can, Jayne. Braumer isn't breathing down my neck anymore, and I made senior detective last month after he put in for retirement."

This is music to my ears.

"Does that mean I won't have the pleasure of seeing him again?"

"You and I both know if you step foot in this department, he'll be back here in five minutes flat. He may have retired Jayne, but that doesn't mean he was finished with this case. He still pops in from time to time, sticking his nose where it doesn't belong anymore."

The music in my ears stopped.

"Alright, I'll call you again soon."

"I'm guessing you're not going to give me a number to reach you at?"

"You guessed right."

I hang up the phone and put the window down in my truck. I put it back into gear and pull up beside a garbage can, tossing it into the trash.

THE UGLY ROSES

It's time to go home, my little cottage home first, then, Ontario.

Chapter Fifteen

I turn onto my lane and note the number of vehicles in Ryder's driveway. I recognize the extra two as both Denny and Cabe's suburban, or at least the suburban his company uses for work. I continue driving, pulling into my own driveway. I pull out my phone and dial his number. He answers on the second ring.

"Elle! Are you alright?"

I brush off his mock concern, or maybe it's genuine. However, after lying to me about Chicago and being involved with another woman, I'm not inclined to take his concern to heart. I may be jumping the gun here, seeing as what happened with his ex-fiancé Anna proved to be false accusations on my part, but this time I know better.

"I'm fine. Is that Denny and Cabe at your place?"

I hear him cover the phone and speak to the guys telling them 'I'm fine'.

"Yes, they're here. Listen Elle-"

I cut him off mid-sentence. "I'll be over in thirty. Please keep them there, I'd like to speak with all three of you."

He's silent for a moment before he responds.

"Sure, we'll be here."

I don't say anything else and hang up the phone. I grab my belongings off the passenger seat in my truck and head into the house. Norma greets me as per usual, but I don't spend long giving her attention.

THE UGLY ROSES

I head straight to the bathroom and turn on the shower. I'm a mess right now, and as much as I know I'm not trying to look good for the men next door, I need my full armor on. I've been made vulnerable twice today and I won't let there be a third. The first was when William Becker entered my life and the second when I learned it's possible Denny knew about Ryder's indiscretions with the political fucking princess.

I scrub fast, not wasting time to shave since I already did this morning. It's a quick wash to get the sweat off me from the gym. I dry off quickly, leaving my mess of hair down in its usual dark brown riot.

I head to my closet and throw on a pair of dark skinny jeans, followed by a black top and the rest of my usual attire. Scarf, black boots, etc. I bend down at the back of my closet and unlock the safe, retrieving my case files. I don't need them where I'm going, and I've memorized what's left in there anyway. I stuff them in my messenger purse along with my cigarettes and shoot a quick whistle for Norm.

Walking toward the kitchen, I head for the fridge. Not for wine, but the bottle of Grey Goose I keep on top of it. I unscrew the cap and pour a healthy portion into the rocks glass sitting on the counter from last night. I don't waste time inhaling or savoring the light liquor. I toss it back and drop the cup in the sink.

Liquid courage.

Norm follows me as I make my way outside, down the steps and across the small beach I've grown to love. I don't dwell on the loss that'll soon come, I just keep moving toward my next destination.

Reaching Ryder's home, I walk up the steps toward his back door and notice the three men congregating around the island, a pizza in the middle and the empty beer bottles piling up. I don't knock since I already told him I was coming, I just open the door and continue what I came here for.

Three heads spin in my direction when I close the door behind me. I follow Norma over to the island where she happily parks her behind next to Ryder, waiting for some love and leftovers. He's dressed in a worn-out pair of light jeans and a white short sleeve shirt. His hair is sticking in every direction. I know it's because he's stressed, running his hands through it nonstop.

I don't ogle him like I usually do, and don't let myself feel anything (if that were even possible.) I open my mouth to get straight to the point of why I'm here but Ryder beats me to it.

"Elle, I heard about Becker's visit today."

It wasn't a fucking visit, it was an ambush.

His eyes hold remorse, and since he's not immediately pulling me aside or trying to defend himself by saying he had no involvement with Becker's daughter, I know he's guilty of it. It's possible that it happened before us, but that doesn't explain his visit while we were together, or the fancy dress clothes when he came home.

If he was innocent, he'd be embracing me right now. He'd be petting Norma or asking me how I'm doing.

Maybe he doesn't know what Becker said to me and he's playing aloof hoping he didn't say anything that would bruise his ego or make me think less of him. I remind myself that either way, I don't care. Not because he wasn't good to me when I needed it, but because there are more important things to deal with than the love affair I had with my neighbor. Regardless of what he said, regardless of him chasing after me, I was never meant to stay here.

I can tell he wants to say more, but mid-thought I hold up my hand to stop him.

"It wasn't so much Becker's visit that caught me off guard, it was the mention of his daughter Claudia."

I can tell he's ready to cut me off so I hold my hand up further. "I'm not interested in what you did before me, and right now I don't care what you did while you were with me. However, I may sign myself up for a health check, seeing as I can't be certain anymore who you stuck your dick in while you were fucking me. None the less, not why I'm here, and definitely not my business anymore.

"You said you'd help me so that's what I'm here for, nothing else. How much does it usually cost for a few days' work with you and a few men anyway? I've been curious."

He's offended at my spiel, but I don't care right now. My emotions are turned off, the numb is back and for once my head couldn't be clearer.

"Small jobs can be anywhere from a grand and up per day, depending on the client and depending on the risk," Cabe answers for me seeing as Ryder is still standing with his hands braced on the counter, eyes closed. I reach into my purse, grabbing the other thing I stuffed in there from my safe.

Money.
Ryder's eyes open when he hears the thump on the counter. "That's twenty thousand dollars."

I reach back into my purse and pull out the case file, tossing it next to the money.

"Got a pen, Cabe?" He grabs one off the counter and pulls a small notepad out of his back pocket.

"Elle, I told you I'd help you, I don't want your fucking money!" Ryder says angrily.

I look into Ryder's troubled eyes with my determined ones. Mirroring his stance with my hands braced on the counter.

"We're not fucking anymore Ryder, and as far as I'm concerned we're not friends. We're working together, that's it. Cabe is your tech guy and I need him more than I need you right now, so if you don't want the money, give it to him. Donate it to charity. I really don't care what you do with it so long as I get what I offered to pay for and what you promised to help me with."

I look back to Cabe, making a motion with my hands for him to get ready with taking notes.

"Everything that happened is in that file, in case you haven't found it all on your computer yet. What's missing is what Ryder still has. As for new information, write this name down, 'Lucille Roberts'. She changed her name to 'Lucy Greer' about thirty years ago. She's a bit of a street rat. She's also the biological mother of the man that attacked me, Andrew Roberts.

"I recently got information that pretty much confirms there were two children she gave up, but it's not concrete. I need you to look into that and figure out where the second child went and why the hell she didn't keep them together."

He continues scribbling before looking up at me. "Alright, I got it. Anything else?"

"Yes. I need you to access border security and figure out if I'm going to be arrested when I use my real Canadian passport to get back into the country in a few days."

Ryder's head swings up, furious. "Jesus, Elle! You're fucking pissed at me! I get it! Hell, I deserve it. But your answer is to just go running back to Canada? The one fucking place that might get you killed?"

I put my hands back down on the bar and lean forward, keeping eye contact with a soulless smirk on my face.

"Don't flatter yourself, Callaghan. I may have left here once, but that was for fear of you blowing my cover. Now, I just don't give a shit."

I turn my attention back to Cabe, noting Denny has been oddly silent throughout this whole exchange.

"Cabe, I already called my detective back home. He knows I'm coming but he doesn't know when exactly. I need a few days on my own when I get there and I can't do that if they know I'm in the country. Find out what you can for me please so I can get back there and tie up some loose ends. There are things I need to do, and people I need to see before I end up in an orange jumpsuit or six feet under."

Ryder slams his hand down on the counter, running the other one through his hair. "This is bullshit, Elle! I thought you were smart, but this is one of the dumbest fucking decisions you've ever made."

I cock my head to the side. Studying him. He has no right to put his two cents in anymore.

"Well then *handsome*, I guess it's a damn good thing I don't give a fuck what other people think of me, or the decisions I make. I'm done running from the police, I'm done running from a killer and I'm pretty much done with you."

I glance over at Denny and note the disappointment in his eyes. Oddly, it's not at me, but directed toward Ryder. Cabe, being the only level-headed one here apparently at the moment breaks the tension a little.

"To state logic here, it's possible that if you were to end up in jail, even for a short amount of time, you could be safe. However, I think we'd all agree it would be nicer just to sort all this shit out, prove your innocence, and be done with it. I know it's easier said than done, but I need the facts Elle, whatever you can tell me that's not in that file."

I look to Cabe, appreciating his all business attitude. Perhaps the stack of twenty grand in cash helps. He's a good man, I can tell. I also know exactly what he's asking me in regard to what's not in the file.

"You want to know if I killed that sick fuck in the basement?"

He nods his head, slightly caught off guard with my boldness. For once in my life I don't give a damn what anyone thinks about my next statement. I don't care what the outcome could be. I place my palms back on the counter and look him straight in the eyes, speaking low and firm.

"You bet your Latino ass I did, Rodriguez. But not before I made him suffer. Not before I tied him up and beat him the same way he beat me. Not before I cut his back open with the same knife he cut me with, and not before I stripped him of every last bit of dignity he had.

"Call it retribution for my mother, my father, my sweet little girl and *her* innocent father. And only then when he begged for his life, did I deliver the final blow for myself."

Three sets of eyes stare back at me, and I peel my eyes from Cabe's to take them all in, the shock evident on all of their faces. I tip my head to the side and say, "that answer your question?"

Cabe is clearly caught off guard again, but he nods and replies, "sure does."

"Good. Want to ask me if I'd do it again?"

I don't wait for him to respond.

"The answer will always be yes."

I reach across the island and pull his notepad closer to me. I scribble down my phone number and push it back across the counter.

"I leave in two days. If you could get the border security info to me first, and fast, I'd appreciate it."

He wastes no time responding, "I'll have it by tomorrow."

I nod my head in thanks and look to Denny. He looks sad, though I don't know why. Perhaps it's guilt for not mentioning Ryder had another woman in Chicago. I don't acknowledge him any further, or the look of despair he's currently directing toward me. He's smart enough to know he won't change my mind.

I give a low whistle and Norm gets up from her dog bed. I try to see if there's a sense of nostalgia left in me. From the first time I came over here and noticed that dog bed. The first night Ryder touched me—a first of many. I take stock of my emotions and realize there aren't any. It's just nothing.

Empty.

Gone.

Numb.

I walk out the door without emotion.

Miserable Jayne is back, and I'm grateful.

This cold-hearted bitch might just keep me alive.

Chapter Sixteen

"Open your eyes you dirty bitch. You want to avoid me? Maybe now you'll learn to pay attention."

Thump!

I crack open my left eye, the least swollen of the two, and stare down at the floor. Not because I want to, but because my neck and back are so fucking stiff I can barely lift my head.

"Nooooooo!"

A heaving sob leaves me as I stare at the lifeless body sprawled across the floor.

"That's what you get Jayne! This," he points to the floor, "is what you get for not fucking paying attention!"

He hauls his foot back and slams it into the back of the body on the floor.

The body doesn't move—no grunt, no whimper.

Nothing.

He's gone.

"W-wh-why? I-I ddddooon't unnddeerstand?"

I shake my head, why why why?

What the hell did I do to deserve this? What did he do to deserve this?
Nothing!

Andrew walks slowly, circling the dead body on the floor. It seems to have given him a little more self-esteem to kill someone, because for once his head is held a little higher, he's not quite as broken. He's not so lost. He's taken pleasure in what he did and he's embracing the sick high he got from it.

"Love is a sacred thing Jayne. I loved you, and you threw it away. You threw it so fucking far that I had to do this, I had to do everything! Now you'll know. Now, you'll learn. You're just as fucking selfish as that bitch you warned me of in school."

He leaves the body and comes to stand directly in front of me. Evil eyes focus on mine, his chest heaves and hands fisted at his side. His face is inches from my own before he gives the final blow.

"He cared too much about you. Nobody should care about someone like you. So he deserved to die."

I look down at Cory's lifeless body, the father of my child. The man that literally gave one hundred and ten percent of his love to his child without once expecting anything in return. He didn't need to be told he was a good dad. He knew it. So did our little girl.

He knew we weren't compatible, but we both held a deep amount of respect for one another and gave our best as separated parents. We focused on what was important, who was most important.

Lilly.

My sweet little Lilly who's no longer with us, but who has now gained a parent in heaven. That's where Cory would go, he's a good man.
Was a good man.

Fuck!

I swing my head forward as fast and as hard as my body will let me, slamming my forehead into his.

Fuck Him!

Andrew stumbles back and trips over Cory's lifeless body before falling onto his ass.

I take advantage of the fallen man, gathering every last bit of strength I have left in me.

For Mom,
For Dad,
For Lilly,
For Cory.

I wrap my fingers around the frayed rope and pull my legs up as far as I can. The gashes on my back re-open. I can feel the sting of the wounds as well as the fresh blood beginning to pour down my back.

I don't care, this is it.

I'm fucking done.

Andrew jumps to his feet, holding his right hip, which took most of the impact from the fall. I don't give him a chance to get close. I'm done letting him near me.

If I die, so be it.

I don't fucking care.

This is it.

This is the end.

I use my arms to lift the majority of my weight while swinging my right leg out in front of me when he get close. He quickly moves his hips back thinking I'm going to kick him between the legs.

THE UGLY ROSES

Wrong move for you asshole, perfect move for me.

Moving his hips back moved his head forward. I continue with my right leg and swing it up onto his right shoulder. My left foot hits him in the back of the left shoulder, forcing him closer to me. He's taller, and at this point it works to my advantage.

He turns his body away from the hit of my foot which gives me enough room to bring my leg completely around his neck and swing it back toward me. He's not expecting my maneuver and before I know it the tall man has my weight suspended on his shoulders which in turn loosens up the slack on the ropes.

I reach my arms above my head to grab onto the beam while simultaneously pushing my left knee into his back, tightening the hold my right leg has around his neck.

"You fucking biiiittccchh," Andrew manages to choke out of his rotten mouth while I continue to crush his windpipe.

His filthy hands grasp my legs and his fingernails dig into my thighs. Not long enough to do serious damage but enough to make scratches that'll take a few weeks to heal.

I want to let up on the pressure enough to move my leg higher, more toward his jaw. If I could do that then I could push my knee hard and quick into his back, while pulling hard enough right with my other to snap his neck.
I can sense what that would feel like, the quick pop, and right now in this moment I'd kill to hear that sound.

Pun intended.

Pop!

It would be music to my ears. The following silence.

But I'm afraid to let up. I'm so fucking weak and the new blood rushing down my back isn't slowing. It's a steady and constant reminder that I may not have a lot of time before I pass out again.

His hands pull strong and I know for a fact that if I let up and attempt to kill him by snapping his neck, he'll get the upper hand.

I can't let him beat me. I won't.

Now, it's all about avenging my family and getting some justice for the lifeless and innocent man that lies on the floor in front of us.

I don't look at Andrew.

I look at Cory.

I squeeze my legs as tight as I can, ignoring the aches and pains channeling throughout my body while I try to kill the man who has taken everything from me. It feels like hours, but it only takes a minute or two until I feel it. His limp body slowly overtakes mine to the point that my arms holding onto the beam are now carrying our weight.

I don't let go until long after his hands have fallen to his sides and my arms can't bear the brunt of our combined weight any longer. I loosen my legs from their hold on his neck and haul myself upward at the same time.

I watch his body drop. His head thwaps against the hard-concrete floor. I have no idea if I killed him, but I know I need to move fast.

I use what little strength I have left and swing my legs up a few times, unsuccessfully, trying to get them around the beam so I can swing myself over.

THE UGLY ROSES

After the third try, I'm almost ready to give up. The blood dripping down my legs has made the beam slippery. I give it one last go while clutching the prickly rope and manage to get one leg over.

I pull with everything I have and don't stop for one second as I allow myself to free fall ungracefully over the other side. I wail in pain when my back comes into contact half with the floor, and half with Cory's body.

I don't have much time!

I crawl over my child's perfect father, slipping in the blood on the floor as I reach Andrew's unconscious body. I pull the side of his red polo up and un-sheath the knife he has kept there. He never bothered to clean it. My dried blood causes it to stick in the holder. I pull hard and it finally comes free.

My blood-soaked hands fight to keep a grip on it as I saw back and forth over the frayed rope binding my wrists. I move as quick as I can, back and forth, back and forth, working tirelessly to cut them off. I place my foot on the slack and pull as I cut, finally breaking free.

I tell myself I would not be a normal person if I didn't shed tears in this moment. I settle for the fact I'll never again be normal, because the first thing I do is drag the slack on the blood-stained rope toward Andrew.

I ignore the pain, I ignore the exhaustion. I pay no attention to my aching bones and bleeding body. I simply stare at the innocent man on the floor and wind the ropes, in the form of a figure eight around Andrew's forearms. I weave and wind and end with boat knot my father taught me.

I crawl on hands and feet, cursing my bleeding back while I untie the rope attached to the floor. Swinging my arm back, I throw the rope over the curved portion of the beam, the same way it was. It takes a few tries, but I get it. I move as quickly as

I can back to the steel loop bolted to the floor, feeding the rope back through.

Using every last ounce of energy left in my body, I pull—for my mom, for my dad, for my daughter, and for Cory.

* * *

I slap his face, once, twice, three times.

No luck.

His head hangs heavy on his shoulders, arms suspended above his head. I grab my empty piss bucket and drag myself over to the spigot on the wall. There's no hose, so I fill the putrid bucket with water, leaving the tap on because my hands hurt too badly to try and close it. I go to pick it up off the ground, but my arms cannot carry it full. The remainder of my strength put Andrew where he currently hangs.

I push the bucket to the side, emptying half its contents, before throwing the rest at his face. He sputters, and spits, before opening his eyes. Clearly disoriented and wondering how in the fuck he ended up where he is now. Hanging and helpless. I greet him with a mocking smirk that I embrace, along with my hoarse voice.

"Welcome back."

He thrashes his feet, pulling on his arms. It serves no purpose; it only makes the sticky rope bind tighter.

"You bitch! I'll fucking kill you! You hear that! Kill you!"

I sway on my feet, "Tsk, Tsk, Andrew. I thought we could play a game. You like games, don't you?"

THE UGLY ROSES

I leave his line of sight, walking behind him. His feet continue to flop like a fish tail out of water. I grab onto the back of his sweat-soaked shirt and bring the knife to the top of it. I push down, cutting the fabric until his back is visible.

The knife pierces his skin as he thrashes, but I have no remorse. Nor do I tell him to stay still. I drag the tip of the blade from his back to his front. I zero in on the lower portion of his body, repeating the same procedure to the belt on his jeans as I did with his shirt. I flick the knife toward the button. His body goes completely still.

I've found his weakness.

"What are you doing? You won't fucking get away with this!"

I push down on the handle and hear a 'ping' when the metal button bounces off the cold concrete floor. I tilt my chin toward his face, enjoying the look of him rendered so helpless.

"I already have, Andrew."

I waste no time in pushing the blade further down his body, ridding him of ever article of clothing aside from his boxers. I want him to feel exactly how I did in this position. I want him to be weaker than me, begging for his life.

His jeans get caught on the rope I tied around his ankles. I wasn't about to leave them loose and able to choke me as I did to him. I leave the jeans where they are and grab my second weapon from the side of the room. He used a two-by-four to hit me with. I however don't think I'd have enough energy to swing the piece of wood hard and fast enough to leave a wound. This is what has me grabbing the four-foot piece of pipe off the floor, something where its weight will do all the work.

"What are you doing with that? You bitch! Let me down!"

"That's not going to happen, Andrew. You should've thought this through better before you brought me here."

"What are you talking about? I watched you for years! I've planned this for years!"

"Ah, but you didn't plan well enough, did you? Because for all the watching you did, including these past three days in this fucking hole, you still failed to learn the most important part of me."

He pulls tighter on the ropes, hoping to gain some slack. Spit flies from his mouth as he begins to yell at me.

"Fuck you! I know everything *about you! I know you spread your fucking legs for just about any bastard who walks into Frank's. I know you never let them spend the night because you're a fucking whore who won't give anyone a chance!*

"You fuck them for what Jayne, a few months before you toss them aside? People in this town think you walk on fucking water! Well you know what? I don't. I saw your true colors. I knew you were just like the rest of them! I know the only type of shampoo you use, so fuck you saying I don't know you!"

His rant is that of a madman, clearly not well in the head. It makes me wonder how someone like him has survived in society for so long. I hold the pipe in one hand, and mindlessly drag the blade back and forth across his chest. Not caring if it makes a mark, but not intending to do so—yet.

"The most important part of me is not who I spread my legs for, or what other people think of me. It's not the shampoo I use or what I eat for lunch. No, the most important thing, Andrew, is that I don't give up and I'm not afraid to die.

THE UGLY ROSES

"You see, you brought me down here, hoping I'd say sorry, hoping I'd beg for my life. I would do no such thing. Ever. You know why?

Spit flies from his mouth as he speaks.

"Fuck you, you crazy bitch! I'll kill you when I get down from here, I'm going to fucking kill you!"

I don't listen to a word he says. Mostly because I don't care, and also because it doesn't matter. I move to his back while he continues to curse me. Pushing what's left of his shirt aside, I place the knife just below his shoulder blade.

"The why, Andrew, is the most important thing. You see, if you want to kidnap and torture someone, you better make damn sure they have something left to live for."
I pierce his skin, watching as the red drips down his back.

"You see, I have nothing left because you took it all from me. So I didn't beg, plead for my life, or say 'I'm sorry' like you wanted me too. No, I did none of that. Because there wasn't one god damn thing you could do to bring them back. The only thing I wished for, and fought for, was this moment right here."

I lean forward, putting my mouth closer to his ear.

"It's called retribution, you sick fuck. And it starts right here" I'm sickly pleasured by the cries coming from his throat as I drag the blade in the same pattern he did on me. I take no pity on him as I watch the blood run from his shoulder to his lower back.

"That was for Gary O'Connor. Father, husband, and grandfather."

I move the knife under his other shoulder blade, dragging it slowly on an angle down toward his spine.

"That was for Susan O'Connor. Mother, wife, sister and grandmother."

I listen to his screams echo off the cold concrete walls. I can hear the tears in his voice, his garbled cries pleading with me to stop.

I don't.
I can't.

I drop the bloody knife to the floor, picking up the rusted piece of pipe. I grab onto it as fiercely as my blood-soaked hands will let me. I test the weight of it in my hands, swinging it around, listening the whooshing sound as it slices through the air.

I walk around the body hanging in front of me. I drag the pipe, letting the screeching sound of it scraping across the concrete grace my ears. I see the tears and snot running down his face. The desperation in his eyes almost causes me to drop the cold metal.

Almost.

"You're going to hell, you evil bitch. You're going to hell for all the sins you've committed and what you're doing right now!"

I smirk as much as my battered face will let me. "I guess I'll meet you there then, won't I Andrew."

I haul the pipe up and swing as hard as I can, hearing the crack when it comes into contact with his ribs. His cries of pain fuel me to move forward like a woman possessed. After everything he has done to me in the past three days, I keep swinging.

I don't listen to him pleading with me to stop. I only hear the crunching of bones and the feel of warm blood raining out of his body. When my arms have grown tired, and my legs begin to tremble, I drop the pipe.

I fall to my knees, feeling around the blood-soaked floor for the knife. I grasp the handle with my shaking fingers and push myself back up.

I will not die, I will not give up.
I'm so tired, but I'm not finished yet.

"Open your eyes," I say, slapping him hard. "I said open your fucking eyes!"

He opens them slowly and spits a mouthful of blood out onto the floor so he can speak.

"They all deserved to die. Your bastard daughter deserved to die."

I don't think, I just bring my right arm up, positioning the knife. "This, you sick son of a bitch, is for Lilly O'Connor. A beloved daughter and granddaughter. She was my heart!"

I pull back, and swing forward as quick and hard as I can, pushing the hunting-style blade deep into his heart, not stopping until the base of the handle comes into contact with his skin. I pull the knife out, walking backwards. Not entirely sure why I feel no remorse, wondering if I'll feel guilty later.

My feet slip on the water that has leaked out from the spigot on the wall, not caring or bothering to turn it off. I take one last look at the room I never want to see again, the resting place of my daughter's dead father and now the man hanging from the pole who's no longer breathing.

I won't feel guilty.

Because I feel nothing.

Chapter Seventeen

I reach over blindly toward the night stand, searching for my buzzing phone. I crack my eyes open and look at the clock. It reads ten in the morning. I didn't go to bed until three; I was too busy packing up my belongings, preparing to move. I can't take everything. It won't all fit in my truck. I debate shipping, or storage, but then I think I could be dead or in jail before the year is out, so that's probably a stupid idea. I settled for sorting it into the few boxes I had in the closet.

I packed up two small suitcases to take with me. The rest I'll figure out later. I open the shitty flip phone and put it to my ear.

"Hello," I say in my sleep filled, raspy morning voice.

"It's Rodriguez. You got five minutes?"

"Ya, shoot."

"Alright, no holds at the border under your name. Only in the town you lived in and a few of the surrounding ones. You're not labeled a fugitive; you're just wanted for information regarding the deaths of Andrew Roberts and Cory Gallagher."

I breathe out a sigh of relief.

"Thanks, Cabe."

"No problem, but one more thing."

I can sense this isn't part of the good news.

"Lucy Greer was found dead a few months after your attack. She was hit by a car."

My eyes shoot open, I sit straight up in bed. This isn't sitting right with me.

"That can't be a coincidence," I say. No way, what are the odds?

"You may be right Elle, hit and run, but there were no leads on the vehicle. No autopsy. She's long dead and buried now."

"Any other information? I still don't know who Andrew's father was either, maybe that's something to look into?"

"He wasn't listed as far as I can tell and I haven't started searching for the brother yet. Other than locating the death of Lucy Greer, that's as far as I got before I called you. Leave it with me, I'll let you know what I find out."

I breathe out a sigh of relief, thankful for this tech savvy man. "I appreciate it, Cabe. Also, I may be getting a new number. I do that a lot, so don't be alarmed if I call you from a Canadian burner in the next few days."

"No problems, Elle."

"Thanks for the help. Talk soon."

I hang up the phone and stare blankly across the room.

Lucy Greer.

Dead.

Something is not right, something is seriously wrong.

* * *

I toss the rest of the spinach into the pan. It's a random dinner made up of things left over in my fridge. Chicken, spinach, peppers, parmesan, garlic—basically whatever wasn't rotting got put into the pan.

I just finish draining the pasta when there's a knock on the front door. Norma waddles her ass over to it, barking. I set the strainer aside and grab my gun off the counter, concealing it behind my back as I walk toward the doorway.

"Who is it?"

"Denny."

I motion for Norm to calm down and open the door. He still has that sad look in his eye, like disappointment or something similar.

"What do you need?"

He shoves his hands into his front pockets. "Can I come in please? I'd like to talk to you...without hawk eyes over there watching my every fuckin' move."

I look left toward Ryder's house and sure enough, he's standing there leaning against his porch railing, eyeballing Denny. Or maybe me. Either way it's not a nice look, but I still don't give one fuck. I open the door, gesturing for him to come in.

I walk back into the kitchen and grab the strained penne out of the sink, mixing it in with my goulash of leftover fridge contents and a little bit of heavy cream.

"I'm sorry, Elle."

I don't turn around because I hate those words. *I'm sorry*. It never feels like it's enough, and I hated hearing it over four hundred times at my family's funeral. I don't tell him that though. I just continue to mix up my dinner that could feed seven.

The last supper.

"I won't lie to you Elle and tell you I didn't expect Ryder to be with Claudia in Chicago, because I did. I just didn't want to believe it. She's a manipulative bitch, Elle. I can't fucking stand her."

It pleases me to hear that she's not perfect. That would please any woman who has been cheated on. I secretly hope she's an overweight ugly whore too, but I don't think I'd be that fortunate.

"I came here Elle not only because I wanted to apologize, but because I wanted to tell you if I knew that's what he was doing in Chicago, I would've told you. Or I would've told him to stop. I asked him Elle, when he got back. All he told me was that he was tying up some loose ends with Becker. I didn't believe him, but he also didn't have a reason to lie to me. We've all fucked around Elle. I'm no choir boy either. But if I knew the truth I wouldn't have let it go on without telling you. I respect you more than that."

I stop my stirring to face him.

"I'm not exactly angry with you, Denny. I'm just fed up. I don't like to be lied to. Brock told me you were a good person, and I believe him, Denny, I do. However, at the end of the day, it doesn't matter what happened. I'm out of here and have bigger things to worry about like whether I'll end up in jail, or *worse*."

"A lot of my loyalty lies with Ryder, darlin'. But that doesn't mean I have no respect for you. To be honest I respect you more than any other woman I've met. You're a good person Elle," He smirks before adding, "and I'll still think you're a good person, and good lookin' even if orange doesn't turn out to be your color."

I whip my head around and do something even I didn't expect.

I laugh.

A full, deep belly laugh that even catches Denny off guard. I wipe the tears from my eyes and the snot off my face. He can't contain the grin stretching across his face, and regardless of what happened, I still really like this man.

I return his smile and turn around, reaching into the cupboard. I grab two plates and dish out my concoction, pushing a plate across the bar to him.

"The last supper, eat up."

He grabs the fork and knife I hand him before digging in, clearly not shy to join in on my impromptu dinner. I'm thankful I'm not eating alone, despite the numb in my body.

"What are you going to do with all your stuff?" Denny asks.

I glance around the little cottage-style home. I love this place, yet I'm eager to get my past life dealt with.
"Leave it. I was going to get a storage unit, but that's a shit idea. I pre-paid a year's rent on this place, so basically it is my storage unit. Maybe Ryder or Tom will find someone to move in, or maybe he'll just maintain it while it sits empty. I packed up all my clothes into boxes, so if I need it, I'll get it shipped to me."

Denny is quiet before he looks at me solemnly. "You mean if you live, or don't end up in jail, you'll get it sent to you."

THE UGLY ROSES

I wipe my mouth off with my napkin and look up at him.
He really is a beautiful man. I wouldn't be surprised if he
descended from some ancient Viking clan. He could certainly
act as one on a television show, in a loin cloth, with his sharp
jaw and light brown hair, his broad shoulders and over six-foot
body.

"Something like that," I say.

I grab two beers out of the fridge, opening them and taking
a long gulp. He does the same.

"If you're alright with it, I'll take it over for a while. If you
come back, I'll move out. I've been staying at The Willow,
this might be a nice change of scenery for a bit."

I nearly spit out my beer, recognizing the name of the
motel. It's not shabby, but it's not a home.

"You're not joking. You live in a motel?"

He shrugs his shoulders. "It has a kitchen and a bed, which
they make every day. Maid even does my laundry."

I shake my head. "Yes Denny, I'm sure she loves to do
your laundry, and make your bed."

He sets his beer down, offended. "Toni is a very good room
keeper."

I let out a small laugh. "Yes, I'm sure she enjoys her job
where you're concerned."

A slow smile creeps across his face. "I tip well."

We both know what kind of tipping he's insinuating, but
say nothing else on the subject.

"I'm out tomorrow afternoon. If you want to meet me here when I go, I'll give you the keys then."

He washes down the rest of his pasta with his beer.

"What do I owe you for the rest of the rent?" I shake my head and start cleaning up the mess. "Nothing."

"C'mon, Elle. That's what? Like six months almost?"

I contemplate his words and realize he's right. How is it that half a year has passed since I moved here, fell in love with the cottage and fell for Ryder, moved from the cottage and then fell out with him? My life has been like a merry go round. Ultimately going back to Canada would be getting off where I got on.

Full circle.

"You heard Cabe, Denny. I'm a millionaire. I don't flaunt it, barely use it. None the less I don't need the money back and I don't want it. If you want to pay me back, help Cabe whenever you can to figure out this fuck up that is my life. *That* means more to me than money."

I turn around from placing the dishes in the dishwasher and come face to face with Denny. His hands are at his sides. He towers over me in my little kitchen and studies my face for a moment, not in an uncomfortable way, but like he's trying to see all of me. I allow him this moment before he speaks.

"When you told us the answer would always be yes, for killing that guy, did you mean it?"

I look up into those piercing blue eyes of his, not hesitating for a second. "Absolutely."

He studies my face for a few more moments before nodding his head. "Good."

He leans down and places a kiss on top of my head, before turning around and heading for the front door.

"Thanks for the food, I'll see you tomorrow."

I give a small pathetic salute goodbye, once again thanking my family and the universe for bringing such awesome people into my life.

Chapter Eighteen

"What color?"

I look at the reflection of the hair stylist in the mirror. She's a little older than me with bright red spiky hair. I love her color. It's daring. It's bold. Knowing I can't venture down that road today, I settle on what I came here for.

"Blonde but leave a little light brown throughout."

She studies me for a few moments before nodding her head.

"Contrast, I like it. I'll go mix up the colors."

By the time the blow dryer starts up, I'm lost in thought. I never thought I'd see something resembling the old me in the mirror. I haven't seen light hair in a long time. I like it, and sometimes I miss it, but I plan to dye it back with a box of dye as soon as I cross the border. I have no interest in looking like I used to.

My face is already different from what it once was. Those sweet cheeks and that southern belle look I had are long gone. Not wanting more questions than I can answer at the border, I settle on my old hair which is the most predominant feature in my passport photo. At the time my hair was in huge curls and nearly down to my ass.

"Well, what do you think?"

The stylist takes the cape off and gives me a reassuring smile. My dark brown is now light in giant curls with lowlights throughout. It's beautiful. She did a great job, but I know I can't keep it.

"It's great. Thank you."

THE UGLY ROSES

I pay in cash and head back toward home. I've tied up all I needed to here. I got my passport out of my safe deposit box and replaced it with my guns, knowing I can't take them with me across the border.

I filled out a slip, listing Denny Black as next of kin in the event I die and my money and guns are still stuck here. Not that they'd really know, since I would die as Jayne O'Connor and not Elle Davidson. But Ryder and Denny would know and I plan to leave the information with Denny just in case. The rent for the deposit box will come out of my account, which has more than enough to cover it. I also stashed twenty thousand in the box; you can never have too much stashed somewhere. You never know when you might need it.

It has certainly come in handy this past year, cash money that is. I silently thank my father for not completely trusting banks and always being prepared. They had a huge safe at their home. A few months after they passed, I located the money, close to a million dollars in cash. It didn't surprise me. He'd been putting it away in there for decades, always living by the rule that you can never be too careful. I took close to half of it with me and transferred some of it via Western Union before I left Canada. It's been more than enough to get me by without needing to use Canadian bank cards to alert Braumer of my location, or anyone else for that matter.

I pull into my driveway, noting Denny's truck is already here. I hop out and meet him at the steps.

"All ready to move in?"
"Yup, got two duffels in the truck."

He won't stop grinning at me. "Diggin' the blonde, darlin'."

I shake my head. "Well, don't get used to it. I have a box of brown dye in the truck for after I cross the border."

"Noted," he replies.

He follows me up the steps and greets Norm when she bursts her healthy ass through the door.

"So, since you don't have much, I don't have to worry about my boxes of clothing taking up too much space in the closet?"

"No worries, darlin'."

I walk into the bathroom and begin packing up my stuff I left out for this morning. There is still no feeling of emptiness as I pack. It's like my mind is set on Canada and nothing else will get in my way. I know I'm leaving, therefore my body doesn't stop to give me time to dwell on the fact I may never see this place again.

I grab my toiletries bag and head back into the main room, looking around, making sure I didn't forget anything.

"You leaving everything in the fridge?"

I peer toward the kitchen, noting the surprise on Denny's face. It's still full of food, condiments and beer. A bottle of wine, or five.

"Yes. Don't drink it all in one night."

He grins at me over the door and comes out with a beer. "I didn't wash the sheets and there's still a load of towels in the dryer. I hate folding."

I start walking out the back door, wanting one last view from my porch before I go.

"Darlin', I've slept on dirt. The sheets are fine. Might call Toni to see if she makes house calls."

I laugh a little and look out at the water. This is it. It's time to go. I turn and look at Denny for what too may be the last time.

"I left my guns and some cash in a safe deposit box at this bank. Here's the slip. I put your name on it, in case I don't make it back here."

Denny looks down at the paper in my hands, not wanting to take it, but knowing I won't leave with it.

"I don't like when you talk like that, darlin'. Why don't you let one of us come with you, watch your back?"

I shake my head at him. I never want anyone close to where I once endured hell, where four innocent people have already lost their lives.

"Enough people have died because they were involved with me, Denny. I don't need any more of that weight on my chest. I'll be fine."

I shove the paper into his hands and stare back out at the water. Only it's not just the water, Ryder is standing there.

"He's right, Elle."

I feel an extra layer of ice coat my chest, not willing or wanting him to show that he cares about me. Sure, he cares about the lives of others in general. He just doesn't give one fuck about the heart and soul of them.

Or maybe he just didn't care about mine.

"Well as much as I appreciate the concern, I don't need it. I paid for information, not a high-priced body guard or pep talks from one, Ryder."

I reach out and give Denny a one-armed hug.

"Thanks."

"No problem. Hey, what about the gym room? Did you look after that?"

"It's yours until the end of the month." He gives me a squeeze on the shoulder and I descend the steps. I look at Ryder as I near him, not bothering to put the sunglasses on my face because there's no emotion to hide in my eyes. I feel nothing. Normally I'd take in the beauty of his body, encased in black boots, dark jeans and his long sleeve shirt pushed up to his elbows.

Normally I'd study the way his almost black hair falls around his face and the darkness of his eyes. They used to make me melt.

I don't do any of that.

I walk on, with my head held high and back straight. I never thought for one second I'd be able to leave without seeing him again. In fact, I expected it.

"It may not mean much beautiful, but you weren't just some random woman to me. You're still not."

I pause in my steps and look at this contradicting man.
"So while I wasn't just some random woman, you still felt the need to run to another one Ryder?"

He shoves his hands through his hair.

"It wasn't like that, Elle. Fuck, I didn't think I'd see you again in all honesty."

"It's okay Ryder. I get it. Just answer one question for me. Did you fuck her after you first saw my scars and took off for work? Or was it when you left me in Indy? Actually, you know what, I don't want to know."

177

He looks down to the ground, avoiding eye contact.

"I didn't think I'd see you again."

I know what he means, and as much as I didn't want to know, I'm thankful for the information. It still confirms what a sack of shit he is. If I were weaker I'd belittle myself and think what kind of man wouldn't want some smooth-skinned beautifully poised woman after witnessing the hell that is my back.

But I'm stronger than that weak belittling woman.

Fuck him, fuck her, and fuck you too.

"Well, that's refreshing. You know, I once said I didn't want to be a job to you. But that's exactly what I was, wasn't it Ryder?"

His head whips up, his black eyes piercing mine. "That's not true!"

I walk closer, so we're toe to toe. I look up into those black eyes for what I'm sure will be the last time.

"You didn't fuck me until I accepted your help. Is that your game Ryder? Bring in the clients, then fuck them? In both senses of the word? Because it sounds like poor Claudia missed you while you were here, working with and fucking me. I guess it's true what they say, isn't it?"

Hard eyes stare back at mine. "What's that, Elle?"

"Don't mix business with pleasure. It's like oil and water handsome, they don't mix. Hopefully not being able to keep your dick in your pants doesn't affect your reputation."

"When did you become such a bitch again, Elle. Huh? Answer that!"

I lean in close, speaking low. "I was a bitch from the day you met me. The only difference now is that you actually deserve to see this side of me. You deserve it and anything else karma fucks you with. I gave you something I never gave anybody, so shame on you, Ryder Callaghan, for taking that for granted. I promise, you'll regret it."

He hisses through clenched teeth. "I already do."

I take a step back and put my sunglasses on. "Good."

I step around him and walk toward my truck. I don't look back when I open the door to throw my bag in. I don't acknowledge that Norma is still sitting at his feet when I whistle for her. I don't let the fact that he looks incredibly remorseful and defeated get to me.

I don't think anything, I don't do anything. I just move, like I'm on auto pilot. I get the dog in the truck. I put on my seatbelt. I turn on the truck. I back out of the driveway. I drive.

All, on auto pilot.

Feeling nothing.

Seeing nothing.

Smelling nothing.

Numb.

Chapter Nineteen

"Identification please, ma'am."

I hate *ma'am*. Almost as much as I hated the last shit motel we stayed at. This trip was not as well planned as the others. Long story short, I slept on top of the covers and debated getting a bottle of bleach to bathe with.

Traveling with a large dog is not always glamorous and a lot of people don't always want them in their establishment. This left us with 'The Nifty Fifty' alongside the interstate.

It wasn't 'Nifty'.

It wasn't clean.

I hand over my passport, plastering on my fake but tired from traveling smile. The young border security guard I don't even think reads my name before he's handing it back to me. Maybe the pricey visit to the salon wasn't needed after all.

"Thank you, ma'am. Where you headed?"

I look at my poor dog in the rear-view mirror and point over my shoulder. "First stop will be a large patch of grass. Second is just north of Toronto."

He nods his head, not giving a shit what I'm saying.

"Okay, drive safe."

I give a small wave over my shoulder and wonder how much money I could've made smuggling a few pounds of blow just now, or how much safer I'd have felt being back in Canada with my hand guns. I totally could've brought them.

Errant thoughts of drug smuggling and weapons aside, I drive on.

I do as I told him and stop at the next rest area, letting my girl out and stretching my legs. I'd like to say it feels good to be back home, or bad. Something, anything. But I still feel nothing.

After a much-needed bathroom break and recirculating the blood back through my body, we reluctantly get back in the truck. I know where I'm going first, it's a few more hours but I don't plan on stopping until I get there.

* * *

I pull up in the driveway and punch in the code for the large wooden gate to the rear parking lot.

Still the same.

The gate opens and I pull in, watching it close fully behind me before driving around back. There's a garage door at the front, but I don't know how full the shop is so I opted for the back lot.

It's not huge, but large enough to park about six vehicles with grass at the rear. There's eight-foot privacy fencing surrounding the lot, which is perfect. Also one of the reasons I chose to come here first.

It's dark out, but the small light on the back of the building allows me to see enough to get to the door. Norma is wagging her tail, knowing exactly where we are. I wait for her to take care of business before punching in the code for the back door.

I open it and smell the scent of my past. *Paint and ink.* Slightly sterile, but welcoming all the same. I don't stick around downstairs. The lights are all off, so I make my way to the apartment upstairs. Not wanting to scare the living shit out of him, I knock first.

No answer.

I open the door, walk in, and close it behind me. Nothing has changed. Beautiful paintings still line the walls, biker memorabilia takes up every shelf and the big black leather couch looks just as comfy as the last time I was here. I walk around the corner and notice the mess that is his kitchen. Take out boxes and a few empty beer bottles. This place is like his junk drawer, the shop is his pride and joy which he keeps clean.

I make my way down the hall toward the bedroom and peer inside. There he lies, sprawled out on his back, boots still on. His dark brown hair is short but messy. He has always been tanned, always has a scruffy face and always looks handsome. He has a sharp jaw and masculine features. He has tattoos on most of his well-toned body and the ladies flock to him like a fat kid running after the ice cream truck.

Norma doesn't waste a minute once she sees him, remembering this is the one house she was allowed on the furniture. She jumps as much as her heavy body can handle and lunges onto the bed. He jumps up, startled, and gets a large white furry dog body plastered to his chest. Norm is whimpering, snuggling into the man she hasn't seen in almost a year. His arms close around Norma and his eyes move up until they meet mine in the doorway.

"If you were a guy, I'd hit you Jay."

I smile at my best guy friend, missing our banter. "I missed you too, Jimmy."

He shakes his head and gives Norm the love she was waiting for. She flops her body down on his lap. I hear him groan.

"When did Norm put on the pork?"

I push off the doorway and move into the room, flopping down on the bed which smells like hookers and cigarettes, staring up at the ceiling.

"When I found it too hard to cook for one."

He too flops back on the bed and we both turn to face each other, our heads about two feet apart. "You park out back?"

I nod my head.

"Didn't hear the buzzer, I was out cold. I painted until three in the morning, then worked all day."

That's definitely something Jimmy would do. When he gets into something, he doesn't like to stop until it's finished.

"How's the shop?"

He stares at me for a few moments then claps his hands, using the cheesy device to turn on his lights. I know why he did it. Sure, the hair and my build is pretty much the same. But being this close, he'd now notice my face. He stares at me for a while, not saying anything. I don't turn away. Jimmy isn't judging me, he's just getting a good view of his new but old best friend.

"You okay with that?" I know what he's asking and I answer him truthfully.

"Not the same woman I was when I left here, Jimmy. I'm okay with it because it's me. The *me* I am now."

THE UGLY ROSES

He lets my words soak in and reaches out to push the hair off my face. "I know. I didn't know it before, but I get it now."

I knew he would and I knew he wouldn't bombard me with a hundred questions when I walked in here. Exactly the reason I came. Well, one of a few.

"I need your help."

He doesn't hesitate. "Anything."

"Get your tattoo gun ready. And beer. Oh, and a pizza from Vinnie's."

A big grin spreads across his face and he sits up, pushing the dog off before standing.

"You know the way to this man's heart. I'm going to enjoy your company first and then we'll talk, babe."

I give him a small smile, thankful that my returning after such a long absence can be this casual. This is what I love about Jimmy. He's just that easy going. Laura will be a different story, but I don't plan on letting her know yet. I can't hide on Laura's busy little street. I can hide at Jimmy's.

I take in a big breath and sit up, ready to experience the pins and needles.

Chapter Twenty

"You sure about this Jay?"

I look down at the pictures I gave Jimmy. I had this idea for a while, and I see no better time than the present.

"Yes."

I set my beer on the small table in front of me, and turn my back to Jimmy. He hasn't seen it since the hospital, and even then I don't think he saw all of it.

I take off my shirt, followed by my bra, and lay down on the towel we spread out over the chair. I'm slightly buzzed; a lack of sleep and a few beers will do that to you.

"You've healed pretty well, but this won't tickle Jay. Especially with all the scar tissue."

My scars aren't wide, but they are long.

"I'm ready."

I hear the buzz of the needle and Jimmy doesn't hesitate to get to work. He knows I'm not into small talk, but that doesn't mean we don't have catching up to do.

"Shop doing good?"

"Yes, it is. I guess somebody really loves me because just before you took off my rent became null and void and suddenly I owned the building."

I smile a little inside. "Yes, I guess someone does love you."

"Funny thing, Laura no longer had a mortgage either. The mall didn't see her coming when her next pay check came in. Neither did Frank's when she bought half the bar's tabs."

I really do smile this time, thinking Laura would definitely go on a shopping spree and buy drinks for random strangers. God, I miss her.

"Thank you, Jay." I don't say anything, I know I don't need to. They'd do the same for me if they came into the kind of money I did.

I bring my arms up and rest my head on them, trying to get a little more comfortable on the table.

"Damn, muscles. Where'd you get those?"

I know he's referring to the size of my arms. My body has changed a lot since I've been gone.

"Personal trainers for the past few months."

He continues with his buzzing on my back, starting up with more questions. "Did you make it personal?" That's Jimmy's way of asking if I slept with them.

"No. It wasn't like that with them."

"But it was like that with someone. Does he know?"

I don't speak, just nod my head. Jimmy is silent for a few moments before he speaks again. "You haven't bothered to bad mouth him yet, which tells me there actually is something to bad mouth. Want me to kick his ass?"

I let out a small chuckle. Jimmy is not a small guy, but Ryder is definitely a lot bigger. "Ex-military, Rambo-type security something or other. As much as I'd love to witness him take a blow, I think you might break your hand if you tried."

Jimmy pauses in his tattooing. Readying himself to say something I know I won't like. "I know about Denver, Jay."

I stiffen, wondering how the hell he'd know about that, seeing as I wasn't there when he was. Jimmy answers my unasked question because he's intuitive like that.

"I was down there four months ago. Spent a week at Remy's shop and stayed at Blacktop again."

I turn my head to the side, studying Jimmy's face. "I trust you Jimmy, but how much do you know?"

He sets the tattoo gun down for a moment and takes off his gloves to light up a smoke. He passes it to me and then gets another for himself.

"We were having a few drinks at The Top (*his short for Blacktop*) and Remy was talking about getting a dog. He wanted a Rottweiler for guarding the yard, but then he talked about this woman who stayed there with a nice white dog. Said she was beat up pretty bad and the dog guarded that woman like he wanted the Rottweiler to guard his yard at the shop, which made him realize it wasn't just the type of dog, but how loyal it was to you.

"Anyway, a fuckload of drinks later and one of the young guys says Norma was a good dog and he missed having her around the bar. It took me a while, but I remembered telling you about those guys and what they did for the women from that strip club that needed new identification and to be relocated. I put it together, Jay."

I take a pull off my beer and set it back down on the table. "Did you ask anyone about that, about me?"

Jimmy shakes his head. "I thought about it, but then I thought if the whole reason you were there was to hide, it wasn't my place. I might've been able to get some info out of someone, but most likely that would need to be Tiny. I don't for one second think he would've told me where you were. That man is loyal to a fault and may have just had me killed for asking about you, thinking it might've been me who did that to you."

I reach out my hand and place it on top of his. "He didn't know where I went when I left, I preferred it that way. He could've told you the name I used, but that would be it."

He looks at me sadly and nods his head. "So, ex-military? Was it Remy? Because if so I'll break that motherfucker's jaw, no matter how big the bastard is."

I shake my head at him, I barely met the guy. "I was only there for a short time when I left here. I went back a few months later, after my surgery and picked up my identification. Left the next day."

I can see the relief flood his face. He's thankful it wasn't his friend who fucked me over.

"Can I ask you somethin' babe?"

I watch him put on his gloves and pick up the tattoo gun to commence my mild torture. "You love him?"

I lower my head and stare at the wall in front of me, wondering if I was even capable of loving Ryder.
"I don't think I'm capable of that anymore Jimmy, or at least not right now."

I absorb the sting of the needle, still not feeling much.

"We've still got about two hours to go. You decide you want to talk about it, I'm listening."

I realize it's been a long time since I just sat and vented to a friend. Years to be exact. I didn't complain about much after my family died. Didn't talk much either. Neither was going to bring them back. After the attack, I just became a body. Moving, walking, eating and drinking. Just not actually *living*. Which means I shut everything off and everyone out.

I decide it's now or nothing. I continue staring at the sketches on the wall and decide to bare it all. Let it all out. From the time I met Ryder, to his finding me in Indy. I tell him about Becker and Claudia. I tell him about Denny and Brock. My voice is pretty mono tone throughout the whole thing, not wanting or able to express emotion with my words.

By the time I'm done, I feel like a weight has been lifted. He didn't ask questions. For once Jimmy was just silent and listened, not putting his two cents in.

"You ready?"

I frown, noting the silence. "Ready for what?"

"I finished about ten minutes ago, babe."

I realize I really must've wanted to get that shit off my chest and I'm more numb than I thought because I didn't notice the needle quit piercing my skin after four hours.

I stand up, holding the towel to my chest. I stretch out my body a bit, noting the tenderness on my back. It's nothing compared to what I've felt before, so I don't complain. I turn my back to the large mirror behind me and look at the one Jimmy is holding in front of me.

My mouth goes dry.

It's beautiful.

The cherry blossom branches completely cover the long marks of my scars. There are a few random branches sprouting out from the big ones, filled with small buds. Among the tree are mostly light-colored flowers, but there are four bright blooming ones representing those I've lost. It's absolutely stunning; Jimmy didn't put a stencil on my back, mostly because he's that good, but also because there's no stencil for my life.

It's not something that could be kept between premeditated lines and colors. This was random, it was outside the box. It was following the nightmares on my back to create something incredibly beautiful. Something I'm not afraid to see. I'll no longer dread someone seeing my back, because from afar you can't see the scars anymore. Only if you're up close—and only if you're touching them.

"It's perfect."

I look up to Jimmy and realize my vision is blurry. Apparently, just because I don't feel emotions right now, it doesn't mean they won't escape my eyes.

He grins down at me and places a kiss on the top of my head.

"Glad you like it, babe."

I grin back at him, once again thankful for the amazing people in my life.

Chapter Twenty-one

I come out of the bathroom and see that Jimmy is still sound asleep. He left a message last night for his clients saying he would need to reschedule his appointments today. He has two bikes downstairs that he's been painting. Since they aren't due to be finished until next week it means we have the building to ourselves.

I head into the kitchen and grab us each a cup of coffee before heading back toward the bedroom. I set Jimmy's on his nightstand and crawl back into bed with my own. This is normal, me sharing a bed with Jimmy. It's never sexual, it's just us. I couldn't count how many times we've fallen asleep in this bed drunk and laughing. He has always been there for me and even kicked a wench or two out of his bed when I came knocking in need of a friend.

He starts to stir. I knew he would once he got a whiff of his morning brew. I look over and his half-open morning eyes stare back at me.

"Brown?" He's commenting on my hair that I just finished dying.

"Blonde sticks out like a sore thumb."

He nods his head in understanding. "What's your plan, Jay?"

Jimmy grabs his coffee and sits up to lean against the headboard mirroring me. I rest more on my side facing him, due to the tenderness of my back.

"I have some guys trying to locate Andrew's brother. I'm going to call them today and see if they found anything."

"What do you need me to do?"

THE UGLY ROSES

God I love this man. There's a reason we've stayed so close over the years.

"I need a burner to keep in contact with them. I was going to stop on the way last night but I just wanted to get here."

Jimmy nods. "No worries, I'll get you one this morning. Anything else?"

"Just don't tell anyone I'm here, not even Laura. Does anyone else have the code to the gate?"

He takes a sip of his coffee before responding. "Laura and my brother."

I think on that for a moment. "If there's any chance they could stop by and let themselves in, do you think we could change it? The less people who know I'm here, the better."

As per usual, Jimmy is accommodating. Within an hour he has changed the gate codes and picked me up a new burner.

"You know, I've had the same code for years. It might be hard trying to remember a new one."

I look over at my handsome friend. He dressed in his usual; black boots, ripped and paint stained jeans, and a short sleeve shirt.

"Oh yeah, what's the new code before I lock myself out of here?"

"654321"

I can't help it, I laugh. "The last code was 123456, so you've just reversed it and you're worried you won't remember?"

Jimmy looks offended. "Hey, many-o-drunken nights I could punch that in blind."

I shake my head at him. Only something so simple could give him such a complex. I move my attention back to the new phone in my hand, punching in Cabe's number. It rings four times before he answers.

"Rodriguez," he says in an all business voice.

"Cabe, its Elle."

Jimmy eyes me from the other side of the island. I told him last night what name I used while I was down there, I'm sure it's just a little different for him to hear it since it's been so long. My grandmother always called me Elle, from the time I was born. If I was in trouble I got the full 'Jayne Elle O'Connor'. Granny was not a woman to mess with, but I didn't always do as I was told so I heard the full name more often than not.

"Good to hear from you, is everything okay?"

I'm sure he's keeping tabs on me for Ryder, not just himself. But I answer him truthfully. "Yes, I'm fine. Any new info for me?"

"Yes, I think I found him."

My heart and my breathing stop, waiting in anticipation for what he'll say next.

"I searched for everyone born around that time with the last name 'Roberts' and got nothing. There was no record of what hospital they were born in and no record for Lucille Roberts ever giving birth to any children.

"I searched for males based on the birth date of Andrew Roberts, which the grandmother had listed on his school records as March fifteenth. I came up with twenty-two hits based on males born that day at hospitals within a fifty-mile radius of Bakersville."

"Jesus Cabe, go on."

"You can Google it Elle, but I'm pretty sure this is our guy. His name is Shawn Flynn, born the same day as Andrew."

"Oh my god, okay why am I googling?"

"Because if you search for 'Baby Boy abandoned at Cornwell Clinic' you'll find out that he was a twin. The mother took off with one baby and left the other one behind."

"Fuck me, how could someone do that?"

"The only answer I have for you Elle is that the boy, Shawn, was in an incubator, fighting for his life. He was much smaller than Andrew and it sounds like they didn't see much in terms of the future for him."

Wow. This is a lot to take in.

"I hacked into the hospital records and got a little more information on him."

"Of course you did, and thank you."

"No problem. Sounds like the Doctor at the time was concerned with possible fluid in the brain, meaning she was most likely stoned for some or all of her pregnancy on god knows what. Long story short, it sounds like she kept the stronger of the two and dropped him off at her mothers, never to return again."

"Wow, I don't know what to say to all that."

"I know, it's a lot. He was in the hospital for over a month, at which time he was placed into Child Services Care. He was given the name Shawn Flynn and spent the next eighteen years of his life in different foster homes."

"Okay, and where is he now?"

It's rather silent in the background and I realize Cabe must have his hand over the telephone mic because I can hear mumbled voices.

"Cabe?"

"I'm here, sorry. I'm looking for him. He hasn't popped up on anything since shortly after university which was almost ten years ago. He did renew a driver's license, but the address he has listed is not where he lives now since it has since been turned into an arts building.

"I have his picture Elle, I'm surprised they are identical because he does look quite different. Although you can't mistake the fact he is his brother. Shawn is smaller. He was held back in school and he definitely looks like a lost little kid. He too went to the University of Toronto for computer science."

This is so much to take in. I never recognized Andrew, therefore if this twin doesn't exactly look identical there's a small chance I may remember him.

"What do you want me to do, Cabe? What can I do from here? Because I have to say, I'm feeling a little fucking useless right now. Aside from looking at the photos you found to see if I recognize him."

"I'll send them, but I don't think there's much that you can do, Elle. The mother is dead, and from the short amount of time he spent in the last few foster homes, I would guess they never learned that much about him. His longest stay was six years, but the woman looking after him died from a severe stroke when he was sixteen. So his last two years were spent in three different homes.

"I'm still digging, I haven't stopped. This is just what I've found out up until you called me. Give me some more time. Can I call you back on this number?"

"Yes, you can. I don't want to hide here forever, so please no matter what time of day or night, you find something, you call me."

"You have my word."

"Thanks, Cabe. I appreciate it."

"No problem. Take care of yourself, Elle."

I hang up the phone and look at a straight-faced Jimmy.

"Is that the guy?"

I lean my head into my hands. "No, that's one of his minions. A talented tech guy helping me out."

I relay everything Cabe told me over the phone to Jimmy.

"Damn, Jay. That's a pile of shit to take in. I want to ask say how the hell Shawn is unable to be tracked down, but I guess if you lived off the grid for almost a year now with a new name, he could be too."

I nod my head up and down, knowing it's definitely possible. I'm living proof.

My phone dings with a text from Cabe. I open up the app to view the attached photos. The first one is a university student photo of a kid I don't know. The second is a driver's license photo. I study them both, hoping for recognition to hit. Sadly, it never comes.

I study the brown hair, like Andrews. His eyes are also the same color. I can only see from the shoulders up in the photos, but I can already tell Shawn is definitely not as big as Andrew. He's thin. Sort of lanky looking. His face still looks boyish and his eyes are completely innocent, a stark contrast from the evil in his brothers.

I hear the rustle of grocery bags and set my phone back down on the counter. "What's all that?" I ask Jimmy, opening up the shopping bags he now sets on the counter. "You're making me stew tonight, since I'm kind enough to harbor a wanted woman."

"You drink MGD. I need Guinness, so I guess the stew is out."

Jimmy decides at that point to bring the large paper bag up off the floor, pulling out a six of Guinness, and three bottles of my favorite wine.

"So, I'm making the stew, and you're getting me drunk?" I ask.

A big grin spreads across his handsome face. "Now you're talkin'."

Chapter Twenty-two

"Damn, you have no idea how much I missed your cooking."

I watch Jimmy, on his third bowl of stew. I made enough so he can eat it for a week or freeze it for leftovers.

"Oh, I think I have a pretty good idea."

I gesture to the garbage can that's now full of takeout containers from every restaurant in town. His fridge art is the menus to said restaurants.

"You know I can't cook shit other than waffles and bacon."

"Yes, so you can make me breakfast in the morning when I'm hungover."

Which I very much plan to be. A good drunk with Jimmy, hopefully a good sleep and then regroup with Cabe in the morning.

* * *

"You are so full of shit."

"No, I'm not. It's over, Jimmy. Leave it alone."

Jimmy brings his laptop out, setting it on the island in front of us. He spends time clicking away and before I know it a photo of a beautiful brunette pops up on the screen.

"Who's that?"

"That, is Claudia Becker."

My heart makes a ridiculous flutter and then the anger starts to build. I hate that I feel anything looking at her photo right now, I prefer the numb. She's an attractive woman, unfortunately. She has chestnut colored hair and brown eyes. Her skin is quite pale and she has high cheekbones with a small nose. She's wearing a cream-colored sheath dress and nude pumps. She's the complete opposite of me while she stands there in the photo—on the arm of Ryder Callaghan.

She looks like someone who'd get along well with Ryder's ex fiancé Anna. They look like they'd run in the same snooty circles, with their pearls and diamond encrusted clutches. Not that Anna could afford diamonds, unless her sugar daddy bought it for her. Much like Claudia, who has most likely had everything handed to her on a silver platter.

I wonder after seeing these two, if this is Ryder's type; a more refined looking woman and not the kind who dresses in black, spending her spare time beating the shit out of a punching bag. The one who drinks way more wine that what's considered healthy and smokes too many cigarettes.

Maybe I was the dirty little secret?

The woman on the side that makes you feel good and feeds you well. Just not the kind you would escort to a public event or put a rock on her finger. I look at the date. It confirms what I thought: it was the night before he came back to the cottage. Still dressed in the clothing he wore to the fundraiser the night before, with *her.*

"What the hell, trying to show me what he left me in Indy for? Or just trying to ruin the buzz I have going?"

Jimmy leans over and puts his arm around the back of my stool. "Jay, the fact that you're angry right now tells me you are in fact, full of shit. If you didn't care about the man like you're letting on, you wouldn't give two shits about this woman."

He's probably right, but I'm not going to tell him that.

"Are you done?"

"No. Did you sit and talk with him? Maybe he had a good explanation?"

I can't keep the sour look off my face. "Did you start taking estrogen pills while I was away, Jimmy? Last time I checked we didn't have these heart to hearts about the men in my life."

"Don't be fucking stubborn. You know as well as I do that you still feel something for that guy."

"Okay! Maybe I do, maybe I don't. It doesn't change the fact he lied to me. You know how I feel about that Jimmy. Can we please just finish getting drunk so I can get a good night's sleep?"

He squeezes my shoulder and proceeds around the island to the fridge. A sure sign that we will indeed, finish getting drunk tonight.

* * *

I hear the ringing, but I can't force myself to move. My head is pounding. I think I'm still drunk from yesterday. I crack my eyes open a little but immediately shut them when I notice Jimmy forgot to close the blackout blinds.

I feel movement on the bed and hear Jimmy finally answering the phone.

"Jay."

He pats my shoulder, but I have no intention of moving.

"Jay, wake up."

"Noooo."

I pull the comforter over my head to block out the sound and the light. I just get comfortable before it's pulled back down.

"No, Jimmy. Close the blinds!"

My voice hurts even my own ears. I crack my eyes when I feel the darkness and see Jimmy in front of me, phone in hand.

"It's for you."

I'm shocked for a moment, until I notice he has my burner phone in his hand.

"Hello." Christ I sound horrible.

"Elle." My body freezes at the sound of Ryder's voice.

"Yes?"

There's a few moments of silence, until I hear him curse. "Dammit."

"What do you need, Ryder? I'm tired."

"Yes, sounds like it. Late night?" he asks with a bite to his tone, suggesting he knows exactly what I did with my late night, considering a man answered my phone.

Oh, how he would be wrong.

Although I don't feel like correcting him right now, ultimately what I do and who I spend my time with is not his business anymore. I could be a better person and let him know who Jimmy is to me, but I feel like I'm done being the better person. It got me nowhere with him the first time except half-humiliated and a little bit heartbroken.

"Yes, it was a late night."

"I don't want to hear about it. I called because Brock has been up my ass because you haven't contacted him in a while. Denny is out of service for a few days and he won't take my word for it that you're alright."

"That's because Brock doesn't trust you. Can't say I blame him."

I hear his breathing on the other end of the phone, I know I pissed him off with that one but I really don't care. "Dammit, Elle. Just call him please so he quits blowing up my phone."

"I will. Bye."

I don't wait for him to return the farewell. I hang up the phone and pull the covers back over my head. My solitude and silence doesn't last long before I feel the bed dip.

"I don't think he took too well to me answering your phone."

A grunt is all I manage for a response before I fall back into slumber.

Chapter Twenty-three

Ryder - Present Day

"Goddammit!"

I pick the phone up off my desk and hurl it across my office. I watch it smash into the slate grey wall before it falls to the polished floor, shattering into pieces. I slam my fist down on the desk and aggressively push out of my desk chair, not certain if I want to hit the wall, or hit myself.

What the fuck was I thinking?

I let her go, not by choice. Now she's shacked up with who the fuck knows, and my hands are still tied from being able to prevent it. I hate to admit the sick feeling in my gut when that guy answered the phone. I know she doesn't have any brothers and the fact she was harping in the background asking him to close the blinds, well, that says it all to me.

Maybe I'm a stupid son of a bitch. Maybe there wasn't a goddamn thing that would've kept her with me. I made my decisions based on the facts at the time and hoped to shit that she would hold out or at least hang on for a little bit longer. Maybe I didn't mean as much to her as she does to me.

"Feel better now, dickhead?"

I swing my gaze back to the doorway at the sound of Ivan Chekhov's voice. He's been by my side for years. Saved me from a few bullets that got too close in Iraq and in return I pulled his ass out of a burning Humvee in Afghanistan. That shit aside, it doesn't mean I won't think twice about pounding my fist into the cocky bastard's fat head.

"Keep your mouth shut Chekhov. I don't want to hear it!"

THE UGLY ROSES

He pushes off the doorway and moves to sit on the black leather sofa along the far wall of my office. He puts his hands behind his bald head, boot clad feet up on my coffee table and makes himself at home. I don't bother to hide the scowl on my face.

"Don't look at me like that boss, I told you from the beginning this shit would go south. It's your own damn fault she's shacked up in Beaver Country, with another man no less."

I look at my big Russian friend and wonder how close we'd still be after I pound his smug face into the drywall behind his head. I also wonder how he knows what my outburst was about.

"What do you know about it?"

"It's not what I know brother; it's what the fuck are you going to do about it."

I kick my desk chair out of the way and storm toward the windows looking out over the water. "Don't fucking play games with me Ivan, you know I did what I had to do."

I hear him huff in annoyance, because he didn't agree with what I did. If he knew everything I wouldn't be put in this goddamn position with my brother in arms. I know it's about time to come clean. I trust my men. I trust them with my life. But there are some things in this business I need to take care of on my own.

The less people who know, the better.

"I take it you don't check in with Maverick?" he asks.

I scrub my hands over my face, annoyed and exhausted. "He has his orders, Ivan. Unless she's in danger, abducted, or taken to jail, he has no reason to report to me."

Maverick is one of my best men. If something were amiss, I'd have heard from him. I don't sit around and shoot the shit much with my guys lately. I've been too on edge and too wrapped up with the most stubborn fucking woman I've ever met.

I can't stop thinking about her, worrying about her. The look in her eyes when she left the cottage gutted me. The Elle I once knew was *gone*. Replaced by the cold numb bitch I first met many months ago. The day I saw that Black BMW cruise through the intersection was the day I knew I was wrecked. I've never had a problem with women. More often than not, I'm the one who turns them down.

I did my best to stay away from her. I knew there was something behind those cold eyes and the crass language that would be the fucking death of me. I thought maybe she'd be a quick angry fuck, get her out of my system and move the fuck on.

I was wrong.

I hadn't touched her and yet for some fucked up reason I found ways to go about spending more time with her. At first, it just bruised my ego that this beautiful woman who was now my neighbor did everything in her power to avoid me. I made up ways to spend more time with her, from playing a damn nurse when she injured her leg, to cleaning her gutters (a task that could've waited until fall).

I never told her any of this, now I'm wondering if it would have made a difference.

Probably not.

I thought I knew what I had, but I didn't realize just how much, not until she vanished into thin air after I saw the unsightly red marks covering her back.

THE UGLY ROSES

I've witnessed men lose limbs beside me in battle. Hell, I've watched them die. It killed me not being able to protect them. But what I witnessed that night, that beautiful woman sitting on her bed. Her once smooth skin marred by slashes from a knife, well that shit *burned* me. It embedded into my bones the deepest pain and fury I had ever felt toward someone. I ached for her. I ached to hold her, protect her and never fucking let her go. It made me want to kill, regardless of what the consequences would be.

Not once in my thirty-six years had I ever felt the need to be so close to someone. Anna was a learning curve. That first real relationship we all have that eventually fizzles out once you pull your head out of your ass. Everyone before and after Anna served one purpose. Sex. That was it. Not once have I felt the need to be close to any of them.

Until Elle.

Before I saw her scars, I'd already spent more time with her than I had with any other woman in almost a decade. She intrigued me, and that's not something that has ever happened with a woman before. After what I saw on her back, it only made me want her that much more. Not just because I wanted to protect her, but because I felt like it was one more piece to the puzzle of uncovering the woman I so desperately wanted to know.

In that moment, it was like the fog cleared. I understood her anger, I understood her attitude. I understood why she seemed to look in every direction, before she left the safety of her home. Little did I know that what happened to her back was just one of the many tragedies that made her the person she is today.

Seeing the photos of her and her little girl is what broke me. How someone could live through so much and still live fighting today is what truly had me hooked. I've met weaker men in battle. Not everyone can handle so much loss.

My only hope is that she doesn't get a wild hair and do something more stupid than heading back to Canada. I hope to hell she doesn't put herself in the path of whoever it is who wants her dead. Call me a selfish son of a bitch, but I need more time with her. The knock on my door pulls me out of my thoughts of the woman who constantly invades them.

"Boss?"

I turn around, acknowledging Rodriguez. Ivan gets up off the couch and heads toward the door.

"Boxing night, Rodriguez. I'm kicking Hunter's ass at seven. Loser buys the crew beer."

We all know Hunter will be the loser, but the cocky little shit won't give up trying to beat the big Russian bastard. Rodriguez gives him a chin lift before Ivan continues down the hall.

"I have the information you asked me to get. I also found something interesting you might want to take a look at."

"How good is the info, Cabe?"

I see a small twitch on his lips. "Solid—and damaging."

I let go of the breath I didn't realize I was holding.

"Get Benson to arrange a flight, I'll meet you in your office in ten. I need to get ahold of Denny."

Chapter Twenty-four

"Don't forget my smokes!" I holler to Jimmy. I've slept most of the day away, not wanting to face the light. I refuse to acknowledge the hurt I heard in Ryder's voice and instead focus on the fact that my headache and hangover are gone.

So now, here I am enjoying a mimosa. The sun is almost down, and Jimmy and I just finished breakfast for dinner, along with a little hair of the dog in the form of orange juice and champagne.

I prop my feet up on the cheap plastic outdoor table and recline as much as possible in the lawn chair I've parked my ass in. Jimmy has never spent much time entertaining. His barbecue probably hasn't been turned on since the last time I was here. Come to think of it, I think the only company he has, aside from his business, would be the one night stands he brings home and immediately kicks out, unless he falls asleep before they do.

I hear the back door open and silently thank Jimmy as he hands me my death sticks and lighter. He settles into the seat beside mine and we both stare out at Norm, chasing a chipmunk through the small compound.

"When are you going to let Laura know you're here?"

I mull over the question, much like I have been the last few days. I can't seem to come up with an answer. I want to see her, but I don't want to put her in danger. I think she could come alone to Jimmy's shop without alerting anyone of my presence, but as good as she is at keeping secrets, I know she would not be able to hold back the breakdown that'll surely follow. It's been too long since we've seen each other, and I have no doubt that she worries about me constantly.

"She'll lose her shit, Jimmy. I can't do that to her yet. Do I miss her? Fuck yes. I miss those kids too. But until I know that no harm will come to her, I can't do that yet. You know she won't be able to hold her emotions in if she sees me. Shit, she'll probably get shitfaced and not show up to work for a week. I can't do that to her."

I light up a smoke, satisfied that even though it feels wrong, I'm doing what's right.

"I'm not saying you're wrong Jay, but if she shows up here and finds out how long you were with me and I didn't say anything? You know what she's like, that woman can hold a grudge."

He is not wrong.

My burner starts dancing on the table. I don't waste any time picking it up.

"Hello?"

"Elle, its Cabe."

"Hey, any progress?"

"Does *ANIG Tech Solutions* ring any bells for you?" I roll the name around in my head, coming up with nothing. "No, should it?"

"Well it's not that it should per se, I was just hoping it would narrow it down for me a little. I've been going through the old bank records of Andrew Roberts. He put money in the account of ANIG monthly. I can't find much on the business; there's no website, which is odd considering it's a tech company.

"What I did find out though is that the business is registered to an M. Downey. This may be a shot in the dark, but I'm hoping I'm right."

I'm practically on the edge of my seat, thanking this incredibly talented man and anticipating what he's going to say next.

"M. Downey is the woman who had Shawn Flynn for six years in foster care. Her name was Marion. Now, I don't think she opened the business, because as far as I can tell it wasn't created until a few years later. Marion left what little money she had to Shawn, but he didn't get the money until he was nineteen-years-old. The will had a stipulation that he only got it if he continued his education after high school, and he did Elle. I think he opened this business with her name in honor of her. I just need to figure out why Andrew put money into it and what they actually do."

Wow.

"Cabe, how would someone open up a business in someone else's name? I mean, I get what you're saying and it all seems to fit. But something's missing?"

"I already checked; you can register pretty much anything online. It's not like he needed to enter a social security number to make a business. If it's not rolling in the cash, then he doesn't have to worry about the IRS picking up on it, or in your case, Revenue Canada. But there have been some purchases so he obviously has some two-bit accountant out of a back alley somewhere that looks after everything for him. I'm not sure how it all works for them, the system up there is a little different from ours so I'm having trouble tracking down my next lead."

"Yes, we're a little further behind up here in our igloos, Cabe." I didn't mean for that to come out as harsh as it did, but shit I hate when people practically refer to Canada as a third world Country.

"I'm sorry, Elle. That's not what I meant. Pretty much everything is electronic nowadays. There was a purchase from ANIG at a property company in Tucker's Point three years ago. I looked at it on a map. Population is only a few hundred people and the local property office is about ten years behind. They don't have any electronic records for their purchases. All I'm able to find is the company name, and I know it was purchased for thirty-two thousand dollars. Someone would have to sign for something. I can't see that on my computer because it's probably locked in a filing cabinet in their office.

"I hacked into their email records around the time of purchase and I can't find anything that way either. Obviously either Andrew or his brother physically walked into that office to make the purchase. They don't have a damn interact machine listed at the property company, so it had to have been done in person."

I don't doubt what he's saying for a second.

"I know where Tucker's Point is, Cabe. That doesn't surprise me. It's not a known town. People mostly go there if they have a hunting cabin located in the near vicinity. It's not a place you go out of your way to visit."

"I gathered that, and the hunting comment seeing as I can only find three business located in the town. One sells hunting shit, and the other two sell booze and food."

"Yes, that sounds about right. So where is the property office located there?"

"It's not just an office, it's a house. The address for the business is the same as the residence of Margaret and Clinton Cooney. They do in fact have a website. It looks like the front of the house is the business and the back is the home. Not sure why they put a photo of their house on the internet with the business because it looks like something out of Beverly Hillbillies. No shit Elle, they have a *moose* head above the office door."

I can't help the bark of a laugh that escapes my mouth. "That's not uncommon in that neck of the woods, Cabe. It's about two hours northwest of here in the bush. Like I said before—hunting country."

"Well, I called the office to inquire about a piece of property."

"Really? Thinking about moving up here to tag a moose for your own front door?"

"Ha-ha, not likely. I called figuring I could get them talking a little, see what kind of property they've sold in the past. I want the location of the property that ANIG purchased. Anyway, they aren't open. Voicemail says they're closed until the twenty-first of this month."

"That's a week from now."

"I know. Like I said though, I'm still digging. I mainly called because I wanted to see if you knew the company, small town and all."

"My town is not that small Cabe, but I'll see what I can find out from here. Thanks for the help."

"No problem, I'll get back to you soon. Stay safe, Elle."

"Will do, Bye."

I hang up the phone, completely floored with the progress Cabe has made.

"Well? What did he say?"

I look over at my good friend, cautiously. "I need to go on a little road trip."

Chapter Twenty-five

"I really wish you would've stayed at the shop."

I half-hoped to sneak out on Jimmy, but I should've known after I mentioned leaving his little compound that he wouldn't let me venture out by myself.

"Fuck off, Jay. I'm not letting you go alone. Nobody is going to recognize us anyway. They'll think we're lost city folk. How did you get this BMW across the border anyway with the Colorado plates?"

"I paid some lot lizard at a truck stop an hour south of the border. Told her to play along if she got a phone call about her truck being borrowed. She gave me her phone number, then I gave her cash and took a picture of her driver's license."

"Why did you take a picture of *her* driver's license?"

"Because she used it to register at the Western Union in the truck stop. I paid her one hundred in cash and told her I'd send two hundred more if I got across the border okay. Figured I better cover my ass after that time you, Laura and myself got held up at the border after high school driving my mom's Cadillac down to Watertown for the weekend. "

"Shit, that sucked. We sat there for like two hours until your mom finally answered her phone. Obviously it worked okay for you this time?"

"Jimmy, I could've smuggled half a ton of cocaine back with me. They didn't ask me shit. He looked at my Canadian Passport and never batted an eye at the vehicle. None the less, I sent her the money."

Jimmy sighs in sarcastic contentment. "You always were charitable, even thinking of the poor pussy lurking around the truck stop."

I laugh a little. Leave it to Jimmy to lighten the atmosphere.

"Speaking of pussy, who's Randi? She's been blowing up your phone ever since I got back."

"Randi is Wednesday's. Sometimes Saturday's. But now she wants to be every-fucking-day and I'm about to cut her off. Even if she is 'Randy'. By that I mean-"

I shoot my hand up to cut him off and shake my head at my good friend. He can be so crass when it comes to women. Not that talking about sex with him has ever bothered me before. It's more like I'm not having any, so I don't want to swap stories right now.

"Almost there."

I see the few small lights of Tucker's Point in the distance. It's off the main highway and the road has now turned into oiled hard pack gravel. It's past ten at night and there are no other vehicles out. There's no bar in this town, nowhere to hang out and nowhere to stroll to. It'll be tough to get in and get out quietly.

I Googled the website for the property company and noted on the map that it was just outside of town. Well, if you could call it a 'town'. I hope to shit they don't have close neighbors so we can get in and get out quietly.

I pass a few homes. By a few I mean five before I see the small hunting store. Right beside it is the food store, and two houses later there's a small trailer boasting that they sell beer until ten o'clock. Most of the lights are off everywhere and there's not a soul in sight.

THE UGLY ROSES

I turn down the next street, heading to where my GPS is informing me to go.

"That's it, Jay."

I look to my right, out Jimmy's window, and note the small little home with the moose head above the door. I continue driving, not wanting to park my vehicle right in front of where I plan to break into.
"We need to find somewhere to park."

I drive down the road a little further, still not finding anything that's out in the open. I only notice a few other homes set back in the bushes.

"Look at the GPS. It says there was supposed to be a wildlife lookout over Pike Lake. We would've passed it when we turned onto this road."

I make a U-turn and head back the way we came, passing the rental office now on our left and a lot of forest area to the right. I see the sign for the lookout area and pull in. It looks like it forks into a few different directions for lookout posts. I don't venture down any of those; I pull my truck in behind a few big evergreen trees and call myself hidden.

"Jimmy, if you want to wait here, you can. I don't expect you to get caught for a B and E. But I need to do this."

As I expected, Jimmy's response is to grab the small array of tools we put in the back seat and get out of the truck. I knew he wouldn't stay back, but I guess I wanted to keep a clean conscience by giving him the opportunity to back out.

We walk toward the road, both of us glancing left and right, making sure we aren't seen. I don't think we would be, being as there isn't a single street light in the small town. Especially not on this deserted road.

HARLOW STONE

I dressed in my usual black armor. My hair is braided to one side, black hat on. I wore a long hooded black sweater, and my black boots and tights.

Jimmy is similar. Dark jeans, black boots, black sweatshirt. All we're missing are balaclavas and guns, then we would really fit the B and E dress code.

We walk briskly side by side, crossing the street toward the Cooney's small office. I noted when we drove past there was no garage, but I plan to check around the back side of the house to confirm there are no vehicles, and nobody present.

We edge along the side of the yard, much like two experienced criminals would do. It amazes me how in sync Jimmy and I are. We don't speak in words. It's just familiar body language and comfort from knowing each other so long. It allows us to maneuver around the property like we've done this a hundred times before.

I want to say it scares me, but then I think about how we used to finish each other's sentences. I think about how he eats my olives and I eat his tomatoes. We do it all without asking, because it's just second nature. We know what the other one is going to do before they do it. That's why we're best friends. That's why we get along so well.

The home is a small bungalow. The carport on the right side of the home is empty and I know from glancing at the outbuilding that it is too small to hold a vehicle.
We slowly make our way toward the back of the small board and batten home. Jimmy leads, looking in a few windows, making sure nobody is here.

We maneuver around a few shrubs and come to a higher window, suggesting it's a bathroom or a bedroom. There's a small amount of light coming out the window that's too high for Jimmy to see through. He motions for me to move in front of him and puts his hands around my waist.

THE UGLY ROSES

I brace my own hands on the wall in front of me before he lifts me up to look in the window.

"Bathroom, empty," I softly say to him and he lowers me down.

We make our way back to the front of the home, careful to stay in the shadows. There's a door directly on the front of the house, boasting a sign for property purchases and with the giant moose head above it. Jimmy motions for the door that was hidden under the carport and I nod my head.

The first thing I see is the small slip of paper, flapping a little in the wind. It's closed between the storm door and the main door. I edge closer beside Jimmy and we pull the paper out. *Tuck's Heating* is written on the top, along with amount of money they owe for having their propane tank filled. I bring it closer to my face and look at the date.

"Three days ago, they're not here Jimmy."

"Good news for us."

Jimmy opens the storm door and we assess the main one. There's no dead bolt, and there's enough room to stick a screwdriver alongside the handle lock to get in. He pulls out a putty knife from a small pack of goodies and within three seconds the door is open. I'm not surprised. Security is never huge in these small towns.

I take a step inside, following Jimmy. My nose is immediately assaulted with the scent of cinnamon and old people. My boots squeak on the old linoleum floor as we make our way toward the front of the house where the office is located.

We first pass through the tiny kitchen. There's a small oak table for four and very cluttered countertops. Every nook and cranny is filled with old lady dust collectors. Porcelain roosters and cow shaped salt and pepper shakers. There are shelves along the upper part of the wall going all the way around the room, continuing into the hallway. Every type of farm animal figurine you can imagine is filling the shelves.

I don't waste time glancing into the living room on our right but continue straight to the end of the hallway where the office is located on the left. There's no door separating it from the rest of the house. Our footsteps become silent as we enter the room with a rust colored carpet.

"Fuck Jay, your mom would've had a heart attack in here."

I give his arm a squeeze, acknowledging he's very right. My mother spent a lot of time helping to decorate my father's architectural masterpieces. One look at the wood paneling and rust colored carpet would've given her a complex.

"Two filing cabinets, Jimmy. We each take one. *ANIG* is what we're looking for on the bill of sale, or a signature with the names I gave you. Shawn Flynn, Andrew Roberts or M. Downey."
"Got it."

We each take a cabinet, hoping to get this done quickly. I note they aren't filed alphabetically but by year of purchase.

"Cabe told me that property was purchased roughly three years ago. That could mean 2012 or possibly 2011. Let's check those first."

"Alright, I have 2011."

We each begin pulling out files, one by one, searching for the appropriate names. Most of the properties sold are hunting cabins, or small trailers near the lake. We've been searching for about ten minutes when Jimmy gives me the news I've been waiting to hear.

"Got it."

I drop the files in my hands and take the ones Jimmy thrusts between us.

"Look, purchasing date November 2011. I wouldn't have recognized the signature. Thank fuck they make you print it too. Shawn Flynn. He signed for it, but the purchase was made through ANIG Tech."

I flip the pages, looking for the address.

"Lot fifty-three, Pine Point. Where the fuck is Pine Point?"

"I don't know, Jay. I don't think we need this. I'll take a few pictures with my phone, leave the file here."

"Good call."

Jimmy flips through the pages, taking photos of each one and a few extras of the survey photo, giving the exact location of the property in Pine Point. We clean up our mess, putting everything back the way it was before exiting the house. We make sure to lock the door behind us and put the propane bill back in the door.

"Are you going to call Cabe?" Jimmy asks as we walk briskly across the road toward where I parked the truck.

"I want to find Pine Point on the GPS before I do. Let's get back in the truck, I'll feel more comfortable calling him once we're on the road."

Jimmy nods his head and puts his hand on my shoulder, giving a mild squeeze. As much as I'm thankful we found what we were looking for, I want to get the fuck out of this creepy dark little town.

We round the bend and cut across the ditch into the lookout area. The moon is almost full, giving us an easy view of our surroundings as we make our way to the truck. I look down, careful not to trip on anything, but let out a gasp as Jimmy's hand wraps firmly around my arm, shoving me behind him.

I stumble into his back, his feet now planted firmly on the ground, not moving. I reach out and steady myself on his arms, peeking out in front of him. The hair on the back of my neck stands up as I take note of the tall man leaning against the front of my BMW.

He too is dressed in dark jeans with a long sleeve dark shirt. His hair is dark brown, I think, and a few inches long around his masculine face.

"Who the fuck are you?" Jimmy asks in a tone I've never heard from him before. It's low, and a little intimidating.

Both men are about the same size, around six feet tall. Not as wide and defined as Ryder and Denny, but still fit.

"Step away from my truck, asshole."

The man steps away from my truck, casually, obviously not threatened by us. He takes a few steps forward, still about fifteen feet away from us. He's not surprised by our presence, probably because he was waiting for us. I don't recognize him, but something tells me he's not out for blood as his eyes settle on mine with humor.

"You're every bit a pain in my ass that they told me you'd be."

I start to move out from behind the wall that is Jimmy, but he keeps his arm there to hold me back. I look into the man's eyes, still having no recollection of who he is.

"You know, I'm getting real fucking tired of people talking about me as if they know me."

I didn't think any of my statement was funny, but obviously he does because his lips twitch and he shakes his head.

"I'm just doing my job, ma'am."

Oh no he didn't!

"I guess *they* didn't inform you I hate being referred to as *ma'am*. But please, enlighten me on who you are and what that job would be."

He sobers and answers, "I work for Callaghan, Elle. I'm Maverick."

If Jimmy weren't holding onto me right now, I think my knees may have buckled.

He sent someone after me?

What the hell? I can't hide the anger in my tone and I don't bother trying to. "I left him and everything else behind. Pardon my language, and I'm sorry you got handed this job, but what the *fuck*?"

Jimmy has relaxed at the mention of Ryder and I move to stand beside him. He throws an arm around my shoulders in silent support, and it doesn't go unnoticed by Maverick.

"I've been here for a few days. Cabe called tonight and asked me to follow up on the lead in regard to the property purchase. You beat me to it."

What. The. Hell.

"Did you follow me from North Carolina?"

He actually looks slightly sheepish before he responds. "No. I was three hours behind. I tracked your truck."

I can't hide the irritation. I step out and away from Jimmy's arm and move to stand in front of Maverick. He's quite handsome this close, even with the scar running from his cheekbone down to his jaw.

"Go home, Maverick. I told him I didn't want anyone here, and I meant it."

I move past him to the truck, unlocking it as I go.

"Jay."

I turn around and look at Jimmy, still standing where I left him.

"Not such a bad idea to have some help."

I stare incredulously at him, my fingers wrapped around the handle of my truck. "You want help with something Jimmy? Make friends with him. I don't want help. I'm done with people dying around here. I told Ryder that but he's to goddamn stupid to listen. I'm leaving, so if you want a ride I suggest you get your ass in the truck."

I see Maverick on his phone, typing something. He's not put out by my attitude. I guess he was right when he said they warned him about me.

I start the BMW and roll down the window, suddenly hot from anger. How dare he? I swear that man thinks he walks on fucking water and can stick his nose wherever it doesn't damn well belong without any consequences. I look out the windshield and watch Jimmy share a few words with Maverick. He doesn't stay long before he moves to the passenger side of the vehicle and gets in the truck.

He turns in his seat to look at me with an emotion I rarely witness.

THE UGLY ROSES

Anger.

"You know Jayne, I fucking love you. Along with a pile of other people. Where you may think this vigilante act is protecting people, you're wrong! Let me ask you something; would you take a bullet for me? For Laura?" He doesn't stop there, "If I was in pain or danger, would you do anything in your power to fucking help me? If Laura was in danger and you could give your life for hers, would you do it?"

"Yes! Of course I would!" I shout.

For the first time in his life, he raises his voice to me.

"Then quit being so goddamn stubborn!" He slams his fist down on the dash of the truck, not caring that it caused the light on the heater switch to go out. His breathing is heavy. I don't think in the many years I've known him that I've seen him so pissed off.

"You're so fucking selfless, Jay! With everyone you know. You'd do anything, for anybody! Yet when anyone has ever tried to give you even a lick of help, you shut that shit down! Do you think that *little* of us? That we wouldn't do the same for you? Pull your fucking head out of your ass!"

Jimmy has never had a temper, so to say I'm surprised at his outburst would be a huge understatement. I don't know what to say, or what to do. I do the only thing I can which is pass him my pack of smokes out of the cup holder and hope to hell the nicotine will make him feel better. I know my words won't.

He doesn't acknowledge me when I pass him the smokes. He doesn't look at me at all. I would say it hurts, but I know he needs a minute. I pull one out for myself and light it up, ignoring the burning of tears behind my eyes. I momentarily forgot about the commando lurking around until I notice the phone thrust through the open window of my truck.

I look up into pale grey eyes, somewhat remorseful. I now know he heard everything that went on between Jimmy and I. I also know he probably isn't fond of his job at the moment. I grab the phone, assuming it must be Cabe with more info, or him calling to ask about the info I found.

"Yes?" I answer wearily.
"I agree with your guy, about letting people help you."

Ryder's voice forces me to close my eyes. Can't there be one day of peace? One where I don't have to second guess myself or the people around me? One where I just don't have any surprises lurking around the next corner. Something in the back of my head says I would hate that, and my life would become too boring.

"Sounds like it. Being as I have a bodyguard even though I specifically said I didn't want one."

He huffs on the other end of line, obviously fed up with my shit. I'm fed up with him too, but I'm too goddamn tired to argue at the moment.

"Deal with it, because he's not going anywhere. You made it into the office first. Cabe called you before he talked to Maverick; he didn't expect you to go all Mata Hari and try to dig this information up on your own, although it doesn't surprise me. If you could let me know what you found, Cabe can get on it."

I look over at my friend, fuming in the passenger seat. He's too good to me and I know he means well. I just can't stand the thought of anything happening to him.

"I'll have Jimmy send you the photos of the file. It was signed off by Shawn Flynn."

Remembering what I wanted to do in the first place, I reach forward to open up the GPS application and set Maverick's phone to speaker on the dash. I access the GPS function on the dash and a big triangle with a warning comes up, informing me of the GPS malfunction.

"Dude, you broke my GPS." Jimmy's eyes finally meet mine, not at all remorseful.

"The stubborn bitch routine finally got on my last nerve, Jay."

He passes me his iPhone and I commence the search on that.

"Ryder?"

"Still here, babe."

I ignore the endearment and power on. "Pine Point. That's where the property is located. It says it's over and hour east of here, closer to where I came from. The country roads obviously make the drive longer than it looks on the map."

"Don't go there, Elle."

I heave out a sigh in annoyance. "I'm not an idiot, Ryder. But thanks for the vote of confidence."

"For fuck's sake, Elle. You know that's not what I meant. You heard your friend, people care about you. I fucking care about you! If you think you have more experience than a bunch of us frogs who practically killed for a living, you're wrong. I hate to say this to you beautiful but set your pride aside and do as you're fucking told for once. I'm a reasonable man, but don't think for one second I won't give Maverick orders to lock you in a goddamn room to keep your ass alive."

Two outbursts, in one day, by two important men in my life. Well, one more important than the other. I don't get to be shocked at Ryder for long before Jimmy joins in.

"I love you Jay, but so long as you remain the stubborn bitch, I'm going to side with Ryder on this one. I've hid you for a few days, fuck I'll hide you for a month. But I won't watch you throw what's left of your life away because you won't accept any help."

I hang my head in my hands, closing my eyes and covering my face to hide the tears that threaten me.

It's too much.

All of it.

I'm tired.

I'm overwhelmed.

I feel defeated.

I feel weak.

Chapter Twenty-six

I don't remember the drive back home. I didn't speak to Jimmy and I have no recollection of what time I finally crawled into Jimmy's bed.

It's funny, the things that our minds choose to block out. The things we're no longer able to absorb. Once your mind hits that place, that rock bottom pit in your head where you just feel like everything you once thought made sense has been shot to shit. Well, that's when you shut down.

I've lived a long time now believing down to my bones that my presence is a death wish to those closest to me. Considering the track record of those closest to me, and the graves I've visited, it's a proven fact.

Is it so wrong to want to keep them out of it?

Am I wrong to ignore my friend's help?

I know I need it. It would be impossible to be where I am now without the help of people like Cabe, Jimmy and Ryder. I know this and I'm immensely grateful for them. I basically kept them on the outside though. They've been giving me information and hiding me when needed, but ultimately, I've tried ensuring they've kept their distance from where the real threats are, not wanting to put them directly in harm's way.

I guess I hoped only communicating mostly by phone calls, and the odd pow wow with a few of them, that I would be able to keep their involvement a secret. Surely wherever Shawn is, he has not figured out I've had any help in getting me to where I am today. Obviously he doesn't even know that I'm here. If he did I wouldn't be spending my entire day moping in Jimmy's bed, thinking about how I got to where I am.

Jimmy is a straight shooter, much like myself. Surprisingly he has been quiet since he lost his shit on me last night. I deserved it, I know I did. I also know how much he loves me because it takes a lot of bombs to be dropped on him before he finally blows up.

It's at a time like this that I wish for Laura. I know I can't call her yet, regardless of how much I want to. So I'm at a stalemate.

I haven't heard any more about the cabin in Pine Point. I figure if there was any important information, it would've been shared with me. I left my phone on the island in the kitchen, knowing that Jimmy will answer it if it rings.

He's been down in the shop painting. I know it's his own form of therapy. Plus it's his work and I'm sure he has a lot to catch up on since I've taken up his time. I don't mind that he's not up here to console me. I managed to shower and to throw on some comfortable clothing since I slept in what I wore last night.

Aside from the shower and a bathroom break, I've spent the majority of my time in bed. I'm sure it must be pushing close to dinner; however I have no desire to eat, and even less to get out of bed.

Is this depression?

Maybe my months of nightmares and lack of sleep have finally caught up with me. Maybe my heart isn't as cold as I thought, and the rants from both Jimmy and Ryder have begun to thaw that chill, enough that I worry about dying and not being able to spend more time with them. Well, more Jimmy than Ryder. I don't think I'll ever be able to trust someone like him again. It doesn't mean I don't still hold a candle for him. Not for us to get back together, more like the way you still think about a first love, the first person to make you *feel* something.

That's what Ryder did, and although I should be somewhat thankful for experiencing something like that, I remind myself not all stories come with a happy ending.

It was, it happened, it's over.

The sound of the door to Jimmy's apartment closing pulls me out of my pity party before I hear the subtle knock on the bedroom door.

Jimmy doesn't knock, ever.

I don't lift my head from the pillow, but I do reach my hand underneath it, just in case. I'm not left in the dark staring at the wall very long before the deep voice washes over me.

"Need your ass kicked?"

I manage a small tip of my lips before rolling on my back. Denny stands in the doorway, arms braced on the frame. I would say I'm surprised at him being here, but I'm not. I never expected Ryder to back down after I told him on Maverick's phone that I didn't want a bodyguard. Although why I have two now is beyond me. Deciding the only way I'm going to get those answers is to ask, I sit up and make myself a little more alert than the zombie I've resembled all day.

"I might, Denver 'Denny' Black. Is that what you're here for? Some ass kicking?"

He manages a chuckle before he pushes off the doorway. He takes a seat at the end of the bed that no longer smells like hookers and cigarettes since I changed the sheets yesterday.

"Can if you want me to girl, but no, that's not why I'm here."

I make a motion for him to carry on and elaborate. He blows out a long breath and pulls his longer hair away from his face.

"I can't tell you everything yet, Elle. That's Ryder's story. What I can tell you is that you do need my help, and that's what I'm here for."

I open up my mouth to both question him further and reject but he holds up a hand, telling me to stop before I cut him off.

"You'll get all the answers soon. I promise you that. But right now we need to focus on other shit. First off is the cabin in the bush bought by ANIG. Did you talk to Cabe today?"

I shake my head no.

"Maverick went there at dawn. No sign of life around and no fresh tracks on the soil around the small shack. However, there was food in the freezer and the heat was left on long enough that somebody must be staying there. Maverick figures it's been about a week since someone was there, but he's keeping an eye on it until they come back."

"Did he find anything personal in the cabin? Anything linking it to Shawn or Andrew?"

Sadly, Denny shakes his head. "Nothing. A few receipts for groceries, but those were paid in cash. There's only men's clothing in the closet. Nothing of value, sorry Elle. But Mav is sitting on it. If someone goes back there, we'll know."

I nod my head, grateful at the moment for the help.

"Were there any other cabins in the area? The image on the survey map looked like it was pretty secluded."

"No other cabins. Maverick stashed his truck and hiked in through the bush."

THE UGLY ROSES

"Jesus Denny, what if nobody comes for days? Where's he going to sleep? What if something happens to him and we can't get ahold of him to know if he's okay?"

Two strong hands reach out and grab onto my shoulders. "Elle, he's done this shit before. He's staying at the cabin. Knowing him he's probably laid back on the couch with his feet up on the coffee table and his gun in his lap. And he has a sat phone, so we'll know if anything happens to him."

This all seems like so much. Why is it so hard to find a twin for shit's sake? I don't get it. And after all we figured out, how can he not be at the cabin? I feel like we've solved a million mysteries, only to be left empty handed.

"Jimmy seems like a good guy." Denny's comment about my awesome friend pulls me out of my head. "Yes, he is. How did you get him to let you in?"

"Ryder tried you on your burner, but Jimmy answered. Told him that I was coming in. I was already parked outside when he called so I guess Jimmy really didn't get a chance to give you a heads up."
"I haven't seen him much today. He needs his space when he's like this, paint and ink keep him sane."

"He's talented. He didn't talk much. He was in the middle of painting one of the Harleys down there and seemed to be in the zone, so I asked him where you were and he pointed toward the steps."

As much as I feel bad for sending Jimmy into the zone, and not exactly for a good reason, I'm glad he has something to concentrate on as opposed to worrying about me.

"Jimmy is the most talented man I know. Wait 'til you see the tattoos he has done. He's not just another pretty face." I joke, shoving Denny's arm. Letting him know he too is much more than his Viking god status. I know he's a very good person at heart, and very intelligent.

"So, how long are you here for and where are you staying?"

Denny doesn't get a chance to answer as Jimmy comes into the bedroom.

"He's staying here, Jay. I'm heading out for a while, for the night."

I get out of bed and walk over to Jimmy, putting my arms behind his back and pulling him in close. I love him so much, and the last thing I want to do is to make him not want to be around me because of my stubbornness. I'd rather be the one to distance myself from him.

"Don't leave your own place because of me Jimmy. I'm sorry. The last thing I want is for you to leave your own home because either you're pissed off at me or you're afraid of getting hurt. If that's the case, I'll be the one to leave."

Mid rant Jimmy's arms come up around my shoulders to return the embrace and he places a kiss on the top of my head.

"Not leaving because I'm worried about getting hurt, Jay. The only time you hurt me is when you refuse my help and everyone else's. Like I said last night, put your stubborn shit aside and let people help you."

I shake my head against his chest. "I know, Jimmy. It's just easier said than done. But I don't want to drive you away."

He pulls back so he can look at me. I take in the paint smear on his forehead and the crease of frustration between his brows.

"You're not driving me away. I love you, Jay. You know that. However I haven't got laid in five days and I need a break. You stay here with Denny, I'm going to crash at Randi's after I tie one on at Frank's."

"I thought you were done with Randi?"

"I am and she knows it, but that doesn't mean she won't open up her legs again."

A deep chuckle comes from Denny and I return Jimmy's earlier scowl.

"Isn't that a little rude?"

"No, and if it feels that way I'll go home with someone else."

Well, he's nothing if not honest.

"Alright. I love you, and be safe."

He gives me one last peck on the head before grabbing a change of clothes and heading downstairs. Jimmy has a shower in his paint shop that he uses when he's especially filthy.

Chapter Twenty-seven

"So, did you drive up here, or fly up?" I ask Denny, while reheating some of the stew I made a few days ago. I still don't have much of an appetite, but that doesn't mean he's not hungry.

"I flew to Buffalo then rented a Suburban to finish the trip."

I push the hearty bowl of stew across the counter to Denny and make a small bowl for myself, hoping to get a little bit of food into me. We eat in companionable silence for a few moments before I get the courage to ask the question that has been plaguing my mind ever since Denny showed up. Or maybe even since I saw Maverick.

"Is he coming here, Denny?" My voice is barely loud enough to hear for my own ears, but I know he heard me because he put his spoon down and rests his elbows on the island in front of him. Denny's intense blue eyes stare back at me, almost apologetic before he responds.

"I don't think there's much you can do to keep him away. He's not here yet, but I expect him to be soon."

I solemnly nod my head. Not wanting to see him, but still wondering why he would personally put so much effort into me. Maybe it's guilt? Guilt for fucking up. Guilt for fucking Claudia, and guilt for not having the balls to give it to me straight. I try not to dwell on it too much and hope I don't have to interact with him when he gets here.

"I appreciate the help Denny, I do. As much as it may not seem like it. You've already gathered why I don't want people near me when all of this comes to a head. I just don't want to see anyone else get hurt at my expense. That being said I still don't want any personal contact with Ryder if I can prevent it.

Call it childish, call it whatever you want. I've just had enough shit to deal with on my plate and I don't need to add any more to it."

Denny reaches a hand across the counter and gives my hand a reassuring squeeze.

"I get it darlin'. But keep an open mind, things aren't always what they seem."

"What's that supposed to mean?"

Denny shakes his head. "Not my story to tell, just know that people make sacrifices for those they care about. In the meantime, I'll field the phone calls."

I sense that I'm not going to get any more out of Denny, so I leave it where it is and continue with my dinner.

* * *

The sun has set, and even though the darkness is beginning to take over, I have no desire to get to bed anytime soon. Most likely due to sleeping the day away, I figure now would be the time to make right some of my wrongs.

"Any more news from Cabe or Maverick?"

Denny looks at me from his spot on the sofa and shakes his head. "Nothing. Mav's fine, still parked at the cabin. Cabe is still trying to track down another location for Shawn. We just sit and wait."

I hate waiting, I also hate the thought of sitting after laying around all day. I have a mild desire to open up a bottle of wine but think better of it and continue with my earlier thoughts of righting wrongs.

"Tomorrow is my daughter's birthday." I clear my throat. "Would've been my daughter's birthday. Was my daughter's birthday. Fuck, I don't know how I'm supposed to say that."

I feel the telltale tingle behind my eyes but blink them back when Denny squeezes my shoulder.

"No right way to say it Elle, but I would stick with *is*. Just because she's gone, doesn't mean you're supposed to forget the day you brought her into this world."

I take a deep breath, absorbing Denny's words.

"Take me there." I ask. I look up and see the confused expression on his face. "The cemetery. Nobody will be there at this time of night, and I don't want to go in the daylight. Tomorrow I risk running into people. I can go by myself if you don't feel comfortable taking me."

Denny grabs my small hand with his much larger one and pulls me off the couch.

"I'll take you."

I nod my head in silent thanks and head into the bedroom to change into warmer clothes before we head out.

* * *

Denny and I are silent in his Suburban, other than me giving him directions to the cemetery on the outskirts of town. I used to spend a lot of time there, laying in the grass, telling them how much I missed them. It was soothing to me. And after months upon months of going home to an empty house, it seemed like the cemetery was the only place I felt at peace. *Closer to them.*

I only visited once after my attack to say I was so fucking sorry for what happened to them. I know if my parents were still around, they would say it wasn't my fault. Unfortunately, that doesn't change the fact it still feels that way.

I still talk to them and I know I don't need to be at the cemetery for them to hear me. There's just something deeper about actually being there, seeing those names on the tombstone that makes me feel a little closer to them.

When Cory was killed, I had him buried with my family. They owned six plots and there was never a second thought as to where Cory should go. Never a second thought as to where he would want to be.

Cory's dad never put up a fuss about it, however he suffered from Alzheimer's and sadly would forget his son was gone. In a way I hope it makes it easier on him, waking up and still thinking his son is still alive. Cory's mom passed away from cancer a few years before I had met him, and he too was an only child which gave me free reign as to where he would be put to rest.

We pull up to Mapleview Cemetery. Denny gives me a questioning look since the gates are now closed and locked. I point in a direction around the laneway and off to the side where he can park the vehicle.

I don't speak when I open my door and neither does he. I follow the path I had used before when I used to come and lay here at night. It leads around the east side of the cemetery where there's just a short concrete wall dividing the path from the cemetery. Not too high, and short enough that Norma could jump over, joining me to lay on the grass during those nights I couldn't sleep.

I move on autopilot in the dark, my only light coming from the moon and the lamp posts standing tall at the entrance. Denny follows at a discreet distance behind me as I make my way through the damp grass toward my family's tombstone.

HARLOW STONE

I enter the sixth row, looking down at my feet. I won't be able to stop the silent tears that will soon streak down my face. The same thing always happens upon my arrival at the marble stone. I don't look up when I reach it, and settle down on the damp grass beneath me.

I don't pay any mind to the wetness seeping into the knees of my tights and I don't stop my hands from automatically moving up, feeling the names of those I loved etched into the cold stone in front of me.

I let the wetness run down my cheeks, keeping my eyes firmly closed. I lean my head forward to rest it on the hard surface. My shoulders begin to shake, but no noise comes from my mouth. My fingers blindly trace the letters that my mind will never forget.

I feel the sharp edge of the letter 'L'. I feel the imperfection of the stone on the letter 'Y'. My trembling fingers follow the deep groove of the numbers. Two sets inform you of a longer span of life, and the last betraying the miniscule amount of time here on earth. A time too short for someone so small to enjoy. A life taken far too early.

A life that never got to her fourth birthday.

A life that never got to her first kiss.

A life that never got to be asked to the prom, or taken on her first date.

A life taken so fast that at this moment the only thing I pray for is that she fell asleep in the car, like she normally did when we traveled. I tell myself she was in fact asleep when it happened. Nobody had to hear her in pain; she didn't have to experience any type of fear before she was taken from me.

I tell myself she went peacefully, in her sleep. Knowing nothing at the time other than the unicorns and rainbows she was most likely dreaming of. I tell myself she wasn't scared and that my mom was in the back seat with her when they went to heaven. I tell myself they were holding hands, and Lilly's little head was resting on my mom while she slept on the way to the hotel.

I tell myself all of these things as I let myself break down on the cold hard ground. I feel the small breeze cutting through the multitude of stones and I smell the dew in the air. I take it all in and breathe it all out. All the while remaining fused to the stone in front of me, wishing to all that is holy I could have had more time with them.

Gary B. O'Connor
1952-2012

Susan E. O'Connor
1956-2012

Only ever a thought away.
I will love and remember you
each and every day.

I do the same thing I always do when I come here, which is rest my finger on that mocking dash between the dates, one little notch that is supposed to represent everything in between the two sets of years. Milestones, birthdays and anniversaries. First kisses, first loves and a first home. I try to focus on the dash and what they accomplished between those years, as opposed to dwelling on the last set of numbers. I trace my fingers down the new inscription I had done after Cory was killed, and I finally let the ugly sobs free.

Lilly Jayne O'Connor
2009-2012

Remembering you is easy, I do it every day,
Missing you is a heartache, which never goes away.

HARLOW STONE

Know that this is not goodbye, just time to rest your head.
The moon will be your pillow, the stars above your bed.

If I could have a wish come true,
I would wish my sweet Lilly, that I still had you.
May you be happy with your dad baby girl,
never sad or blue.
Until the day I get to heaven, and make my own debut.
Love, Momma.

I don't bother to try stopping the sobs that wrack my body; I know it would be an impossible feat. After spending so long trying to be the strong one, bottling up all of my emotions and running my life on auto pilot, it has finally reached its breaking point.

I have reached my breaking point.

I don't bother to turn around and guess whose arms have come around me. For once instead of fighting and pushing people away, I fold myself into the warm embrace and let it all go. The anger, the tears and the deeply rooted loneliness I refuse to give into.

I don't know how long Denny holds me in his lap on the cold ground, but eventually he breaks the silence when my sobs and ugly crying subside to small whimpers. I feel the tightening of his arms before he speaks.

"What do you want, Foley?"

I'm confused and disoriented. I pull my head out from under Denny's chin and notice the man standing about fifteen feet away. Denny obviously feels no threat from this man, but regardless I crawl out of his lap and stand on my own two feet.

THE UGLY ROSES

Denny doesn't let me get far and stands partially in front of me, blocking my clear path to the strange man.

"Mr. Black. Perhaps we don't need to worry about her and Callaghan any longer, seeing how close you and Ms. O'Connor have become."

I jolt at the use of my real name and get a better look at the man in front of me. He takes a few more steps forward and recognition hits. This is the guy who was with Becker, the one who waited outside of my private training room back in Jacksonville.

"I'll ask you again, what the fuck do you want Foley?"

The man known as Foley shoves his hands in his pockets, shaking his head with a mild smirk on his older wrinkly face.

"It's not what I want, Mr. Black. It's what works best for all parties involved. I couldn't very well take Mr. Callaghan's word for it now could I? Certainly not without an insurance policy of my own."

I grab onto Denny's arm. "What the hell is he talking about?"

I look between the two men, watching the standoff unfold in front of me, more confused than ever as to why William Becker's right hand man from Chicago is standing in the middle of a cemetery in Ontario.

Denny doesn't answer me, but holds onto my arm and begins to lead us back the way we came as he speaks over his shoulder. "Not up for yours or Becker's games. Get the fuck back to Chicago. If you don't, we both know what'll happen."

Denny and I climb over the concrete wall and almost make it to the truck before I see the flashing lights coming in the distance.

"As I said, Mr. Black. Insurance." I spin out of Denny's hold to face the prick coming up behind me. His pace is confident and the smug look on his face conveys his message. He got what he came here for.

"What do you want with me? I have no hold over Ryder! Leave me the fuck alone!"

Foley shows no emotion, no remorse at my outburst. Simply cocks his head to the side wondering what my game is. "No hard feelings, Ms. O'Connor. Mr. Becker trusted you would stay out of Ryder Callaghan's reach. This is just a precaution to ensure *he* stays out of *yours*."

"What fucking 'precaution'?" I don't know why I'm asking, I hear the sirens getting closer.
"My apologies, but you serve our cause best behind bars at the moment."

Denny bursts in front of me, storming for the smug prick and grabbing him by the lapels of his suit jacket.

"You stupid son of a bitch! You think this will stop him! You think you're going to win? Huh? You might as well tell Becker his time as a mayor is fucking finished!"

He shoves off of him and comes back toward me. "Get in the fucking truck Elle! I'll get you out of here."

I don't move. I just stand frozen to the spot, wondering how the hell what started out as finding a killer has turned into such an act of vengeance. All because Becker wants Ryder? I don't get it.

"Move, Elle!" I move toward the truck, but not to get in. I place my hand on Denny's arm, squeezing a bit to get his eyes to focus on mine.

THE UGLY ROSES

"It was coming sooner or later. I'll be alright." My voice holds no hope, or sadness. It's just monotone as I watch a police cruiser come to a stop at the entrance to the cemetery. I'm not afraid, I'm not worried. I knew I'd have questions to answer sooner or later. My only hope was that we caught Shawn first so he could fill in some of the blanks, and I could rest easier at night.

I lean up on my toes, ignoring the sound of footsteps heading my way, ignoring the selfish prick named Foley, and not paying any attention to the look of anger and despair on Denny's handsome face. I lightly kiss his cheek and wrap my arm around his neck while speaking softly so only he can hear. "I put thirty thousand in the safe at Jimmy's. If you guys need it, use it."

His giant arms embrace me back and he too speaks low enough that only I can hear. "Don't need it girl, and we'll get him. I promise you that. One of us will be waiting for you at the station. We'll send in a lawyer."

I nod and give him one last squeeze before letting go and not looking back. The footsteps have long since stopped and I see Bryan Miller standing about twenty feet from me, kind enough to give me space and sweet enough to give me time to say goodbye.

His eyes roam over my body, my dark brown hair, my new face. It's been a long time since I last saw him, and as much as I wish it were under different circumstances, he still is a friendly face—even though he's here to take me in.

I study the man I haven't seen in a year. He's tall, around the six-foot mark. Chestnut colored hair and deep brown eyes. A slight scruff on his jaw, but still clean enough to warrant that sophisticated all business persona. I don't waste any more time and walk toward him, hands at my sides.

"How does this work? Do you read me my rights, cuff me and throw me in the back seat of your car?" I tilt my head to the side in question and I don't miss the small flash of desire in his eyes before he masks it behind empathy.

"I heard the call come in of your whereabouts. I wanted to take it myself. Not because I want to bring you in, but because I didn't want you to be treated that way."

Bryan Miller.

He always was the one with the soft heart toward me.

"How about we just start with walking side by side to my car. Unless you want a head start?" he asks while quirking an eyebrow at me. I solemnly shake my head.

"I told you I was done running. Not that I was ready to come in yet, but something tells me it's time."

He reaches his hand out and gently holds onto my arm while guiding me toward his black undercover police cruiser.

"As much as I hoped this was over for you Jayne, it's good to see you alive and seemingly well."

"Seemingly is accurate, but I'm far from well Bryan."

The caress of his thumb against my arm is his answer before he opens the door to his cruiser and guides me into the back seat. He motions toward the camera on the dash, and I nod in understanding and keep my mouth shut.

He gets in the front seat of the car and we make the journey toward the station. I look over my shoulder and watch the cemetery fade into the distance. It could be the last time I ever got to see my family in their resting place. It could be the last time I see my dog and the new friends I have made.

THE UGLY ROSES

Knowing there is one more person I need to see before I potentially become a prison inmate, I remind myself to speak to Miller once we're out of the camera's view.

Chapter Twenty-eight

We pull into the small police station and Miller helps me out of the car. He still didn't put cuffs on me, thank god. Not that it really matters, but I fear having flashbacks to when I was kept prisoner in the basement.

"Bryan?" I softly ask, so as to not attract attention from any other potential police officers in the lot.

"Miller from here on out, Jay." I nod in understanding. "I need you to call Laura, as soon as you can and let her know I'm here. Please. I didn't get to see her yet."

"I'm going to take you in and put you in a secure room. I'm sorry, it's procedure. I'll grab us a coffee and call her once I get you in there."

"Thank you."

Feeling somewhat better, I let him guide me into the station. We pass through the double glass doors, drawing little attention seeing as it's like a funeral in here. One tired looking woman behind the desk filing her nails at ten thirty on a week night. A few officers hunched over paperwork on their desks. All in all, it's a quiet night in a small town.

Miller leads me through a secure door past reception which enters into a large room with about ten desks. The left side of the room has a few offices and from here I can see Miller's name on the door of one of them.

"Congratulations," I mutter, pointing my head in that direction.

He gives me a small smile and a quiet thank you before guiding me into a room on the right side. There's a window facing the main room with blinds and there's also a window on the inside which is clearly a one-way mirror. I sit down in a plastic chair in front of the cold metal table and Miller tells me to wait for his return.

I'm only left staring at the cold grey walls for a few moments before Miller comes back with a coffee and leans against the table.

"The cameras in here are not on, and there is no one on the other side of the glass. I called Laura and I'm going to put off calling Braumer until the morning." He sighs and continues, "You need a Lawyer here, Jayne. I know you'll ask for one. Braumer wants in on the questioning and I can't shelter you from that. If you think you can get a lawyer here tonight, then I'll call him. If not, I need to keep you until morning when you can do that."

"I don't know when I can get one here, but I know one is coming. How about that one phone call? Then I'm guessing I'll go hang out in one of those fancy rooms with bars in them?"

Clearly finding no humor in my tone, Miller stands up and guides me out of the room toward a phone. Ryder might be the best one to call at this moment. However, after what happened with Foley, I want nothing to do with him. I pick up the phone and dial Denny instead, knowing he'll most likely know what's going on.

"Black."

"Hey. What time for the lawyer?"

"He lands in Toronto at zero six hundred. Are you okay?"
"I'm fine. You could just call a Lawyer around here. I have the money Denny, I just haven't needed to use one before so I have no idea who's good."

"Don't worry about it darlin', worry about you right now. And this guy is the best, so I'd suggest you wait for him."

"Thanks, Denny. I'm here for the night and I'm guessing they don't allow visitors. So, I'll talk to you later."

"Hang in there."

I hang up the phone and continue with Miller down the hallway. It comes to a T, on one side is a door with a pass code lock, and on the other is a set of stairs, leading down. I slow my steps, not because I mean to but because I can't help it. I feel my breathing getting shallower and the sweat begins to form on my face and neck.

"What's wrong, Jayne?" I shake my head frantically back and forth, my unruly brown hair getting stuck to my sweaty face in the process. I know my words will come out jumbled but I do my best to try. I focus on the confusion in his eyes, letting him see the fear in mine before I speak so quietly I can barely hear myself.

"Basement."

He puts his hands on my shoulders and puts his face level with mine.

"It's mostly case files and storage. Breathe Jayne. There's one old cell down there but it hasn't been used in years, and I'm not taking you there. Breathe."

I focus on his face, breathing. In an effort to get away from the stairs I push us toward the door. He quickly enters the pass code before getting us to the other side.

I lean against the wall, gathering my breath, deep in through the nose, out through the mouth. I repeat a few times until I no longer feel like death is looming and begin to walk down the hallway.

THE UGLY ROSES

We come across a desk, which is empty, and another door with a pass code which is currently hanging open. I follow Miller through the open door and finally see the two holding cells. They aren't as big as what I've seen on television, probably because this is a small town on the outside of a big city with a much bigger precinct. Still, there are two. One has a double bunk, nothing to write home about. And the other has benches along two of the walls. I'm assuming the difference is people are only held here for an hour, versus people who are kept overnight.

He walks me to the one with the double bunk and I make my way over to the lower bed, sitting down with my elbows on my knees and my head in my hands. I knew I'd get here eventually, I'm not upset. Maybe I'm just a little overwhelmed after seeing those stairs leading below.

I feel the warmth of Bryan's hand on my shoulder and look up.

"I'm truly fucking sorry Jayne. But I'm still glad it was me that brought you in here and not someone else, especially Braumer."

I nod my head, thankful too for the same thing and manage a small smile.

"The cameras are off when nobody is in here, but I have to switch it back on when I go out. Before I do that, is there anything you want to tell me? Or any info you want to share? Maybe who those guys were when I showed up at the cemetery tonight?"

I lean my head back on my shoulders, staring up at the only man in this department who could potentially help me. I don't want to tell him too much, mainly because I think Ryder and his team have more pull than he does. In fact, I know they have more pull, but he still deserves a little bit of information for all he has done for me.

"The older man was not my friend. He's the one who orchestrated this arrest, not for the greater good, but a personal vendetta against someone who was close to me. I can't tell you why, because ultimately it doesn't pertain to why I'm here tonight.

"The other man is a close friend and someone I trust. Let's just say he and his friends protect me and work for a company called Callaghan Security."

He nods his head, motioning for me to continue. "They're good people, should you come in contact with them Bryan. They're intelligent and they'll help you with the case. Most of them are ex-military personnel or something similar and they do their jobs well. I'm sure they won't get in your way but please don't stop them, or tell Braumer about them. If they want Braumer to know they're here to help me, then that will be up to them. In the meantime, consider them an ally, not a threat.

"Should you encounter the man you saw at the cemetery, Foley something or other, or another man named William Becker, be sure to let whatever they say go in one ear and out the other. They aren't good people."

"Becker? Why does that sound familiar?"

"You follow American politics?"
He nods his head. "A little, why?"

"Because he's the Mayor of Chicago."

Wide eyes greet my serious ones. "I'm not lying, Bryan. That man is fucking evil. Avoid him and his cronies if you can help it. However, I'm sure he and Braumer would get along great over a single malt and a few cigars. They both share a mutual dislike for yours truly."

"I don't think you're lying, Jay. Jesus, what the fuck happened since you left here?"

"Too much, and not enough."

Bryan paces the cell for a few moments, lost in thought. I barely told him anything, but to him I'm sure it's a lot. I didn't tell him what I found out about Shawn because at this point I don't think it'll help. If Ryder and the guys choose to share that, it'll be up to them.

I move to lay down on the board they call a mattress, knowing I need at least a few hours of sleep before I face the evil prick known as Braumer in the morning.

"A guard will come down soon to man the desk. If you need anything, let him know. Or if you need to speak with me again, I'll let him know to take it seriously and send me back here."

I give him a small salute in acknowledgement before I roll my back to the wall, curling up with the pillow. I don't like it in here and I refuse to sleep without seeing who's coming in and out of this room.

"Oh, one more thing. I found Lucy Greer. She died." I can see the defeat on his face, upset that he doesn't have something more substantial since my absence and phone call.

"I know."

* * *

With nothing to look at, I've kept my eyes closed, but I can't fall asleep. I heard the guard come down the hallway, but he said nothing to me. I can see his back from where he sits at his desk at the end of the hallway. He didn't bother to greet me, and I'm thankful.

I hear the door open again just a few moments later, and the sound of shuffling feet.

Great, a drunk person.

Hoping I don't have to share my cell, I keep my eyes closed and feign sleep in the hopes they'll keep me and the newcomer separated.

"If you don't wake up right now Jayne Elle O'Connor, I promise to vomit all over your selfish ass for not coming to see me as soon as you got back!"

I bolt upright in bed and can't stop the happy tears gathering in the corner of my eyes. Miller opens the gate to my cell and kindly shoves Laura through before closing it again. I make my way to embrace my best friend who is closer to a sister to me, but stop short when I feel the burning slap across my cheek.

"That's for not telling me you were home! For leaving me for so long and not letting me know you were okay! You damn well deserved it too!"

I don't move. Jimmy wasn't kidding when he said she can hold a grudge, and as much as I want to correct her and let her know it was for her own well-being that I stayed away, I don't. She's been drinking and she's slightly wobbly. So I stand my ground, waiting for her to unleash whatever it is she needs to on me.

I know I would do the same if I were in her shoes. I've lived for nearly a year knowing that she was well and truly okay. She has lived in fear that I could be dead or dying in a ditch somewhere.

THE UGLY ROSES

She hasn't taken her eyes off me. Much like everyone else from my past who I've encountered, she studies me intently, taking in my new much firmer body, my purchased face and dark brown hair. After what feels like an eternity, and mostly likely due to the alcohol, she loses it.

Her chin quivers and her face falls, along with the tears gathered in her honey colored eyes. I pull my dear friend close and hold her tighter than I'd been able to the last time I hugged her. Too many stitches prevented me from giving her a proper embrace.

I let her weep onto my scarf for however long she needs to, knowing she needs this reassurance that I am in fact alive.

After a small eternity, she pulls back. She reaches behind me to grab the pillow off the top bunk and motions to the small bottom one. I climb back onto the bed, knowing this is our time to share.

I get in first, with my back once again to the wall, and she settles herself on the outside facing me. She adjusts her too-tight jeans and pulls her grey cardigan around her body before she settles onto the pillow.

We stare at each other for a few moments, much like we used to in this same position. From high school and on, this was the way we would have our heart to hearts. Vent about first loves, teething children and insufferable men. This is how we shared our secrets and stories.

"You're still beautiful," she says after a long perusal of my face. "Where were you? Why are you back? You know everything I want to know, so just start from the beginning, I have all night."

I laugh a little. "How did you get in here anyway? What did Miller say when he called you?"

She gives me a smile before diving in. "He was smart enough to tell me that being an unruly drunk in front of the police would land me in the drunk tank. He told me that my blood alcohol content would be taken and he'd be outside of the station around eleven o'clock." She huffs, "Of course he told me all that shit *before* he dropped the bomb you were in here. After I lost my shit, I told Brad to hand me the tequila and watch the kids. So, here I am. Half-drunk and here overnight so long as I, and I quote, '*behave myself and dry out by morning*'."

She follows this up with a tipsy smile before sobering, at which point I lay it all on her. It takes a few hours and a lot of questions from her. But I start at Denver and end with Canada. Not surprisingly, her choice words for Ryder are more colorful than mine. And after a good curse fest of her proclaiming him *'that lying sack of shit cheating whore of a hooker's son'*, we finally find slumber.

Chapter Twenty-nine

"Knock, Knock!"

I feel Laura move on the bed and I crack my eyes open to greet the dick behind the voice. There's no clock in this cell so I have no idea what time it is, but I feel like I just got to sleep. Laura sits up on the bed, holding onto her temples from what I'm sure is a massive headache, courtesy of the tequila she drank last night.

I finally let my eyes settle on the sorry excuse of a detective standing on the other side of the bars. I wish our places were reversed, but there's not much I can do about that right now. Wish in one hand, shit in the other—we all know which fills up first.

"We meet again, Ms. O'Connor. Up and at 'em. We have a lot to talk about." He's almost giddy, his pudgy cheeks heavy over his smile and his ill-fitting suit much tighter around his midsection.

"Is my lawyer here yet?"

"No, but he should be shortly. You and I can get started."

"You and I will do no such thing until my lawyer is present."

He sighs, as if it's a big deal to him. He's only upset because he knows his presence bothers me and he'll do whatever he can to make my life miserable. I'm sure of it.

"Very well. I thought we could have a coffee and catch up, but stay in here if you wish."

I know his game and I'm not about to play. The lousy fuck doesn't want to have coffee with me. He wants some sort of a confession as to what happened, anything to nail me to the wall.

"I hate that prick!" Laura nearly growls.

"You and me both, Laur'."

We don't sit long before the desk guard comes down the hall.

"Monroe?"

Laura stands up. "Yes, that's me."

"Time to go Curly Sue, your night at the hotel is over."

I embrace my girl one last time, knowing there's nothing else I can do to keep her in here with me, and not wanting too. Well, sort of. But I know she needs to get home, and it won't be long until I'm called back to the interrogation room.

"I love you, Laur'. Give the kids a hug and kiss for me."

"I will, I promise. I'll call Jimmy as soon as I get out to find out what's going on."

Once again, I'm left alone in my little cell. I stretch out my legs, fighting the urge to pee but refuse to use the open toilet where anyone could see me. I had my privacy taken away from me once, it won't happen again.

I do my best to wash my face and rinse out my mouth just in time to hear a set of footsteps coming back down the hall.

"O'Connor, lawyer's here."

I'm led by another young rookie cop to the interrogation room. Miller greets me outside the door and I notice the distinguished gentleman inside the room through the blinds.

"Really, Jayne? He's your lawyer?"

I give a slight shrug of my shoulders. "I don't know, who is he?"

"That's Andrei Patrov."

"Is that supposed to mean something to me?"

"If you associate with the Russian mob it should."

This is news to me. Seeing as I don't know any Russians that I can think of.

"Well, is he any good?"

"You could say that," he says.

I can tell by the expression on Miller's face that he must be good, but maybe not entirely legal in his endeavors.

"Well, that's all that should matter."

I open the door and enter the room to greet an attractive man. I'm assuming in his late thirties to early forties with light brown hair and sharp midnight blue eyes.
"Ah, Ms. O'Connor. Pleasure to meet you."

I note the light Russian accent and extend my hand to greet him. "You as well."

"Detective Miller, could you please allow us the room so I may speak with my client confidentially."

Miller wastes no time in closing the door.

"Alright, we'll cut the shit and get straight to the point. I'm Andrei Patrov, if you have not heard of me, you will." This statement is followed by a shark of a smile, which I don't find scary but definitely threatening if he wanted it to be.

"I know most of what you are dealing with, having been briefed on the flight here. Mr. Callaghan joined me midway through my flight as well as my cousin, Ivan."

The look I give him must show my confusion.

"My second cousin, to be exact. He works for Mr. Callaghan and served with him overseas. Now, we need to go over what you are going to say. They no longer wish to hear a recount of what happened to *you* in the room, they know this already. They wish to find out how each of the men ended up dead."

I lean back in my chair and rub my hands over my tired face. I've thought about this a million times. I know what he would want me to do in this situation, but he's not here anymore to confirm it for me.

"May I call you Jayne?" I nod my head in the positive.

"Jayne, this not my first case involving murder, in fact I have done this more than a dozen times. You will say part of what you originally did. You were knocked out, the contusions on your head and lack of blood supporting that claim. You heard a struggle, you heard the men in the room. And when you woke up, they were both dead and bleeding out on the floor."

I look Andrei in the eye through all of this, knowing this is very much similar to what I had planned to say, but in the same sense I feel as though lying taints Cory's death. Would he have been okay with that? With what I'm possibly about to do? Lying to the police?

Probably.

But he's not here to confirm it for me. Since I no longer have Lilly, or any immediate family to worry about, what's keeping me from spending time in jail?

I know what's keeping me from there; it's that I don't feel as though I deserve it. I feel like I should be free because justice was served no matter how long I drew out Andrew's torture. The sick fuck deserved it and then some. He killed my family and he tried to kill me for Christ's sake. He ruined my life.

Fucking right he deserved it!

That thought in mind, I nod in acknowledgment to Andrei Patrov.

* * *

I've been in this tiny interrogation room for two hours. I was let out to use the washroom, for which I was thankful. But being back here is like listening to a broken record.

I've learned that Andrei Patrov is a lion in battle. He fights when it's needed and calls Braumer's bluff more often than I expected. He definitely knows his way around the law and what to do to get me out of here. I'm only half listening to what is being said around me, not because I'm not interested in my fate, but because I can't be bothered to listen to the same thing over and over again.

Braumer's questioning once again pulls me out of my head. "Please explain, Ms. O'Connor, why partials of your fingerprints were found on the knife used to torture and kill Andrew Roberts?"

"I told you before, I used it when I woke up to cut the bloody rope off of my wrists."

He slams his hand down on the table.

"Here's what I think! I think you used it to kill him after Cory used it to cut you free. I think, Cory was too weak to fight anymore from the stab wound to his chest, he died and you then took the opportunity to avenge his death by killing Andrew Roberts! Isn't that how it went down?"

"That's enough! My client will not be badgered or belittled by you or anyone else in this department. Unless you are here to charge her with the death of Andrew Roberts, then this conversation is over. If you need to speak with her again you will contact me directly."

I'm led out of the room. My feet don't move me quick enough. I have no belongings to collect since Denny drove last night and I never bothered taking my bag with me, my pockets too were empty. At the moment even if I did have belongings to collect they would have to be pretty damn important for me to stop and pick them up.

I storm out the front door and take a huge lung full of fresh air. In doing so I start to crave a cigarette to taint the freshness—and a whole lot of alcohol.

"You need to stay close, O'Connor. I will do what I can to help you and also try to find out why that man despises you so much."

"No need to put it kindly, Patrov. He fucking hates me."

Andrei chuckles at my choice of vocabulary and does nothing to correct me.

"Thank you, for your help. My ride is over there and I desperately need a shower."

"You go. If I need you I will be in touch."

THE UGLY ROSES

I walk down the sidewalk, cutting through the parked civilian vehicles when a black town car cuts off my path to Denny. The window is rolled down by the time it comes to a stop and there in the back sits Foley.

"Be smart, Ms. O'Connor," he says.

"Go fuck yourself, Foley."

I move to go around his vehicle but his words slow me down. "Claudia Becker is pregnant. I trust you won't get in the way, or contact Mr. Callaghan. If you do I will make sure you regret it."

I waste no time in rushing over to Denny's Suburban. I don't wait for hugs, I don't say hello.

"Get me the fuck out of here, please."

He wastes no time in doing just that.

Chapter Thirty

I sit low on my haunches when Norm comes barreling out the back door of Jimmy's shop. I missed my girl, clearly she felt the same. We have not for one night been separated since the attack. The only thing that kept us apart was me being in the hospital. Before that, she was with me every day since my family died—she even attended the funeral.

I give her as much love for as long as I can before I head inside to shower. I feel like a layer of filth is on me, not knowing who stayed in that cell before Laura and I did. I climb the steps up to the apartment and am greeted by Jimmy and some other large male who I've never met before. I don't get a chance to speak before Jimmy has me in his arms.

"Fuck. Had I of known you were going to end up in jail I wouldn't have gone out last night. Worst fucking part is I didn't find out until this morning, and those cunts at the station wouldn't let you have any visitors aside from a lawyer."

"I'm alright Jimmy. But I need you to let me go so I can shower. I feel like I caught an STD in that place."

He gives me a quick kiss on the head before letting me go. "Laura called, she'll be over soon."

"Alright. Give me thirty, or an hour please."

I let him go and walk toward the hallway. I realize I forgot to ask who the big bastard on the couch is.

"Who are you?"

"Ivan. You met my cousin today." His accent is much more pronounced than Andrei's. He's also about one hundred pounds heavier with a huge head. I wouldn't want to piss him off.

"Yes I did. Nice to meet you, and thanks. But I need some time."

I point my thumb in the direction of the bathroom and don't bother with any other pleasantries as I head to the heaven that is the shower.

* * *

I soak, scrub and shave every nook and crevice on my body, not stopping until the water runs cold. I blow dry my hair and paint my face. Not because I need to, but because I crave to be in control of what I put on and how I look, ultimately hoping it'll change how I feel.

The only thing I want to do when I leave the bathroom is sleep, and maybe manage something small to eat. I also need to talk to Denny and see if Maverick made any progress at the cabin. I hope they did, but somehow I know he would've told me on the drive back to Jimmy's if anything substantial were to come up.

I put on a loose-fitting pair of worn in ripped jeans and an old worn out long sleeve black top. I have no desire to impress, I have nowhere to go. I just need comfort and armor at the moment.

I hear arguing coming from the living room and what I most certainly can tell is Laura's voice. I have no idea what rant she could be onto now, and at the moment I don't care. I take my time in the bathroom and quietly cross the hall into Jimmy's bedroom.

I sit down on the edge of the bed and stare out the window, reminding myself most jail cells don't have windows and the one last night was a small exception. I allow myself a minute to be thankful for the help of Ryder's men, and people like Bryan Miller.

I absorb the sunlight coming in through the window and the feel of it warming my skin. I noticed my bag on the floor next to the bed when I sat down and waste no time in digging out my smokes. I never smoke in my bedroom, but this one isn't mine and it already faintly smells of them. Most likely because the first thing Jimmy does after nailing some nameless woman is light one up.

My solitude is short lived when I feel a large body sink down to sit at the end of the bed. I was going to look, but I don't. I can smell him. I can feel him. I know who it is without turning around to verify it.

He says nothing as he sits there, but I sense him looking at me. Studying me. Wondering when I'm about to crack.

Soon, I think to myself.

My breakdown last night is evidence I can only hold strong for so long before I finally need a break. One might think living the way I have for the past half a year or so is a break. But it's not. When that time is constantly spent assessing your surroundings and watching your back, there is no real *break*. It was like a full-time job. Add in a few nightmares and a lot of paranoia, what you have left is a woman who most certainly will fucking *break* at some point.

My emotions are bleeding through and essentially corrupting the cold-hearted bitch I had become. Some think the mind runs the heart. Some think the heart runs the body. Essentially I think everything works together. My heart was cold, but my mind was focused enough to keep me alive.

Now my heart is unfocused, all over the place, not knowing for one second what I should feel. In turn my mind is trying to make sense of all these new emotions and not knowing where to stick them to keep myself on the cold-hearted track. It's like my brain has run out of space to hide everything I care about and now it has just come crashing in all at once.

My dead family.

Laura.

Jimmy.

And now, Ryder.

"I never fucked Claudia while we were together, Elle."

His words give me a bit of shock, but not enough for my half-empty soul to process at the moment. Being mentally and emotionally drained has taken its toll on me.

"Do you have anything to say to that?"

My voice is low, tired and beaten. "I'm tired Ryder. I spent the night in jail after being apprehended at my daughter's grave. I'm all out of words. I'm just...I'm just all out of everything."

I put out my smoke and continue with my blank stare out the window. I don't look at him, I can't right now. Or maybe I don't want to burst this small little bubble of pleasure I have at staring out the window. The bright sun in the sky is completely at odds with how I feel. Ryder's next words catch me completely off guard.

"I was blackmailed. Becker blackmailed me which caused me to leave Indy. I didn't want to worry you with what he said, so I went to Chicago to be his fucking dog for a week and escort his daughter to a fundraiser. He figured out who you were, don't ask me how. But he did, and he used it against me, telling me he would basically hang you out to dry if I didn't cooperate with him. I promise you babe I never touched her, I didn't want to touch her. I haven't been with anyone since I met you, and I'd like to keep it that way."

I soak in the news with a mild bit of hope and then I remember Foley's parting words when I left the station.

Do I think the child belongs to Ryder?

No.

He's too smart for that.

But what about me? What about his life too? What if Becker pulls something on him like he did with me? Ultimately if it were not for him, I would not have slept in jail last night.

If it weren't for me, Ryder would not be in the middle of this mess with Becker right now. Becker would have no leverage over him, nothing to make him cooperate, because at the end of the day, it has always been Ryder and his men. Ryder has never cared enough about a woman for her to be used against him.

Now I fully understand the term 'love hurts'. I guess if it didn't, it wouldn't be love. But what the hell am I supposed to do with this information? I can't very well go back into hiding. We still haven't found Shawn and Ryder runs a business he can't hide from. He can't very well go into hiding with me.

How would it work?

Someone wants me dead, and an influential person wants Ryder to play his daughter's baby daddy. If Ryder refused, then Becker would probably begin his own hunt to find Shawn to ensure I did in fact, die. Thus freeing up Ryder, but essentially losing his leverage on him.

The only win here is if I die, Ryder is free. Or I need to let Ryder go and suffer the consequences.

"Claudia is pregnant, Ryder."

He jumps up from the bed and moves in front of me, pointing in my face. "That's not fucking true! And if she is it sure as shit isn't mine!"

I move my hands in a motion of surrender.

"I know it's not, Ryder. You're not that reckless."

Seeming placated by my words he settles down, if only a fraction.

"You need to go, Ryder. You can't stay here."

He bends his legs and gets down to my level on the bed.

"If you think for one fucking second after everything we've been through and how much it fucking *killed* me to be away from you that I'm going to leave just because you say so? Well wake the fuck up beautiful because it's not going to happen.

"I may have played along, I may have did what he asked, but that does not mean I didn't lie awake in bed every goddamn night hating that I hurt you. Hating that you were there, alone, next to my own fucking house and I couldn't come to you.

"I'm done! I'm done playing Elle! I had to do it until I got enough dirt on the bastard to get myself out of that mess, but here I am. And I'm not fucking leaving just because you're too tired to put up with me. I told you I would help you, I told you I wouldn't stop. This is me not stopping Elle. Even when I was in Chicago I was working on a way out of it. When I was home, I shipped Denny or someone else to Chicago to get me what I needed.

"I'm done! And I'm here. So please don't be so damn stubborn for once and fucking keep me!"

"I can't!"

His hands come up to grasp me on either side of my face, his only inches from mine. "Why? Why can't you Elle? Give me one good reason!"

"You know as well as I do. If Shawn doesn't find me, Becker will make sure he does. He needs me out of the picture, Ryder. And for whatever sick fucking reason he wants you for his daughter."

"I don't want her Elle! I never fucking wanted her. I fucked her a handful of times over the past year before I met you, and many other women in between. I never let her stay the night and I never asked her for more. She *knew* what the score was with me from the beginning, just like anyone else I fucked.

"The only time I ever ate with the woman was at a few business dinners hosted by Becker. I never, not once, gave her any idea we would be something more."

I shake my head as much as his hands will allow. "Well she obviously wants more Ryder, because Foley showed up last night and again this morning to solidify the fact I need to stay away from you, or there will be consequences."

Ryder punches the mattress beside me, then stands up and angrily grabs his phone out of his pocket. He punches something in and holds it to his ear.

"You have twelve hours to get Foley out of the fucking Country and to call off the rest of your dogs."

"No Becker! I've had it. It's not my fault your whore of a fucking daughter can't keep her goddamn legs shut. That's your problem to deal with, along with the bastard grandchild.

THE UGLY ROSES

Get off my back, and stay away from my woman. You have twelve hours to confirm or I'll make sure those photos go public. You can kiss your seat on the high chair goodbye."

He tosses his phone onto the bed and hauls me up by my arms. "Nobody will keep me from you, babe. Not Becker, not Shawn, nobody!"

I don't get to respond before his lips come crashing down onto mine.

The feel of him, the smell of him, the taste of his minty mouth in mine. I absorb it and shut down everything else other than the man who's currently holding me in his arms. I don't listen to my head, telling me this could go horribly wrong. I don't listen to my heart, telling me this could potentially break it.

I run my hands across the scruff that's much more than two days of growth and continue into his long inky dark hair. I can't help the whimper escaping my mouth when he puts his hands on my back, forcefully pulling me closer to him. He immediately lets go, even though I don't want him to.

"What's wrong beautiful?"

I come back to the present and vaguely note the bedroom door is wide open. I decide to address that issue first, since there's nothing but silence in the upstairs apartment.

"Where is everyone?"

"Downstairs, I told them to give me an hour after your friend called me every name in the book. She apologized after I told them what happened and why I had to do it."

I knew I heard Laura's harping from the bathroom, and now it all makes sense.

"You're off topic though, babe. Did someone hurt you in jail? Why does it hurt when I touch your back?"

I give Ryder a kiss on his scruffy jaw before turning around to close the bedroom door. I walk back to the side of the bed and grab them hem of my shirt, pulling it over my head. He reaches out to do it for me, but I stop him with a small shake of my head.

I unbutton my jeans and slowly lower them down my legs. I can already see the evidence that Ryder is aroused through the front of his jeans as I reach behind my back to undo my bra. I toss it on the floor with the rest of my clothes and do the same with my thong.

I look to Ryder, still dressed in his usual garb of dark jeans, black boots and long sleeve black shirt before I turn around.

I hear his intake of breath behind me before I feel the tips of his fingers on my back. They lightly trace the small flowers at the top of my back, before following the branches down to the top of my ass. His lips begin to follow the path of his fingers and I close my eyes, absorbing the feel of his skin touching mine.

"I still thought you were beautiful with your scars babe. They didn't define you, they were just a part of you."

I open my eyes and let the first tear fall, half-hating myself for letting so many go lately, but knowing regardless of where my head or heart is at, this man has a way of bringing the emotion out of me.

His strong hands work their way over my hips, up my rib cage, alongside my breasts and over my shoulders. He adds pressure to turn me back around and moves them up my neck to hold my face. His eyes tell me what words cannot and I lean forward to tell him with my lips what I can't say with my voice.

THE UGLY ROSES

Ryder sheds his clothes in the quickest way a man can before laying me down on the king size bed. He wastes no time in reconnecting himself with my body and I let my hands wander every inch of his that I can reach. His hands and lips travel every inch of my body, from my hips to my toes, and back again.

No part of me is left untouched. No erogenous zone is left un-kissed. The only way I can describe this moment is being worshipped.

Ryder got to know my body in Indy. It was a moment of discovery, in all senses of the word. Not just getting to know my body, my scars and my flaws, but spending time to discover what makes me moan.

The act Ryder is doing is pure worship. I've never felt anything like it and I don't suspect I would again with any other man. There are pheromones and chemistry, and everything else beautiful in between.

By the time he enters me, I have already come twice from his touch alone. His lips have not left my body until he finally makes it back to my mouth, devouring me in a passionate kiss deep enough to leave me breathless. He nibbles on my lower lip before letting go and planting himself to the root.

"Keep me. No more games, Elle. No more running. Just fucking keep me."

I look into his beautiful black eyes, running my hand around the back of his neck into the thick hair I'm insanely jealous of.

"I'm scared."
The deep roll of his hips leaves me momentarily speechless and I close my eyes on a deep moan.

"You don't have to be. You had me on the beach with *'fucking peachy, neighbor'*. Hell, you may have had me when you almost run me down in the middle of the street. I didn't need to clean your gutters babe, and I sure as shit didn't need to fix a sink that you may never have come back to. But I needed to, because I wanted to be near you. You're mine, babe. I'm not going anywhere, and neither are you. So fucking *keep me*, beautiful. Because I sure as fuck am not letting you go."

His lips crash back down onto mine, and I pull his hair, tight to the roots. I wrap my legs around him, keeping him as close as I possibly can for however long this messed up life of mine will let me.

"Ride me, beautiful."

Strong arms close around my back and he sits up on his haunches, taking me with him. His hands firmly grasp my thighs, his fingers digging into my ass. I place my hands on his shoulders as he lifts me up and drops me back down on his long hard shaft.

Repeatedly.

"Fuck you feel so good, too fucking good."

He releases one of his hands from my rear and moves it up my back, burying his fingers in my hair. He gently pulls back to expose my neck before he attacks the sensitive flesh like a man starved for the taste of my skin.

When his teeth hit that sweet spot above my collarbone, I come undone. Soaring towards bliss and one hell of a climax. It doesn't stop, just keeps going as he continues to drive deep, never letting up, never slowing down.

My internal muscles contract around his cock as he places both hands back on my hips, holding me close enough that his groin hits my clit in the most incredible way. My body is shaking, my skin is dampened with sweat and in this moment I can truly say that I would never want to be anywhere else than right here, watching Ryder's handsome face as he too comes undone inside of me.

"Keep me beautiful."

I stare into those beautiful black eyes, absorbing the sincerity. I keep eye contact as I lower my head and bring my mouth to his.

"I'll keep you, handsome. Just don't let me go."

Chapter Thirty-one

I slowly wake to the feel of warm kisses dancing across my shoulders. I let out a little hum in appreciation.

"I missed you, babe."

"Missed you too," I softly say, still half in slumber.

I'm rolled onto my back, and the kisses from that wonderful mouth give the same treatment to my collarbone, neck and face. When his gentle lips finally meet mine, I'm ready.

Jesus I missed this. Missed him.

As usual I was just too stubborn to admit it.

Ryder positions himself on top of me. At the same moment the bedroom door bursts open.

"What the fuck?" Ryder curses, while trying to cover up my body.

Jimmy rushes into the room and turns on the side lamp since the sun has now set. Or maybe it's almost morning, I don't know.

"The cops are here to arrest you Jay. They said you have ten minutes to get downstairs."

What the fuck?

"Do they have a warrant? "Asks Ryder, always the smart one, even while he unabashedly jumps out of bed naked and begins tugging on his clothing. Boots and all. I follow suit, a little more discreetly, and thankfully Jimmy has turned his back to give me privacy.
"Yes, they have a fucking warrant. Denny is on the phone with the lawyer and Laura is down there half-licked, doing her best to end up in the cell with you again."

"Jesus! What the hell did I do? I thought that shit was over this morning, I don't understand!"

Jimmy cuts me off mid rant. "It's not the shit with Andrew. They say it's an assault charge."

Ryder is long ahead of me, storming out the door and down the stairs.

"What do you mean, assault. On *who*?"

Jimmy wastes no time now that Ryder is gone, embracing me in only my jeans and bra.

"I don't fucking know Jay, they said some woman came into the station and said you assaulted her. And the only reason she knew it was you is because the goddamn local news website already posted a picture of you, saying you were back in town for questioning regarding the Roberts case."

"Who the hell would recognize me now, Jimmy? Unless they knew me before?"

"I don't fucking know. Finish getting dressed and I'll bring up whatever the hell it is she saw on the website."

I find my shirt on the floor and head to my suitcase for socks and boots.

"Here."

Jimmy shoves the tablet in my hands and there I am, me, many months ago. The photo is a close up of me and I don't mistake the background. I recognize the Italian place where I used to get my favorite dinners from in Indianapolis. It doesn't take long for me to know someone was following me, and it wasn't Shawn.

William fucking Becker.

I recognize my still shiny face from sweat after I left Brock and Ryder at the gym. This is just more proof of how much he wants Ryder, and how much he wants me out of the picture. It also means I wasn't a fool all those times my paranoia kicked in. I should've listened to my instincts better.

Ryder chooses this moment to come back into the room.

"This is fucking bullshit, I'm not sure why that fuck Braumer has it out for you so bad but-"

I cut him off. "It's not Braumer."

I move to shove the tablet toward him.

"He's downstairs Elle, it fucking is!"

"Look!"

He finally glances down at the photo, clearly not seeing what I am.

"That photo was taken the night I left you and Brock at the gym. Not too long before Becker called and summoned you back to Chicago. That's where I got the Italian food that night."

I've never seen Ryder so mad when he tosses the tablet onto the bed and follows it through with a punch to the wall. "Jesus fuck! Why? Why can't he leave you the fuck alone?"

I walk up and place my hands on his back, then wrapping my arms around his torso.

"Because he wants you, but not as much as I do."

THE UGLY ROSES

I place a kiss between his shoulder blades. He turns me around in his arms and forces his mouth onto mine. Squeezing me so tight I don't think I could breathe if I tried.

"I can't stop them right now, babe. I can't. I don't know how they got so much, so fucking fast. Well I do know, it's Becker. But still. This is too fast, they have too much help. And I can't fucking help you right now unless I haul you out the fire escape and hope we're quicker. Fuck babe!"

I grab onto his face with both hands, oddly feeling like I'm the strong one here.

"It's bullshit, and I have all of you here to vouch for me. Patrov will get me out. Everything will be okay."

I place another kiss on his lips before I hear the pounding of footsteps coming up the stairs.

"I'll do everything I can. Stay strong babe."

I let go of the man who has become my world and walk into the hallway where the officers will be at any moment.

A young rookie cop is who I see first. Behind him is Braumer who's failing at trying to hide a grin.

"Ms. O'Connor, you have the right to remain silent-" I cut the prick off. "I know the Miranda Rights spiel, no need to waste your breath. Sorry I took so long getting dressed but I was asleep. Now, I'll gladly follow you fellas down so we can get this misunderstanding taken care of."

Braumer gives a sick shake of his head before addressing his little deputy. "Rookie, what do we do when we apprehend someone being charged for assault, who's presumably armed and-or dangerous?"

"We use force if needed Sir, and we use cuffs to ensure our own safety."

Braumer pats him on the back. "That's right boy. Now although Ms. O'Connor is cooperating, I think it's a wise decision to cuff her seeing as she has a history of violence. As with any repeat offender, this is procedure."

I scoff at him. "Repeat offender? Are you kidding me?"

"Rookie, do as you're told and escort Ms. O'Connor down to the car."

I can tell the rookie feels out of place and uncomfortable, and clearly doesn't want to cuff me. I take a few deep breaths, hoping I don't lose my shit when I feel my arms pulled behind my back. Andrew never pulled them behind, only above. But it still freaks me out.

He makes a motion for me to turn and face the wall, and I do, all the while listening to Denny bark on his phone, Ryder bitch to Braumer and Jimmy telling the young rookie not to harm a hair on my head.

I breathe in and out, over and over as my arms are pulled behind my back, albeit gently. The cool metal of the cuffs settle on my wrist bones. I picture myself somewhere else, away from here, on a beach, in North Carolina where it's just me, my dog, the water and my handsome neighbor. I replay those images over and over and over again in my mind while trying not to hyperventilate.

I hear voices, but they're muffled. I feel my feet moving, but don't remember telling them to. I feel foreign hands on my arms and a hand on my head as I'm lowered into the car. I keep my eyes closed and keep the happy memory playing. All of it on a never-ending loop.

* * *

THE UGLY ROSES

I don't look down. I look up, trying to portray the strong woman they think I am, but deep inside I'm breaking. I'm led through the same doors, taken down the same hallway and finally pushed toward the end. Braumer holds one arm like I could run, while the lowly rookie trails beside me with a hand placed loosely for support. At the end of the hallway I push left to head toward the cells when Braumer pulls me right. I shake my head frantically which seems to make him happier. He tugs again.

I don't think, I just drop to my knees.

I will not go down there.

I cannot go down there.

I can't.

I won't.

I'll die.

"Top cells are almost at full capacity and since the one you were in last night hasn't been cleaned we need to put you down here so that can be done. We also don't want you harming anyone else."

I remain a deadweight, screaming in my head. Hell, maybe I'm screaming out loud. I don't know. I have no idea. There's no one else in the hallway aside from the three of us. I don't let that stop me.

"No Basement! NO!"

"Use force if needed son! You're in charge here and we need to get her down there."

"Sir, I'm pretty sure Bates cleaned out the cell already, I'll go check." He doesn't wait for Braumer to answer. I don't begin to cooperate. I curl up in a ball with my hands restrained behind my back, refusing to go down those stairs.

"Get up! Get the fuck up and go down those steps!"

I don't speak back, because I can't. I don't fight back when he forcefully grabs my arm and drags me down the first few steps. I don't kick him because I don't want to be here any longer than I have to. I just remain limp, allowing my forehead to bounce off the steps as he tries to get me down them, wishing I could stop the shakes that are taking over and hoping to hell I don't vomit all over myself.

"It's clean, Sir!"

I breathe out a silent sigh of relief and tell myself one day I will make this bastard cop pay for the way he has treated me. I also waste no time in rising on shaky limbs to accommodate the rookie who's now helping me to a much nicer area of the station—one above ground.

I don't listen to anymore words I hear coming out of Braumer's mouth. I don't thank the rookie even though I want to. I move as quickly and quietly as I can toward the cell and let him deposit me inside. There are only two people in the cell with benches. The one with beds is empty. I wish plenty of evil karma on Braumer as the cuffs are taken off my wrists and I dive for the toilet.

I don't make it in time. Half of my sickness ends up on my jeans before I finally get my head over the toilet. I pay it no mind as I empty everything into the bowl I haven't eaten in the past two days. I rinse my mouth out in the sink, and do my best with the toilet paper and water to get it off my jeans, then I crawl onto the bed and curl up in the fetal position.

Back to the wall.

Chapter Thirty-two

"O'Connor, your lawyer is here. O'Connor! Wake up!"

I slowly come to, not that I'm sure I was actually asleep. I see the same guard who was here last night, or maybe that was the night before? I have no idea.

I sit up on the bed and wait to be escorted from my cell, only this time it opens, and the guard steps aside for Andrei Patrov to enter.

"What in the hell happened to you?"

Andrei doesn't waste a moment and is on his knees in front of me. Not at all grossed out as I sit, a once semi-sophisticated thirty-year-old woman half-covered in vomit and most likely bruised judging by the way he looks at my arms and head.

I follow the path his eyes took and confirm that I do in fact have multiple finger mark bruises on my arms. I have no idea what my head looks like because I don't have a mirror.

"Talk to me, what happened? We have thirty minutes before we need to leave for court."

"Court?"

He rests a hand gently on my arm. "Your bail hearing. You're entitled to one."

I'm so tired. I slowly shake my head, closing my eyes when I realize how much of a headache that small movement causes.

"I don't know why I'm here, Andrei. Other than Becker and maybe Braumer. Why?"

"A woman came in and said you assaulted her the other night. Not the night you were at the cemetery, the night before that. You were with Jimmy, but because he's a close friend and only one person his statement may not be enough. This woman has bruises on her face, says that you attacked her while she was jogging, blamed her for something or other."

"What? Who? I don't understand Andrei."

"She claims she used to date Andrew Roberts and you attacked her out of jealously."

"What! I don't know anyone he was with, he tried to kill me. Why-"

He holds his hand in front of my face. "I know, it's bullshit. Which is what I will go in there and prove. I had Ryder bring you a change of clothes. We'll go and change quickly once you tell me why you look the way you do."

I take a cleansing breath of air and tell Andrei what happened when I was brought here, not being able to help the trembling in my voice. He curses a few times and types something out on his phone before we leave the cell and head toward the bathroom.

* * *

"What the fuck!" This is the first thing I hear when I enter the courtroom, dressed in cleaner clothes. Ryder gave Andrei a three-quarter sleeve loose grey top and black tights. Not that I had any courtroom clothes in my suitcase, and Andrei thought it better to show the marks on my body as evidence to what has been done in the past.

I hate it, I feel naked. But I also know I wouldn't have been allowed to wear my cuffs and scarf along with the rest of my armor in the courtroom. Least of all my knife packed boots. So here I stand, in the short sleeve but long peasant top and tights with gladiator sandals.

THE UGLY ROSES

The judge is not in the room yet, which I'm thankful for, and I allow Ryder to assess the bruises I now know that are on my forehead and temple (courtesy of the mirror in the washroom). I watch him take in the finger mark bruises on my arms.

"All will be taken care of, Callaghan," Patrov assures him.

The judge begins his grand entrance into the courtroom, and we all take our seats.

I listen to the beginnings of my bail hearing, someone saying I should not be granted bail because I'm a flight risk. I have too much money and not enough ties to the community. I listen to Andrei bicker back and forth about police brutality. I half listen, knowing there's nothing I can do to help myself.

'Speak only when spoken to', Andrei had warned me.

So here I sit, quietly.

My ears perk up when Miller enters the room.

"Your Honor, if I may?"

He seems put out by the kind officer's request but grants him regardless. "I have personally contacted Special Investigations in regard to Detective Braumer's conduct in the police service. I have many men behind me who agree his actions aren't justified, nor are they condoned. This is not the first instance and I'm sure it will not be the last where his fellow officers have witnessed his ill behavior.

"In the instance of last night when Ms. O'Connor was brought into custody, the rookie involved also noted that Detective Braumer used more force than necessary. From this point forward, in fact, as of twenty minutes ago, Detective Braumer is once again on leave from the department pending further investigation.

"I ask that you take this into account before you make your ruling today and discredit any information that has been given to you by the detective."

I thank all that is holy as I listen to Miller, wishing this would've happened before I rolled into town. I wondered and was a little upset that Miller wasn't there for me last night, but obviously he was busy with bigger and better things.

"I will take your words into account, Detective Miller. However I have been in the courtroom for a long time. I have seen a lot of justice done at the hands of Detective Braumer. I will also remind you that we are not in this courtroom today because of the actions of one detective. We are here because of the actions of one woman. A woman who has not fully been cleared from a previous murder investigation involving two men. And while that may be unsolved, and she may potentially be innocent, we need to remember that she is here because of an assault charge on the ex-girlfriend of the deceased from a previous crime no less.

"While you may be concerned with the detective's motives, I see plain as day a continuation for aggressive behavior. Ms. O'Connor did not stick around before and I don't suspect she will stick around now."

Andrei stands up to address the judge at this.

"All due respect, your Honor. My client was in hiding from a killer who is still out to get her. Kill her, more accurately. Evidence being-"

"That is neither here, nor there, councilor. We are here on an assault charge and we will focus on that. Ms. O'Connor, I believe Detective Braumer and the counsel are correct. You are a flight risk; you have too much money to be left on your own. I would freeze your accounts and let you stay with a friend, but I do not believe that that will stop you, given your history of assumed violence and fleeing the country. You are hereby remanded into custody and you will have a chance to plead your case again in four days' time. We will resume on Tuesday at ten a.m. Court is adjourned."

I don't hear the profanity.

I don't feel the hands pulling at my arms.

I don't recall the look of disgust on the judge's face like I deserved the marks that are on my body.

I only hear the sound of the gavel that lands heavily on the hard wood.

Chapter Thirty-three

"Take off your clothes and set them in the bin."

I follow the female guard's instructions, thankful that she sounds professional. I strip off what I was sent here in, all the way down to my birthday suit. She's done this before and I tell myself this is just procedure, this is just what needs to be done.

I remain silent through this new routine, taking the clothes she gives me after the pat down. I feel her hands slow when they move over the raised ridges on my skin. I don't speak or dwell on it as I follow her through a series of rooms. If you could call them that, being as they're not really separated and provide no privacy.

I'm issued a towel and a toothbrush, a pair of canvas shoes and scratchy bed linens. I don't speak back, but I respond when spoken to. I show no disrespect because they've not done anything to warrant it yet. These people are here doing their job and *they* didn't do anything to put me in this place.

I've noticed a few male guards. I avoid eye contact and stay close to the female guard. I follow her through another series of bars before she leaves me in front of cell number D13.

The door opens and she puts me inside, telling me when check times are, when I will be fed and a series of other shit I pay little attention to. I nod my head in silent thanks before she leaves the room.

"O'Connor?"
I look up to the slightly bigger woman in uniform for the first time. She's in her mid-forties maybe and a little rough around the edges. She isn't wearing make-up, but kind eyes lie beneath the professional exterior.

THE UGLY ROSES

"I read what happened to you. Keep your head up, your mouth closed and stay out of trouble. You don't belong here. Follow those rules and you'll be home before you know it. You get me, girl?"

I nod my head. "I get you."

With one last look she closes the door behind me. I look from right to left and around again. The eight-by-ten cell has a double bunk, but I'm the only one in here which I'm thankful for. There's a toilet without a camera above it and a small sink with a mirror.

I remember reading stories about a few certain sick fucks from my area who ended up in Kingston Penitentiary in Ontario. I remember reading about child molesters being given a television and murders being given access to computers. I look around my damp drab cell and wonder where those are now?

I'd like to say they were just rumors, but I had a friend who became a guard at the prison and confirmed the rumors to be true. I wonder who the hospitality came from, because aside from how professional my guard was, I don't see me getting a television or laptop anytime soon.

I don't know how long I sit there lost in thought before a flap on the door opens and a food tray is pushed inside. I reach out to grab it, only to have it pulled back. I know this game and I don't plan to take any part in it.

I look through the glass and my eyes meet an evil set of brown ones, belonging to a larger, mid-thirties looking man. I rest my hands on my lap and wait for him to finish eye balling me and leave before I grab the tray.

I'm not hungry, my appetite is long gone. But I'm thirsty. I grab the orange juice and chug it down while surveying the plain looking sandwich and apple. I tear it all apart, looking for anything out of place.

Finding nothing amiss, I start with the apple and eat the bread from the sandwich, not trusting the cheap looking deli meat. I set the tray back in the door and curl up on the bed. Praying, hoping that somebody saves me before Tuesday.

* * *

I listen to the sounds in the prison. The clanking of bars, the unmistakable sounds of hushed voices, all the while avoiding the scent of damp concrete, for it will bring back my darkest nightmares.

I lie awake for the better part of the evening, drifting in and out of consciousness. I have no idea what time it is. Perhaps if I'd listened better to the kind guard who brought me in here I would have a better understanding of when the check times were, which would help me figure out how long I've been laying here.

I hear them every time they pass my cell and each time I instinctively reach under my pillow for the gun that's not there. It's an endless cycle and habit I have not quit. Every time my hand comes back empty, I feel weaker.

The sound of footsteps causes me to do it yet again, as I hear them slow outside of my cell.

"Breakfast, O'Connor."
Thankfully, this is a woman's voice. Not wanting to disrespect her or cause any friction between me and the staff, I dutifully get up and take the tray.

Once again, I have orange juice. My food consists of a banana, scrambled eggs and toast. I once again eat the banana and bread, washing it down with the juice before setting the tray back in the door.

I'm assuming this must be maximum security, not that I really know. I never saw any women grouped in cells on my way through yesterday but having no clue about the ins and outs of jail, I'm not sure.

The tray is taken and I use my spare time to stretch and workout. I have no energy to do either, but I feel like I need to keep myself centered and fit to keep up in a place like this, hoping my stay is no longer than four days.

"O'Connor, you've got a visitor."

I turn toward the opening door of my cell and follow yet another guard. She leads me through the same series of hallways I came through, ending up outside of a small meeting room.

She opens the door for me and I see my lawyer sitting at the table. As much as I wish it was a more friendly face of the dark-haired variety, I'm still happy to see him.

"How are you holding up?"

I shrug my shoulders, not much to say.

"Listen, I am sorry I could not do more for you yesterday. I assure you, this was completely out of my control. This has everything to do with William Becker and nothing at all to do with you."
"I know that Andrei, I'm not upset with you."

"Okay. Look, I don't think it is just Becker. Ryder and his team have been working around the clock. We don't have proof, but we are certain it was Braumer who found the woman and possibly paid her to make those claims. Cabe found a list of priors for her. Not a long list and not much stuck but it was mostly petty crime and drug charges. Want to guess who the arresting officer was?"

Fuck.

"Braumer."

"You are right. If I'm not mistaken, Braumer has become close with either Foley or Becker. I can't be sure, but my gut tells me so."

What are the odds that I would end up in the middle of this mess? I'd like to say that karma has come back to kick me in the ass, but haven't I been knocked down enough? Haven't I lost enough? Sacrificed enough?

"Denny followed the woman who is charging you, Bonnie Macintosh, after they left the police station. He has been on her ever since. She lives with a friend in a low-income apartment building and has a two-year-old son. I have no doubt that Braumer had leverage, or William forked out some money. We have no idea which is correct, so Denny and Ivan will take turns watching the apartment to see who comes by, or who she goes to see."

I rest my elbows on the table and put my head into my hands, wondering how my life went from worrying about someone who wants me dead, to keeping good graces with a mayor.

"What happens on Tuesday, Andrei?"

He closes the notepad in front of him. "It will depend on what Denny and Ivan find out. If this woman follows through with charging you, I need to work on figuring out ways to prove that it was not you. She has priors, but they believe you have a history of violence. I have won all of my cases but a handful when I first became a lawyer. My skills are good, but when people are bought it makes it hard for me to plead a case on deaf ears.

"I assure you that Ryder, his team and myself will not stop until we get you out of here. That's a promise."

I nod my head. Hoping the men can figure this out. If not... "You're aware of how much money I have?"

"Yes, I'm aware," he says.

I clasp my hands in front of me and lean forward, speaking in a hushed tone. "Then if you have to pay her, or someone else more than what they are getting—you do it. Just get me the fuck out of here, Patrov."

I don't wait for him to answer. I know our conversation is finished.

I head to the door and knock twice for the guard to escort me back to my cell.

Chapter Thirty-four

I don't know why I dream. Maybe the same reason everybody else does, to picture ourselves somewhere else. Somewhere far, far away from where we currently are.

Somewhere with sunshine and water. Hell, who am I kidding? Somewhere in the cold bush with a fucking rainstorm would be a dream right now. This bed is dry, the room is warm, but I still would rather be anywhere but here.

I take that back. Not anywhere. I once would have wished for this place over the basement at Andrew's. Regardless, I dream. Daydream that is. I'm still very much awake and not comfortable enough to fall asleep.

I hear cries of other women. I hear swearing and other voices. I hear the squeak of shoes up and down the hallway. What I don't expect to hear is the opening of my cell while the lights in my room are off.

I feign sleep, hoping this is one of the checks the guard woman told me about.

I'm not that lucky.

"On your feet, O'Connor."

Shivers run down my spine and the hair on my neck stands up. I crack my eyes and move to my feet beside the bed, coming face to face with the guard who teased me with my dinner.

"You will remain quiet and not wake the other inmates. You will follow me to block B and you will not act out of line. Is that understood?"

I would love to act out right now. I would love to use the moves Brock taught me, but I know none of that will help me.

THE UGLY ROSES

"Yes."

His evil eyes look me over from top to toe, making me want to find a heavy sweater to cover myself with. I know if I reach for the thin one on the top bunk he'll stop me. So I settle for shrinking myself down into the shirt I have on.

"Let's move. No noise, O'Connor."

I nod my head and follow him out the door and to the left. He grabs onto my arm and leads me through a series of hallways I've not been in before. I look to the wall outside the empty guard station and note the time.

12:13 a.m.

I follow him down a set of steps, albeit very open and airy ones. I can see into the courtyard through a window in the stairwell so I know we're only on the ground floor. Hoping that's as far as we go, I let him steer me down yet another hallway. This one is much darker than the one I came from. He opens a door at the end with a key and pushes me forward into darkness. I hear the door lock behind me and a motion sensor light comes on.

"Keep moving O'Connor."

I see the steps in front of me. Only four. Half underground. I could do it, but the damp smell sets in and takes me back there. I close my eyes, feeling his sweaty hand grab onto my arm.

I won't fall.

I won't break down.

I don't look as he leads me down, I don't pay attention. I keep my eyes closed and my mouth shut like a good little inmate. I focus on the sound of blood whooshing through my ears and the way my hair feels on my neck. I focus on the sound of my canvas shoes on the floor.

"I'm getting paid a pretty penny to bring you down here, not that I wouldn't do it for free. I hear you're afraid of the dark? Or is it just going downstairs?"

I cringe and slightly cower away from him but unfortunately it doesn't go unnoticed.

"Scream, complain, and tell somebody what I told you. It doesn't matter. Nobody cares. You see, it will always be the word of the upstanding guard against the inmate. And you know what O'Connor?" he asks, breathing heavily into my ear. "The guard always wins."

I hear a door open before being roughly shoved forward into another tomb of blackness. I pray and hope he didn't follow me in, but I learned a long time ago that what I want is rarely what will be.

The light in the hallway reflects his silhouette in the doorway. I don't take in much of my surroundings, only note this room is smaller than the one I was in. There's a bed at least, although at the moment I wish there wasn't.

"I only have a minute or two before I need to get back, so this will be quick. I'd tell you to be quiet, but I don't think anyone will hear you."

His words are the only notice I get before his fist comes at my face. I stumble backward and scold myself for not being more prepared. I haven't hit the wall yet and his fist comes back full force into my eye. I move my arms up to block his next hit, wanting so badly to beat him but afraid of the consequences that could bring in this place.

"Ah, Ah, Ah! Hands down. I'm finished, for now. Now stay still."

THE UGLY ROSES

I see the bright flash of a camera before my eyes squeeze shut at the blinding light. I hear the squeaking of rusty hinges before the room is in darkness. My face throbs, my eye burns, and I feel blood running down my face. I remind myself I wasn't raped, or tortured. I can overcome this.

I have endured worse, I have been hurt more.

I crawl toward the bed and lift myself up onto it. I don't lay down, I'm too afraid to sleep. I put my back to the wall and pull my knees up to my chest. The concrete is cool at my back, but I don't dare move.

My body begins to shake, and my hands start to tremble.

I will not cry.

I will not give in.

RYDER

"What do you got, Ivan?"

I sent him to relieve Denny, watching over the woman who claims mine beat her. One look at Bonnie and I knew this was not her doing. Hell, I knew it before then. This woman may not be a great one, but she sure as shit didn't want to accuse my woman of beating her.

Bonnie has a few petty theft convictions and a minor drug charge. From what Brock told me she spends more time with her kid at the park than she does drugs. This screams Becker. Or Braumer. Fuck I can't keep those two straight anymore with the amount of shit they cause.

"Same as Denny. No visitors. She took the kid for pizza and went straight back home."

"Alright, we'll sit on her one more night. If she gives us nothing by tomorrow afternoon, we go in and figure out who the fuck is pulling her strings."

"Got it, Boss."

I hang up the phone and pace Jimmy's apartment. I should have left by now. I should have got a room at the hotel. For some reason I can't. I feel closer to her here. Jimmy has a spare room that I've stayed in. Not slept, but stayed. I'm still confused as to why Elle—*Jayne? Fuck it, she's my Elle*—slept in the same room with him, but after a long talk with the guy he assured me it's just always been their thing.

I'm a guy and I'm not fucking stupid. Elle is beautiful. What man wouldn't want a piece of her? I told him this and he actually told me they haven't slept together in over ten years, and only the one time because he said if he had a sister, he assumes that's what it would've felt like to fuck her.

THE UGLY ROSES

After that fucked-up conversation, I let it go. It didn't take me long to figure out why she loves this guy so much. He's one of the most grounded of people I've ever met. Solid guy, and intelligent. Two good things in my book.

My ringing phone stops me from wearing a hole through the floor.

Unknown number.

"Callaghan."

"Since you are answering your phone, I can assume you are not on a plane back to Chicago?" Fucking Becker.

"You'd assume right. Your contract with Callaghan Security is over. I will not now, or ever, fucking work with you again. Now get the fuck out of Canada, your time's up."

Hearty male laughter comes from the other end of the line. Why this prick wants me with his daughter so bad is beyond me. There are dozens of qualified security specialists who would die to work for him and have no fucking problem dropping their jeans for his bitch of a daughter.

"Mr. Callaghan, you mistake me for someone who will do as they are told. I can assure you, if someone is to give orders, it will be me."

"That's where you're wrong, Becker. I will ruin you, mark my words. You may make it out of Canada with your dignity intact, but by the time those wheels touch down in Chicago, well, let's just say the media won't be your only nightmare."

"You would do well not to threaten me, boy. I'm parked on the street, meet me downstairs and you will see just how serious I am."

I don't get to respond before hearing the click of the call ending.

Chapter Thirty-five

I jog down the steps into the shop, passing Jimmy and Denny on the way. I don't stop when he calls my name. I continue past them and storm out the front door. Becker's black town car is parked across the street and I waste no time striding toward it, seeing his smug face through the open window.

"Now before you do something that I will make you regret, I have something for you to look at. You would do best to listen to me."

I ball my fists at my sides, it's taking everything in me not to drag this piece of shit out of the car and beat him into the sidewalk. I hear two sets of footsteps behind me, heavy on the concrete. I had no problem being out here alone, but I'm grateful for the support.

"I expect you to be on a plane by noon tomorrow, Ryder. If not, I assure you the outcome will not be pretty."

He holds the phone in front of my face. I do all I can to not rip his arm off with it.

"NO! You son of a bitch I will fucking kill you!"

Two sets of arms grab onto me, but it doesn't stop me from moving closer to the screen. Elle's beautiful face is swollen. Her eye is barely visible and there's blood running out of her nose. I have no idea where she's being kept in the prison, but it looks like the hole. The bare concrete wall behind her and the unfinished floor remind me of the basement she was once kept in. If that's the first thing I think of, then she's probably having a fucking panic attack right now. And I'm not there to hold her, help her through it.

Fuck! What have I done?

I never should have started working for this fuck! I should've kept my goddamn dick in my pants. Now my actions have caused this fucking shit!

"Now, now Ryder. Unless you want the lady to endure more than a beating you will do as I say. That guard enjoys what he does, enjoys taking advantage of the women who enter the facility, for a fee of course. Or I can tell him not to harm a hair on her head and make sure he is compensated for doing so.

"Now, I don't like to order people around. Surely we can come to an agreement. I am not one to condone rape, Callaghan. But I'm afraid I can't stop him once he gets started. Especially with one that looks like your sweet Elle."

Jimmy fumes at my side and Denny works hard to keep us in check.

"So tell me Ryder, would you be able to live with the fact that she has been taken in every way imaginable? Against her will no less. Or will you be a good soldier and do as I ask. Because all it is going to take is one text or phone call. AH! Here comes another photo now. Keep in mind the first one was sent almost an hour ago."

He once again holds the phone out in front of me. Denny and Ivan give it their all to hold me back. She has more blood on her beautiful face and there's a large hand wrapped around her hair, holding her head up. Her fucking shirt is torn.

Hang on beautiful! Don't let go, just hang the fuck on.

Chapter Thirty-six

The sound of my raspy voice echoes off the concrete walls. I sing softly, mostly to myself, but for some reason hoping he can hear me. I know the song is roughly five minutes long, so I tell myself if I sing it on a loop it will help me keep track of time.

I don't know if I've been sitting here for five minutes, or five hours. Time travels slowly in the dark, it always has. I know deep down that time is not of importance. But with nothing but my morbid thoughts keeping me company, I know I need something else to focus on.

I'm not sure if it was another man's hands on me, or the darkness that took over (both literally and figuratively). Either way, I came to the same conclusion.

I'm madly in love with Ryder Callaghan.

I want to see him, smell him and touch him.

I want to feel his arms around me and his voice in my ear telling me to keep him. I want to run my fingers through his hair and tell him I am sorry for doubting his commitment to me.

I want to apologize for running because it took away valuable time we could have spent together.

I just *want him.*

I pull my legs tighter toward my chest with my shaking arms, trembling inside and out. I ignore all those things and just sing the fitting song by Kings of Leon. For Ryder, for me, for us.

Love is a beautiful thing.

HARLOW STONE

I will not run, hide, or leave him. I will not allow William Becker, Detective Braumer, or anyone else to get in the way of what I *know* is the last beautiful thing I may ever experience in my life. Regardless of the war going on around us. So I just sing, on a loop, praying he can hear me.

I say love
Don't mean nothing
Left them something
Worth fighting for
It's a beautiful war

I feel the words as I sing them. Deep down in my soul and again when I start over. It's relentless, but therapeutic. I sing in a voice I do not recognize. One I've never heard before. It's new to me, made deeper by my once bruised and battered throat. It's raspy like Janis Joplin and echoes back from the cold bare walls.

It's my beautiful melody to the man who I think about. The one person I can focus on that adds some sunlight to my otherwise dark tomb.

I hear the sound of a door opening and see the motion sensor light activate on their arrival. I stopped my singing as soon as I heard the door, not wanting them to be a part of my moment with the person I deeply care about.

Thanks to the light in the hallway, I see the shadow when it stops outside my room. This time, he uses a key to open the door, indicating he locked it on departure. I sit still on my spot in the corner of the small bed, not moving.

He opens the door and once again the light illuminates him from behind. I would say he's maybe one hundred and ninety pounds. Not in muscle, he has no definition for that. He is just shy of six feet tall and nothing to write home about. His light hair is unkempt. His uniform is ruffled. He's not handsome, but average. He's unremarkable and every bit of evil.

He doesn't shut the door behind him, but moves into the cell. He reaches out and grabs me by the front of my shirt, causing it to rip as he hauls me off the bed. I try to cooperate, not wanting to anger him anymore, but for some reason he still slaps my face when I'm not fast enough.

I'm shoved backward into the cold concrete wall, the force causing the air to whoosh out of my lungs and my trembling legs to weaken. The guard reaches out and grabs a fist full of my hair, holding me upright.

"Stay still."

I don't know why he asks, it's not like I can move. I don't understand until the flash of the camera blinds me once again. I blink, repeatedly, trying to regain my sense of sight.

"You must be popular, princess. Or worth something, because our little photoshoot is over."
He releases my hair and I let out the breath I was holding, hoping to hell I can now go above ground and back to my cell. I will my legs to take me there, one foot in front of the other, but his hand moves to my shoulder and his mouth moves to my ear. The sick hushed voice sending chills down my spine.

"That doesn't mean that *I'm* done with you."

He moves away from my ear, remaining close enough that I can feel his breath on my cheeks. Regardless of the lack of light, I don't miss the evil smirk on his face. The calloused thumb on his left hand moves from my neck into the hollow of my collarbone. He applies enough force in the pressure point, using his hand to push down, leaving me no choice but to drop to my knees.

"Now be a good inmate, number 67413."

Author Notes

This is not the end!
The final book, *Blinded By Fate* is available now in both
eBook and print on Amazon.

Thank you so much for reading the second book in
The Ugly Roses Trilogy! If you enjoyed it please take the
time to leave a review on Amazon or Goodreads

Want to chat about all things books?
Connect with Harlow:

www.facebook.com/harlow.stone.author

harlow.stone.books@gmail.com

Instagram.com/harlowstone

www.harlowstone.com

Acknowledgements

Thank you so much for making it this far with me!

To the readers— you guys rock! Without your reviews and constant questioning for book two's release we would not be here today.

To my mom and dad (who calls this venture his retirement fund), thank you for the support to get me where I am today.

Erin, you're my rock in this venture. You appreciate my no-nonsense attitude and push me forward. Your criticism is constructive, and our mutual love of the written word will always give us something to talk about.

To my beta's (Jen and Kim) thanks for reading my mess of a manuscript and helping me along the way!

Rachel, my fellow raunchy book lover; thank fuck you're perceptive!

My editor Greg, thanks for putting up with my endless questions and correcting my horrible grammar.

Christine Stanley. I'd still be a like a lost kid on her first day of school with toilet paper stuck to her shoe if it weren't for your help.

Keep it classy,
Harlow
xx

Made in the USA
Middletown, DE
02 January 2020